OBSIDIAN

BOOK I OF THE MYSTIC STONES SERIES

BY KAYLA CURRY

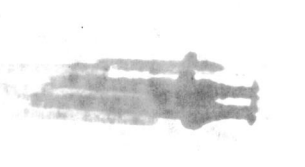

THE MYSTIC STONES SERIES

Obsidian (Mystic Stones Series #1)

Copyright © 2015 Kayla Curry

Editing by Samantha S. Lafantasie

Formatting by Jason Sharp

Songs by James Warburton Music

www.KaylaCurry.com

Paperback ISBN: 978-0-9916684-3-4

Ebook ISBN: 978-0-9916684-4-1

DEDICATION

To the friends and family members who may have raised an eyebrow when I told them I was writing a novel, but never said I was crazy for dreaming big. Also, to my husband and sons who put up with the constant keyboard tapping.

TABLE OF CONTENTS

PROLOGUE

The sound of the world has changed since its creation. Today, we hear notifications going off in public places from all directions. Smartphones are ringing in every pocket, and our reliance on them grows. The simplest of tasks has been reduced to diodes and wires. The human race uses technology to communicate, entertain, control, and organize. Our smartphones and tablets have become our lifelines. We use them to socialize, and they are part of our everyday lifestyle. Computers control everything from buildings to the electricity that pulses through them. Each passing year brings new technology, and in five years, the technology used now will be considered ancient. Each model of the newest gadget surpasses the last.

Most of the newest technology depends on the many satellites orbiting the earth to send and receive data. If something were to happen to these satellites, the modern way of life would be dismantled. If all the satellites were out of commission, some places would even be without food. Islands, like the Hawaiian Islands, receive most of their daily supplies from ships that navigate with GPS. Of course, human life would sustain for a while. Eventually, food would run out and riots would begin. Soon, world panic will set in. Worldwide assumptions of the apocalypse will cause chaos.

Our dependence on technology grows every day. Imagine what life would be like a few years from now. Imagine how much more we will rely on our technology.

Unfortunately, we're in too deep. At this point, we are so reliant on technology that if we were unable to use it, we would be lost. This story begins on February 2nd, 2020, when our dependence on technology has grown so immense that a simple task, like getting to work on time, is much more difficult when technology disappears.

CHAPTER ONE

The chiming of my old alarm clock woke me. The ancient object had become my backup in case my phone ever let me down. It had been years since I'd needed it.

I sighed. Another day at the office awaited. I went to the bathroom to shower and get ready. My Dayinfo Planner, which usually reminded me of important events and recited the weather to me each morning remained quiet. The screen showed blank except for the word "ERROR" blinking under the Psytech logo.

"Must be some kind of glitch," I said to myself.

I walked through my empty house, half expecting one of my parents to greet me even though years had passed since their accident. I thought about the drunk driver who killed them before they could watch me graduate. The anger I had fought since the police told me the bad news resurfaced and then receded once again. I always buried it before it could take hold of me, and turned my thoughts to other things.

I finished my morning routine and then consumed my bagel, banana, and juice breakfast in minutes. I grabbed my phone before I locked up.

On my way into work, I passed people with new cars still in their driveways with the hoods up and stress lines on their faces. I reached into my purse for my phone at the next stop sign to check for any missed calls or text messages, but the screen was white.

No menu. No apps. Not even the time displayed—just a blank screen.

The phone, the cars, and my Dayinfo Planner were all acting up. I turned my attention to the sky for signs of volcano smoke or something else. Nothing.

In Hilo, humidity could be blamed for some of these things, but that didn't account for the people with car troubles.

Driving should have been my main focus. I put the issue out of my mind until I got to work.

My car came to a stop at a light flashing red. An officer attempted to direct traffic but seemed to fail miserably. One car almost hit the officer through all the chaos. I managed to get through the intersection and the others without a collision. My outlook for the day didn't look good.

Ten minutes later, I finally made it to work, but the security guard at the gate was manually checking badges. Apparently, the SecuriScanners were offline too. When my turn at the gate came, the guard recognized me and waved me through. I stopped briefly to ask him if he knew what was going on.

"I don't know, Miss Tanner. I think all electronics went haywire today. No TV, no cell phones, no GPS, no SecuriScanner—I'll be lucky if I make it through the morning without some corporate guy punching me in the face. I hate manually checking badges, it takes so long," he said.

His name was Todd, I think. The security guards at Herrick-Peyton all blurred together with their cliché mustaches and baseball caps.

"Well, hopefully, all the really arrogant corporate guys won't make it in due to having trouble with their BMW's GPS system," I said.

"I can only hope!"

A polite smile and a wave from me took me past the gates and into the parking lot. The area had only about half the cars it normally did. The blue Mini Cooper I drove fit perfectly into the stall. I was thankful I bought it a year before all new cars came outfitted with GPS as mandated by the government. I had dodged at least one bullet today, thanks to my distaste for GPS.

Inside, chaos disrupted my day further. Herrick-Peyton had been my place of work since shortly after my graduation. The building had 120 office spaces and ten warehouses rented out to companies needing space to conduct business. I managed 12 office spaces and one warehouse. As a building manager, my job happened to be pretty easy, but keeping the tenants happy today might be difficult.

I had all my spaces filled and my tenants kept me busy even when technology worked fine.

I was surprised to see most of my colleagues made it to work, although it seemed no work was actually being done. A quick assessment told me all the computers were down— 90 percent of the job was using a computer. Some people banged on their computers, some talked on the phone with tech support, I assumed, but most stood around sipping on their morning coffee and got paid to do nothing. At least the landlines still worked, I thought, and then the phone on my desk rang, almost as if it said, "Don't worry! I'm still here for you!"

"Aloha from Herrick-Peyton, this is Ava Tanner. How can I help you?" I said, with my best phone voice.

"Hello, Miss Tanner, this is Tom Walker from Psytech."

I recognized the smooth voice right away. My heart jumped a little in my chest.

"Hello, Mr. Walker, what can I do for you on this hectic day?" I asked.

"Ah, so I guess you guys are having electronic problems as well. I hope you will still be able to get some security passes for me. Some high-up corporate executives are coming in tomorrow," he replied.

"Well, as long as you provide names, a copy of a photo ID, and socials for me, I should be able to use our backup system to print out some temporary badges," I said. My attention flickered to the storeroom that doubled as a catchall. I dreaded having to go in and dig for the backup computer, but I always did everything in my power to help a client.

"That sounds perfect. I'll ask my secretary to gather the information for you. I'd ask her to fax it down, but—well, I don't know if those are working," Mr. Walker said.

"It's no problem, I'll come up and get them in about an hour," I offered.

"They'll be ready. I'll talk to you later, just let me know when they're done."

"Will do, Mr. Walker!" I chirped. I annoyed even myself with my phone voice. I wondered what he thought of it.

"By the way, when are you going to quit Herrick-Peyton and come to work for me?" Mr. Walker asked.

6

He'd asked the question many times before, and I always answered the same way.

"I've told you a million times, Mr. Walker. I'm loyal to Herrick-Peyton, and until they go down the tubes or give me a reason to walk away, I will stay loyal," I said with a smile he couldn't see. Of course, I'm sure he could imagine it since it was the same one I showed every time I answered him in person.

"That's exactly why I want you. Loyalty is essential at Psytech."

"Unfortunately for you, loyalty means I'll be staying right where I am, Mr. Walker," I said.

"Yes, it is unfortunate, but at least I still have the pleasure of having a competent account manager like you to handle our business with Herrick-Peyton. I suppose that will suffice—for now."

"Don't get your hopes up, Mr. Walker. I'll let you go for now so I can work on getting the backup system up and running, it's a program from the Middle Ages," I replied.

I hung up the phone with a quick good-bye and went to sort out the mess around me. My boss walked in looking exasperated. His thick hair seemed muddled and his tie hung loosely around his neck. His ordinarily tucked in shirt was half out of the waist of his pressed slacks. I remembered he had one of the newer cars with GPS wired in.

"Hey, Simon, glad you made it in," I said, "We have a bit of a problem."

"Obviously," he said looking around, "STAFF MEETING IN FIVE MINUTES!" he yelled.

Everyone looked up from what they were doing. Some started to make their way to the boardroom. Time wasn't on my side, so I followed them.

Exactly five minutes later, Simon rounded up the stragglers then headed into the room with a radio. He'd used the last five minutes to compose his appearance. He set the radio at the head of the big table then plugged it in before tuning to any station with a signal. 108.5 came in loud and clear, and the whole room quieted down as the station broadcasted an important news bulletin.

"Moments ago, we here at KCTN received news that a virus has been planted in all satellites orbiting the earth. The virus has shut down cell phone service, internet service, and any device that uses satellites to transfer data around the world. This also includes all commercial aircraft, most ships, boats, and many new cars equipped with GPS.

This virus has traveled from the satellites to any device that uses them rendering the items useless. As of midnight, our time, all electronic devices connected to the satellites were infected, causing them to display a blank screen or an error message. It is still unclear how or why this virus was planted. It is also unclear who is responsible for this act. NASA scientists and other scientists around the world are working to shut down the virus, but all communications with the satellites have been cut off.

At 5p.m. President Sampson will address the nation and give any further information on this matter. Please tune to KCTN at that time to find out if there is any more information. Until then, please remember to drive safely as most stoplights are out. Also, all commercial flights out of Hilo International have been canceled due to planes not functioning, so if you are visiting, you may want to extend your stay. Aloha!"

The room was still silent when the broadcast finished. Most people had wide eyes as if they didn't know how they'd survive without technology. Simon was the first to speak.

"Well, no use in paying you all to sit around, so anyone who doesn't have something they can do without a computer may leave—come back when everything works again."

"What if it never gets fixed?" Sally from accounting asked.

"Then the world will go to hell and you won't need a job because money won't be worth anything anyway. It will be like the dark ages again," Simon replied cynically.

He always had a generally pessimistic attitude. He was a decent boss, but never saw the glass as half full. The energy that came with him spread and made the people around him the same way whenever he was in the room. There were times it was almost toxic. I wished he could just relax. Apparently, his career choice stressed him out almost to the breaking point. Simon had worked hard to get to his position, and he sacrificed nearly everything. He had no family, no social life outside of Herrick-Peyton, and no ambition to achieve those things. It sometimes bothered me when I thought about it. My worst nightmare would be ending up like Simon.

I stood. "Well, Simon, I need to make some passes for Psytech and then I'll be out of your hair."

"Alright, anyone else have something to do?" he asked, looking around at the lethargic group of individuals. Some people spoke up, but I was already leaving the room. Time to pick up the documents from the Psytech office.

Psytech rented three spaces from Herrick-Peyton, two office spaces; one for the tech department and one for the corporate department; and one warehouse. All three were my accounts and they had been loyal tenants for the last three years, which was the majority of the time I had been working for Herrick-Peyton. My four-year anniversary was coming up in July. I could hardly believe it.

The office spaces were about 4500 square feet. The warehouses were twice the size of the office spaces and three stories high with climate control. With six office spaces on each floor of the twenty-one story building, Herrick-Peyton was one of the largest buildings in Hilo.

The elevator took me to the 17th floor to Psytech's corporate office space. The secretary at the entrance swiveled around in her chair, answered phone calls, wrote down notes, and looked up at each person that walked by.

Psytech lived on technology. The fact that they were even functioning at all was amazing. The company was a major pioneer in technological advances—they invented a majority of the gadgets considered to be essential—but right now they were all useless. I assumed they were receiving a lot of complaint calls, and the poor secretary had to direct them somewhere else.

I approached the desk. "Hello, I'm Ava Tanner, I believe Mr. Walker left some documents with you that I need to pick up."

The secretary glanced up at me and arched her brow as her eyes roamed over my clothing and appearance. She had golden blonde hair carefully wrapped in a bun, and her eyes were bright green. They reminded me of two perfect limes. Strangely, I remembered making her badge at the beginning of her employment, but the picture Mr. Walker had sent didn't do her eyes justice.

"May I see your badge?" the secretary asked.

I smiled. My badge hung from my neck on a long lanyard. She couldn't see it over the desk, so I lifted it up.

The young girl took a quick glance then picked up a manila envelope with my name on it and handed it over.

"Thanks," I said, "Would Mr. Walker happen to be around?"

"No, I believe he's gone to the warehouse. We have some important things in there and he wanted to make sure that the climate control still worked with all of the virus problems."

"We don't have the fancy system that's in tune with the weather quite yet. We were planning on getting them, but after today, I'm not sure we'll follow through," I said with a little chuckle.

The secretary didn't seem interested in what I said, but replied, "Yeah. Technology is overrated anyway. I better get back to work. Mr. Walker said to call him if you had any questions."

"Alright, well, have a nice day! I'll get in touch with Mr. Walker and let him know what his corporate guys are going to need before coming in tomorrow."

I hopped back on the elevator and glanced back at the woman who was already back to her manic morning. On my way down, a thought crossed my mind to go to the warehouse and check in with Mr. Walker. It would be easier to track him down on site since cell phones were down. I reached the ground floor and went out the entrance. Psytech's warehouse was the closest one to the main building, and I headed straight for it.

Despite the stress from the technology issues, I enjoyed the atmosphere of the outdoors. I lived in such a beautiful place and rarely got the chance to enjoy it.

Once I reached the door of the warehouse, I rang the buzzer that freight truck drivers use. In moments, Mr. Walker came to the door.

"Hello, Miss Tanner, is there something I can help you with?" he asked, as he stepped outside and closed the door behind him.

Mr. Walker was a tall man with a muscular build. His short dark hair was always combed back. The suit he wore fit his body with perfect lines.

"Oh, I just wanted to let you know that I'll leave the passes at the gate when I leave tonight. Your guys will need photo I.D. to pick them up in the morning, so if you have any important meetings, you may want to tell them to arrive early, especially if the SecuriScanner is still out."

"Thanks, that sounds great. I'll tell them to get here about an hour before our first meeting then," he said, before pausing. "You know, you didn't have to come all the way out here, you could have just left a message with my secretary."

I smiled and looked to the distance. I didn't want to give him the wrong idea. Mr. Walker was a good-looking guy. With a clean cut style, amazing eyes and a charm that he laid on thick, it was hard to resist hitting on him. I had to consciously keep myself from being too flirtatious.

"Yes, well, I like to be more personal than that with my clients. Talking to them directly always ensures that the message is delivered and everything is understood," I replied, "Not to mention she acted a little frazzled with all the calls coming in, I didn't want anything to get lost in translation."

Mr. Walker nodded with understanding. "I see. That's an excellent work ethic. I should remember that when you quit your job and come work for me," he said with a chuckle.

"Nice try," I said. A grin spread across my face. His chuckle was punctuated with his own devilish grin.

"Well," he began, "the advantage of you not working for me means I can ask you out without any potential for office drama. So, would you consider going to dinner with me tonight?"

A sharp inhale noted my surprise, and then I tried to come up with a quick answer. "Do you think anything will be open?"

"Oh, that was the wrong thing to say. I can't date a client. I can't' I thought.

"Probably not, but I can cook if there isn't."

"Are you sure you can cook, or is that a euphemism for box dinner?" I asked mischievously. The words came out before I could stop them, I didn't want him to misinterpret them as an acceptance.

"Oh, I can cook. Maybe even better than you," he said with his sly grin.

"That's not difficult to do. I've been known to have trouble with ramen noodles."

"You're changing the subject," Tom replied.

"I'm not sure I should. I mean—Simon has never said anything, but I'm sure dating a client is frowned upon," I said. I forced a serious expression.

"One date couldn't hurt. Besides, if you get fired, you could just come to work for me. That would work out nicely. It's a win-win situation," Tom said.

I didn't want to jeopardize my reputation by going out with a client. Of course, if the restaurants were closed we would be in the privacy of his home, which was another kind of risk.

I hadn't dated since my parents died. I always dreaded the awkward conversation that began with, 'so what do your parents do?'

"Alright," I heard myself say, although my mind wasn't completely convinced, obviously my voice was. Might as well go with it at this point.

"I'll be ready at 7. Meet me at Montrell's?"

"I'll be there," Tom said. The devilish grin returned.

I smiled and turned to walk away. I couldn't believe I had just accepted his invitation. I couldn't believe I was going on a date with a client.

Then a thought came to me that would have been handy a moment before. *What if someone from the office saw us?* It would be an awkward conversation and my reputation would be ruined. I told myself I'd put it off as if it were a business dinner if suspicion arose.

CHAPTER TWO

Time passed with ease as I worked on and finished the security passes. I dropped them by the gate and went home to get ready for my . . . date. Every time the word ran through my mind I clenched my fists on the steering wheel and thought, *I should not be doing this.*

Nonetheless, once I arrived home, I found myself zipping up the back of my best little black dress.

The dress showed off my cleavage—just a little. I left my long, dark hair in neat waves, and put on some smoky eye shadow to highlight my blue eyes.

I stared at myself in the mirror. Thoughts in my head competed for attention. Some shouted to call and cancel. Others shouted I needed to go on a date. One reminded me I'd been attracted to him since the first day I took him on as a client.

Ultimately, I took control and told myself that I was almost 25, and I did want to get married someday. Today was as good as any to start dating again. My best friend, Alani would be proud. I forced myself to get in my car and drive to the restaurant.

Montrell's was open. Thankfully, we wouldn't have to eat dinner at Tom's house. A sign in the window said "CASH

ONLY." The satellites affected credit card machines too. I hoped Tom carried cash.

"Hello, Miss Tanner."

I heard his voice from behind me. My body reacted and I spun around to see him in an exceptional suit—probably Armani. His short hair laid perfectly swept back, and he had a huge smile on his face and a gleam in his eyes. A force of nature derived from his charm pulled me in as I stepped toward him. He looked stunning.

"You can call me Ava. After all, it's a date," I said with a smile.

"Alright, Ava. I've got cash, but if you'd rather go to my place--" he said as he gently took my hand and motioned toward his car.

"Slow down there, cowboy. I think it would be best if our first date was in public."

"As you wish," he said with a devilish smile across his face again.

He opened the door for me, and even pulled out my chair. It had been a long time since I'd been on a date, and even longer since I'd been with someone so well-mannered. Tom ordered a vintage wine, then we ordered our meals and started into some easy-going conversation.

"So, what do you have in mind for our second date?" Tom asked mischievously.

"You're confident, aren't you?" I countered.

"Would I be President of the Hawaiian Branch of Psytech if I weren't?" Tom said as he flared out his napkin and laid it in his lap.

"I suppose not," I replied.

"How long have you been with Herrick-Peyton?" Tom asked. He set his elbows on the table and clasped his fingers together.

"Almost four years now. I got the job right out of business school. How long have you been with Psytech?"

"It's been a long time. Seems like a hundred years," he said with a chuckle, "But, I love it. I've worked my way up. Did you know, we have corporate offices in every state and all major countries?"

"I didn't. But, I guess your business is in demand right now. Technology is growing as our generation comes to power," I said then took a sip of my water.

"You know what I like about you? You're beautiful and brilliant. There aren't many girls like that around these days."

I smiled and averted my eyes. He was full of compliments today. "Well, I do enjoy the intellectual conversation now and then."

"That's why I wish you would come to work for me, you would make twice the pay," Tom said trying to sway me. I was starting to think of this as more of a business dinner.

"Yes, you've mentioned that many times, but I'm comfortable where I am and with the amount of money I make," I said.

"That's modest of you. It's refreshing to meet someone who isn't out for all they can steal, you know?" Tom said as he looked into my eyes.

"I'll take that as a compliment," I replied, "I do like the way things are right now. I'm happy with what I've accomplished and how hard I've worked to get to where I am."

"Hard work is the best road to a thoroughly appreciated reward. It's the only way to live without any true vices," Tom said.

"Well, I'm sure I have my iniquities, but I think that my good deeds greatly outweigh my bad ones."

"I'm sure they do. You're extremely honest and good at heart—and let's not forget stubborn. This is why I must confess something to you, Ava." Tom leaned forward and brought his hands closer to mine. "Part of the reason I asked you out is to tell you that my company is preparing to offer Herrick-Peyton a lot of money. The executives coming tomorrow are trying to buy the Herrick-Peyton building and all the warehouses."

A gasp escaped my mouth. Words tried to gather and form sentences in my mind, but I kept them at bay because I knew they'd come out in a jumbled mess. Then I was hit with a wave of anger. He definitely had audacity.

I couldn't believe he asked me on a date just to tell me this news.

"So, it's not a date, but a business meeting as well. I should've known," I said. I crossed my arms and leaned back in my chair.

I was a little annoyed that I'd gotten so dressed up for the date. I should've worn business attire. My first date in years was wasted on a man who was unworthy.

"No, I really wanted to take you out. I've wanted to do this for a while. I never could get the nerve up to ask you, and then when the corporate heads told me what they were doing . . ."

His sentence cut off while he searched for more words.

"I just wanted to tell you so it's not a shock to you," he finished

"Why do you need the entire building? That's a lot of space for one company, especially in Hilo. What about all the people I work with? What about the other companies who've been renting from us for years?"

"The companies will find other buildings to rent from, and your co-workers will be considered for jobs with us if they wish. They will not take a pay-cut if they decide to stay with us. As for the building, we are expanding, and we grow tired of renting."

I raised my voice above standard restaurant level. "You grow tired of renting? Why not build a new place? Why go messing with the way people live their lives?"

"We've considered that option, but our expansion plans are rapidly growing, so we need a place that already exists. Building a 21-story building would take much too long, and the Herrick-Peyton building fits our needs perfectly. Plus there's a lot of red tape to go through in order to build on the island. You know that. Space is at a premium here."

"Your needs? What about the needs of other people? All corporate companies are the same. Crush the little guys and move on to overtaking the world."

Tom fought off a grin.

"Maybe I should leave," I said as I stood up. His hand moved for my wrist, but I was quick to avoid it.

"No, please. I didn't mean to upset you, Ava. It's not even my decision. It's over my head," he spoke quickly and quietly. Heads were now turned in our direction.

"I may be the President of the Hawaiian branch, but they make the major decisions like this. You went to business

19

school, you know how it goes. Please, sit down and let's try to make the best of this evening," he pleaded with a gaze so intense that I decided to give him the benefit of the doubt. My compassion kicked in and I eased back into my chair. With my guard up.

We waited for our food in silence.

Once our meals were placed on the table, I took my eyes from glare mode to stare mode. Tom's charm was too much. It was almost as if I couldn't say no to him.

That worried me.

"Are you okay?" he asked after a moment of watching my face.

"Yes. I'm just thinking. Maybe I over reacted. I'm sorry for causing a scene. I really like working for Herrick-Peyton. I care about that place, Tom."

"It may not last. Don't you ever want something new?"

"Sometimes. Sometimes I wish I could put my degree to better use," I admitted. Uncertainty surfaced, but I felt the need to confide in Tom.

"You could do that at Psytech, Ava. I would give you any job you'd feel comfortable in. Any position you wish— except mine, of course."

"If Herrick-Peyton sells, I may have no choice," I said as sadness cracked my voice. I cleared my throat.

"When will Psytech make the offer?"

"In two days. A meeting is already set with the shareholders of your company for Wednesday. The shareholders are aware Psytech wants to meet with them for a business proposition, not that they want to buy. So, if you could refrain from telling anyone, I would greatly appreciate it. You and I are the only ones that know outside of the men coming tomorrow."

"You haven't told your employees?" I asked.

"They know something big is happening, but not what."

My heart raced. I was astonished that he would tell me before anyone else. He could lose his job if they find out. "Why risk your career to tell me this?"

"Because, I have had feelings for you for a while now, and I don't want you to think that you have no place to go if this deal goes through. My gut tells me it will. The men coming tomorrow are persuasive; that's how they got to the top."

"I guess we'll find out on Wednesday," I said purposefully ignoring the comment about his feelings for me.

Defeat crossed his face, and then with determination he said, "I'm betting we'll have an answer before noon. I've seen it happen before. It's likely there will be a staff meeting after that. Come find me after the meeting. I'll be in our warehouse. If you want the job, that is. If you turn it down, I'll understand." He seemed to swallow a lump in his throat. A strong urgency coated his voice.

"Okay, I have to think, I guess. I'll come to the warehouse either way, to tell you what I decide. I don't want to leave you guessing."

At least he trusted me and cared enough to tell me everything. I would have been angrier if I found out on Wednesday after we'd just had a date.

"I would appreciate the extra effort," Tom said.

I thought I saw, for a split second, Tom trying to fight his smile again. I ignored it and cursed myself for being paranoid. I proceeded to attempt to save the evening from total failure.

We finished dinner—and the wine. The whole bottle, that is. My mood had led to me drinking more than I should have.

Feeling a little tipsy, I walked out of the restaurant with Tom. He walked me to my car, as I pretended to be perfectly sober. He seemed to buy it, but before opening my door he noticed me stumble a little, "Would you like me to drive you home? Or maybe you'd like to come to my place for a while? I don't know if you should be driving tonight."

"I don't think I'm ready for that yet," I replied.

"Well, at least let me give you a ride home. I couldn't live with myself if you were hurt because I kept filling your wine glass."

Swirls in my thoughts and the sensation of not wanting to hold my head still made me rethink my plan of driving myself. I came up with the conclusion that I shouldn't. The accident came to mind and my hatred for the drunk driver who caused me so much pain made me even more decisive. "Okay, a ride home would be nice."

We walked toward Tom's Audi. It was a beautiful black car with curves that reminded me of a Ferrari. It was an older model though, most likely without GPS.

"I bought this car just before they made GPS mandatory in all new vehicles. I have a portable GPS, but thankfully it's not connected to the mainframe in the car," he explained.

"I like it," I said as Tom opened the door for me and offered a hand. I couldn't believe he was still being such a gentleman after our little spat in the restaurant. He was so polite and charming, and his looks were definitely a ten. My thoughts got the best of me again.

Doubt told me I shouldn't be with someone whose company was trying to buy the company I worked for. The last four years at Herrick-Peyton had made me who I am.

Working there helped me get past the loss of my parents, or at least kept my mind from going crazy because of it. I almost felt as if I were betraying myself and the company by getting into the car.

I shook my head. That was silly.

Tom walked around the car then got into the driver's seat. He looked at me with longing in his eyes. I could tell he didn't want the night to end. My thoughts were starting to conspire with his.

"Are you sure you won't come over? I'll be a perfect gentleman and I will drive you home the second you want to leave, I promise."

I didn't know him all that well, aside from dealing with him at the office for the last three years. During that time, he was always an upstanding gentleman. I wondered if it was some kind of act. It crossed my mind that his intention may have been to get me tipsy enough that I'd have to let him drive me home, but no one forced me to put the glass up to my lips.

Trust had been an issue for me. It was time to get passed the doubts and fears. I needed to take control of my life. Besides, the pocket knife in my purse was all the insurance I needed. The knife was a gift from my mother on my 16th birthday and I'd never used it, but it was comforting to know I concealed a sharp object.

Before I could convince myself to revert back to my old ways, I forced the words to leap from my lips, "Okay."

The excitement on his face flickered and disappeared as he once again gained his composure. The man had a poker face like no other.

We drove to the more ritzy side of town, where he pulled into a driveway longer than my house—times two. The house itself was about five times the size of mine. It had beautiful architectural style, which was modern, but with a flare of some more traditional details. He pulled up near the front door on the circular driveway, got out, and then went around the car to help me out.

Inside stood a grand entryway with a beautiful chandelier and a spiral staircase. He led me into the great room which housed a lounge area and a bar. The kitchen and dining area occupied the space as well. There was a large TV with what I estimated to be an 80 inch screen. Tom told me I could sit wherever I wanted then went to make drinks.

"I'm not sure I should have anymore," I said at the sight of a wine bottle.

"I was thinking I'd mix it with some Sprite, that way you would come down a little slower and have less of a chance of waking up with a headache tomorrow."

"Oh. Okay," I said. The reluctance in my own voice echoed through my words.

He finished making the drinks then set them on the coffee table. Mine was more of a light pink color while his was dark red, which made me a little more at ease. Then he picked up a small remote and turned on some music. It was classical. I didn't recognize the song, but I also don't listen to classical often.

In fact, music hadn't been a part of my life since my parents died. My mother was always the musical instigator in our house. The memories of the times we used to sing together were too painful for me to relive on my own.

"So, Ava, tell me about yourself. I feel the whole night was wasted talking about business and I've gotten no closer to knowing you," Tom said, leaning in closer to me.

"Well, I grew up in California, but I moved here with my parents when I was 17. They wanted to live somewhere even more carefree than California, so we came here. They loved waking up to the ocean in the morning. I took it all in until I graduated High School, then I got serious about going to business school, so I did that. They were so supportive and paid for all my schooling."

"They must be proud of you, I'd like to meet them someday if I get the chance," Tom said.

"I'm afraid they died in a car accident about four years ago, the day I got my Business Administration Degree. I would have liked for you to meet them too."

"I'm sorry for your loss, my dear," he said gently.

"I miss them every day. What about you? I'd like to know your story too."

"My story is long and boring, Ava. I suppose I could summarize though. I grew up on the East coast. My family and I traveled a lot. Mainly in the older parts of the US, where the colonies began and the history is strong. I also outlived my parents, like most children, but like your parents, their time came too soon. My mother died of cancer, and my father followed shortly after with an unknown illness. I went to business school and the School of Technology. After that, Psytech recruited me to be a Texpert and I worked my way up from there. See? Boring."

"No, not at all. Living on the east coast must have been interesting."

"It was certainly much different than Hawaii. Have you ever been to the east coast?"

"No, I've only been here and California. My mother didn't like to travel far from the ocean. She always said the ocean meant too much to our family to leave it behind," I said.

"We are so compatible, Ava," Tom said with a look in his eyes that said he wanted me. The way he said my name was like music. Even his voice was sexy. His charm was unquestionably turned on as his hand moved closer to mine.

"I only wish I'd asked you out sooner. Time is a terrible thing to waste," he said, seizing my hand and kissing the top of it. My stomach immediately filled with butterflies. Tom stroked my hand with his thumb, and turned it over so that my wrist was exposed, then kissed it.

"I hope you don't think I'm a violent person after I tried to take your wrist at the restaurant," he said, kissing it again.

My breath turned heavy.

"I meant it out of passion, not violence."

"Of, course," I managed to say, "I realize that."

The way he kissed my wrist made me want him to kiss my lips. I moved closer to him and met his eyes. His gaze intensified, and suddenly his lips were right where I wanted them. I kissed him back, then pulled away gently to catch my breath and his lips found my neck. He kissed it gently which sent my heart into a frenzy.

I put my hand on his chest and pulled away from him. I needed to gain my composure. This was headed for something I simply did not do on a first date.

"I'm sorry, Ava. I've broken my promise and have been less than a perfect gentleman. If you want me to take you home, I understand," Tom said.

"It's not that I didn't want you to kiss me, Tom, I need to take things slow. It's been an eventful night and my emotions are all over the place. I need some rest, so—I think I should go home, but I would like to see you again—outside of Herrick-Peyton that is."

"I would be delighted to be in your presence again. Let me take you home, I'll be on my best behavior."

We went to his car, and his gentleman ways did not disappear, he opened the car door again and helped me in. Then he went to his side, and started the car.

"Where do you live, my dear?"

I gave him my address and soon we were pulling into my driveway.

"I like your house," he said, "It's whimsical."

"It's the house my parents bought when we moved here to Hilo. It was left to me after their accident. My parents were lucky to get this house right on the beach with so much beautiful vegetation sprouting up everywhere. I'm so glad to carry on their dream of living this lifestyle."

"I would like to see the inside someday, but for tonight I'll walk you to the door and make sure you get in safely, and then I'll be on my way."

"Okay," I said, and with that, Tom got out of the car and let me out.

He walked me to the door with my hand in his. After unlocking my door, I locked eyes with him once more. He kissed my forehead softly and said, "If you give me your keys, I'll ask my personal assistant to bring your car here tomorrow morning so you can get to work."

"Okay, thank you, Tom," I said. I unclipped the car keys and placed them in his soft hand. He held onto mine and kissed the top of it before letting go.

"Good night, Ava. Sweet dreams."

"Good night," I said, as he walked to his car.

I closed the door behind me and a wide smile took over my mouth. I sighed and decided it was time to get ready for bed.

I turned on the radio. There was a re-run of the President's address to the nation and it said that they were no closer to finding out how to fix the satellites, or to figuring out who planted the virus.

Tomorrow would be another long day. I couldn't help but leave the radio on overnight. The music at Tom's house had unearthed something I'd buried deep inside, and I fell asleep listening to the midnight classical block.

CHAPTER THREE

The next day, I looked outside to see my car parked right where it should be. Tom's assistant had put the keys in an envelope and slid it into the mail slot so they landed on the floor inside my front door.

I continued to get ready for work even though I probably wouldn't be there long. The notion that I might see Tom meant I still wanted to look stunning. Excitement welled up inside me until I thought I might burst with a girly scream. Of course, I secretly hoped to see Tom and my mind began to think up possible reasons to go up to his office or ways I could bump into him. The previous night awakened something in me. I hadn't felt like a girl with a high school crush in such a long time.

On my way to Herrick-Peyton, I drove with care since stoplights were still out and the local police had given up on directing traffic. A long line awaited me at the security gate. It took about 10 minutes to get through. Simon was already walking into the building when I pulled into the lot. I assumed he carpooled with someone.

"Hello, Ava!" he said as we walked in together. He was in a slightly better mood than the previous day. "Staff meeting in half an hour!"

"Okay, boss."

I went to my desk and pulled out the paperwork I'd been neglecting. The disturbing thought that this may be the last time I'd have to fill out my revenue report came to the front of my mind. Then I remembered no one else knew.

They were all so unsuspecting of the coming events. Even Simon, whose whole life revolved around his career, didn't know what was coming. I wondered about the reaction Simon might have to Herrick-Peyton selling. I imagined he'd be upset by the news.

The meeting itself was pretty short and sweet. He talked about things we could do without our computers and the possibility of pulling out some old ones that would work as long as they weren't hooked up to the internet At the conclusion, Simon turned on the radio and told us to work in the boardroom if we wanted to keep updated.

I didn't want to hear it. Word would travel fast once the virus was fixed. One thing that wasn't traveling fast was supply ships from the mainland, so I made a mental note to stock up on groceries after work.

My paperwork took less time than I thought, considering I didn't use a computer. My hard copies of receipts provided all the information I needed, allowing me to complete my paperwork by lunchtime.

Simon was in his office when I went in to say I was done for the day and he gladly let me leave early. I clocked out and went to the lobby. I lingered so that I might catch Tom going out to lunch. Amazingly, he walked into the lobby about two minutes after I did. He immediately noticed me and approached with a smile.

"Ava, how are you today?" he asked.

"I'm doing great, how about you?"

"Much better, now that I've seen you," Tom mused.

"You aren't having a bad day are you?" I asked.

"No, it just lacked a certain spark until now. You light up my days, Ava," he said with that sly grin that came across his face frequently.

"That's sweet of you to say. Would you like to eat lunch together?"

"I wish I could, but, regrettably, I have a business lunch to attend with our, uh, visitors," he said gesturing to a group of pale men in suits.

I imagined they were most likely from New York and spent 24 hours a day in their offices.

"May I take a rain check?"

"Yes, that would be fine," I replied.

"How about I take you out to lunch tomorrow, after the big meeting?"

Tomorrow just seemed so soon for my life to change drastically, but at least he told me before everything happened. "Yes, then maybe we can discuss a few things I've been thinking about today."

"If you wish to talk about business we can, but I prefer to wait until after lunch to do that. I'm hoping to make up for our nearly disastrous dinner," Tom said.

I saw by the apology in his eyes he meant what he said. "Okay, I'd like that too, no business until after lunch then."

"Alright, my dear, I must leave you, but I will meet you here at noon tomorrow."

We parted ways, and I dove into my thoughts. Tom always seemed to be respectful. He was well-spoken and used manners from the last century. Maybe it was the way he was raised, but it was almost as if he were a time traveler. Something else about him—possibly the sly grin—made him seem dangerous.

I shook my head. I needed to stop thinking about Tom. Groceries should be my main focus right now. Not my budding romance with a client.

The grocery store was packed, but I'd gotten the idea soon enough that the shelves were still half stocked with food. The lines at the check-out were even worse than the aisles full of people. It took thirty minutes to get checked out and everyone had to pay with cash. I was glad that I kept a little cash on hand for emergencies. The banks were still down.

My home welcomed me at 5 p.m. as I dragged my bags of food inside and put everything away. Since I didn't have much cash, I had bought the cheap stuff in order to get by. So, I started with some ramen noodles and laughed to myself about the reference I made about them to Tom. I turned on the radio only to find that no new developments came up.

Psytech. Did I really want to work there? Working with Tom would be a bonus unless anything ever went bad between us. Then I'd have to find a new job. I did enjoy the prospect of picking my own position. At the same time, I wouldn't want the other employees to think I'd gotten the job just because I had a thing with the boss.

For every negative, a positive popped up beside it.

The money would be good, and I'd still work with the same people if they decided to stay. After much contemplation, I decided to give it a try, and if things didn't work out, I would get another job somewhere else. All that was left for me to do was tell Tom.

I finished my dinner with a sense of relief. The decision was made. Relief turned to determination, and I put that to good use by doing a little spring-cleaning. After cleaning virtually every room in the house, I ran out of steam. Sleep came on fast as I finally hopped in bed.

A strange dream interrupted my sleep. My mother appeared before me, but she seemed to drift away. I ran to keep up, but no matter how hard I tried to get to my mother, I couldn't gain any ground. The nagging feeling that my mother was trying to tell me something woke me in the middle of the night. Perturbed, I laid in bed, trying to get back to sleep; back to the dream. I knew it wasn't real, but finding out my mother's message seemed important.

Eventually, I fell back asleep, but the dream didn't wait for me. When my alarm sounded, I woke in an even more disturbed mood. The connection with my mother in my dream felt so real. I missed her. In an effort to clear my mind, I took in a deep breath.

The time had come to get ready for work. The day ahead was sure to be an interesting one. It was the day that Psytech would offer to buy the Herrick-Peyton building, not to mention my lunch date with Tom and my decision to work for Psytech if the deal went through..

The line at the gate wasn't so long this time. I wondered if most people gave up on even coming to work. Simon greeted me on my way in and relayed that there would be a mandatory meeting with the shareholders at one o'clock. I nonchalantly asked him what it was about and he told me that he didn't know. Deep down, I wanted to tell him, but to do so might get Tom in trouble, so I refrained.

Someone unearthed a few old computers from the storeroom and were using them to type up reports. Of course, those who used them were careful not to connect them to the internet. Because there weren't enough to go around, everyone had to take turns. With none free, I had to ask William, who seemed to be wrapping up, to let me know when he was finished. He nodded and asked if I knew anything about the meeting.

"I have no idea what's going on. I'm sure it's probably just about the recent events and what we're supposed to do about it," I said. The lie tasted like metal in my mouth.

He shrugged and continued on with his work, and I went to make a list of the things I needed to do on the computer. Most of my tasks were limited by the lack of internet connection and the fact that none of my files were on the old computers. After William let me know he was finished, I took over the computer and worked as quickly as possible. I wanted to finish before lunch so I wouldn't need to work after the meeting.

Finishing with a little time to spare, I filed more paperwork, and then got a few things in line, just in case they decided to sell. I resolved to help my clients find somewhere else to go. As noon rolled around, I was free to go to lunch with Tom. I met him in the lobby. His eyes found mine just as I entered the large open room. A sly grin crossed his face as his gaze touched me.

"Ava, you look lovely today, as always," Tom said, crossing the room to meet me.

I tried to conceal a smile. As if I could keep it away when Tom was around. "Thank you, Tom. You're so sweet. Are you ready for lunch?"

"Yes, where would you like to go?"

"Oh, somewhere simple. How about that café across the street?"

"That sounds good to me. Are we keeping with our no business deal?" he asked as we began to walk out. He placed a light hand on my lower back.

"Yes, we can talk business later. After the staff meeting, I'll come to the warehouse. We can talk there," I said.

The café was close to the main gate of Herrick-Peyton, so we walked to lunch, as we commented on how beautiful the day was. The floral aroma of Hilo was in the air. I loved the way the gardens perfumed the whole city when the breeze gently blew.

Tom bought lunch. It came as no surprise to me considering he was always the perfect gentleman. We sat at one of the outdoor tables with our sandwiches and talked.

"What is your middle name?" Tom asked, somewhat out of the blue.

"Mae, what's yours?" I said. A giggle escaped my lips.

"Lorence. Who is your biggest role model? The person who's influenced you the most?" he asked. He leaned forward as I thought about my answer.

"My mom, I suppose. She always taught me to follow my dreams no matter what anyone said. She supported me in everything I did. She helped me find myself."

The conversation went on as we asked each other more questions; anything to keep the conversation from veering towards business. Too soon, we had to return to Herrick-Peyton. In the lobby we said our good-byes. Tom stopped me from walking away too quickly.

"Technically, it's not lunch anymore, so I'm going to tell you. Herrick-Peyton took the offer. Act surprised when they announce it at your meeting, and I'll see you soon, okay?"

Tom said. Our eyes stayed locked together as he boarded the elevator.

Once he was gone, I steadied my mind. This was actually happening. I was going to be changing jobs.

I turned and then went into my office where the meeting was about to begin. Everyone had gathered in the big boardroom. I imagined everyone expected instructions for the time that the satellites were going to be out, or maybe they thought we were all in some kind of trouble. Of course, I knew better than that.

One of the shareholders stood at the front while the rest of them sat on each side of the table. He was the prime shareholder in the company, Joe Herrick.

"Alright people, let's get started," Herrick announced in a monotone voice.

Everyone quieted down and turned their attentions to him.

"Today, the shareholders attended a meeting with Psytech, a worldwide company that has a rapidly expanding branch here in Hawaii. You may also be aware, they are Ava Tanner's clients. It is so rapidly expanding, in fact, that they need a building our size, and so they offered to buy our building and the ten warehouses. After much discussion, we decided to accept their offer."

Everyone gasped, and I did too just to play along. Whispers filled the room.

"Calm down everyone. Now, Psytech has extended a welcoming arm to our employees here at Herrick-Peyton. If you wish, you may take a position in their company at the same or higher pay. There will be a sign-up tomorrow from 9 a.m. to 5 p.m. if you wish to accept this job offer. They will place you where they believe you would do best, and if you wish to accept, please do so with a free conscience as we will no longer be active as a company and will have no need for your services. Simon will find places for your clients to move to and has been offered an exceptional position within the Psytech Company."

I looked to Simon. Apparently, the news of a job offer from Psytech was a surprise to him as well. Everyone else fell silent after the whispers died down. The other shareholders seemed like they were under some sort of spell, probably trying to contain their excitement over the money they'd just come into.

Someone asked, "What if we don't want to take the job from Psytech?"

Joe Herrick responded, "If you do not wish to work with Psytech, you will be paid two month's severance from Psytech, and you can take your chances finding another job elsewhere."

After that, I tuned out. I didn't care what everyone decided right now. In my opinion, they'd be stupid not to take the job offer. I desperately wanted the meeting to be over so I could go talk to Tom. After a few more grueling questions from my co-workers, the meeting adjourned. The shareholders left first, and I was caught up by my co-workers asking me what I would do. Everyone seemed to think it was a huge scandal, but the truth is, things like this happen every day. I reacted just as strongly when I first heard the news, but I didn't control the company. Sure things like buying a company building didn't always happen so fast, but I knew what my future held. When I was finally able to disengage myself, I rushed outside and made my way to the warehouse.

Tom waited for me outside the door of the warehouse. When I neared him, his smile changed from happy to his sly grin he used so often.

"Ava, I'm so glad you made it. Come on in, we're discussing the companies' new direction right now," Tom said as he motioned for me to enter.

I wondered why they were discussing it out in the warehouse instead of in the comfort of the office. As I crossed the threshold, I felt uneasy. I hoped to talk to Tom privately, but the group of men that came to buy Herrick-Peyton were all gathered around a table with a laptop on it. I wasn't sure why. It wasn't possible for the thing to work. When I neared the table, I realized the laptop was connected to a live stream of some sort. On the screen, another businessman spoke via video chat. He saw me and smiled. The rest of the men turned their attention to me.

The laptop had a strange device connected to it that resembled a flash drive, but much smaller. A glowing purple gemstone was embedded into the black plastic.

"How did you get it to work?" I asked Tom. "Are the satellites fixed?"

"Ava, we are the most technologically advanced company in the world. What good would we be if we couldn't figure out something so simple?"

"But, why haven't you told anyone you have a solution?" I asked, still confused about what I saw.

"Because, sweet Ava, we caused it," Tom said with a chuckle as if it were obvious.

Things started to make sense now. Of course, they caused it. They had so many experts and made more technological advances than any other company, so they were the most capable of infecting the entire world with a computer virus.

"Why?" I asked as I backed away. All he represented now was betrayal. He'd obviously known from the beginning, and even before.

"In this day and age, technology is power. If you control technology, you control the world. Psytech has been planning this for a very long time, and we're glad you decided to join us. Now you can share the power."

"I don't think this is right, Tom. How could you do this?"

"Ava, our kind has been waiting for power like this for centuries now, and you joining us in this expedition will make us even stronger," Tom explained.

"Our kind? I'm not in the corporate game, and I don't want to be in your company anymore. You are not the person I thought you were." I turned to walk out of the warehouse, but Tom moved to block my way.

"You know very little of me, but soon, everything will make sense. When I said 'our kind,' I meant me and my associates. You are not yet one of us, but we can make you just like us, and once you are, you'll want the power. The need will grow within you. You'll be the perfect addition to our team."

"What is the point? Turning everything back to the Middle Ages is just cruel, you'll have no control over anyone, and they will run wild."

"We don't intend to turn the world to turmoil like that— at least, not for long. We do intend to control everyone. In the end, everyone will make a choice. Either submit to us or live without the luxuries."

"Submit? I don't understand. What is it you need from us?"

"Not from you, my dear, no. I want you to be with us. You'll be like royalty. The need we have is from those who will become like slaves to us."

"Slaves? You want everyone to work for free in return for technology? You're delusional."

Tom and the other men laughed. Then, he showed his sly grin, once again, only this time he showed something more . . . fangs.

My mind raced. What on earth did I just see? Was it real? Was it even possible? Could he really be a . . . a vampire?

I could hardly even think it. It seemed so absurd. My adrenaline coursed through my veins.

I looked around the room. They were all vampires. I wasn't imagining things. All of them brandished their fangs. My heart beat faster and I prayed for it to slow down so I could get up the courage to get out of the warehouse. My feet wouldn't move.

I quickly tried to use my breathing to steady my heart and then slowly backed away toward the door. Tom saw what I was doing and walked toward me slowly, but faster than I was backing toward the door.

"My, you connect the dots quickly don't you?" he said, showing his fangs once more.

"What are you? You can't be a . . ."

"Vampire? Yes, I can be, and you can be too." Tom disappeared into a blur and popped up behind me. He circled me, but kept a little distance between us. He was like a shark getting closer to his prey with every rotation.

"You see, we're going to use technology to get the blood we need from humans. Their donations will ensure that their lives stay relatively normal."

He stood within inches of me. Shivers traveled along my spine and I started to panic. I stumbled over words to say in order to distract him. The only thing that came to mind was, "But--you were out in the sunlight; all the legends say you can't go into the sun."

"Oh, Ava, those legends are spread by us to make humans who believe in us think they're safe. We exaggerate things so that it seems we can't possibly exist." He went for my hand.

I froze at the thought of him touching me. He held it gently just as before. He pulled me farther into the warehouse, toward the other vampires. I had to distract him. He wanted me to be one of them and I shuddered at the thought.

"The time of hiding and keeping our secret will soon come to an end," he shouted to the room full of vampires as they all clapped.

Finally, a clear thought came to me. I needed to get more information and then escape. If I had enough information, I might be able to find someone who could stop them. If I could get anyone to believe me.

"So, when you said you'd been working for this company for what seemed like a hundred years . . ."

"I meant it," he finished for me. I searched for a way to escape. A ladder led to the upper level of the warehouse only ten feet away. I remembered the pocket knife in my purse. My mother's notion to give it to me had finally come in handy.

"Enough stalling, Ava. We must do this now. Trust me. Our side is the one you want to be on. You don't want to be a slave to us." He motioned for one of the men to bring a chair. "You may want to sit down for this. At first, you will be weak, but when we get some blood in you, you'll be stronger than you ever imagined."

I sat on the swivel chair, but only because Tom was so close that he towered over me. I needed room to think.

He turned around for a moment to address his associates. "And so begins a new era for vampires. An era of prosperity. An era of power beyond our wildest imaginations."

I slid my hand into my purse as he gave his little speech. When he turned back, I was waiting with my knife. His fangs came at me as I flipped open the knife and stabbed him in the chest. I turned in the chair and dashed for the ladder, and then climbed without looking down. As I reached the top, Tom laughed.

"There's nowhere to run," he called out. "I'm not sure you want to be up there anyway, we're keeping a few, uh, meals up there."

I observed the boxes I hid behind. They were more like coffins. The one next to me had a name on it: Joe Herrick. Another said: David Peyton. As I turned my attention to the others I recognized a few more names. Shareholder names.

"They should have read the fine print!" Tom laughed and the others laughed with him. I wanted to burst into tears, but if I were to succumb to my emotions, I would not leave the warehouse alive, or at least, not human.

"The contract they signed also signed over their blood to us. They are no longer human, nor are they vampires. Once you sign a contract like the one they signed, you become a zombie. There are ways of making people sign those. You don't want that to happen to you, do you? They will spend the rest of their existence doing our bidding and providing us with blood. That's not what I want from you. I want you to be a full-blooded vampire, but if you're going to be difficult, I'll hand you the same fate we handed them."

I bit back tears. There was no way out. I was trapped and the future I'd been so sure of before disappeared. Now it was either eat or be eaten.

"Come down here now and stop this foolishness. I could easily come up, but things might get . . . violent. I'll overlook the fact that you stabbed me if you come down on your own."

I was scared and I didn't know what to do. The ladder I came up was the only way up or down besides the hydraulic lift that was no help sitting in the down position.

"Please, don't do this to me. I can't be like you. I'm not cut out for it."

There was a long silence and then Tom spoke. "I can change your mind. I know it seems scary, but I'll make you a deal. I'll wait three days to change you if you promise to keep an open mind. If you give me three days, you'll see that you could have everything you ever dreamed about. You will stay with me at all times and see what your life could be like. I'm sure after the first day you'll be begging me to change you."

It was likely a trick, but I had no choice. Maybe I bought myself some time. I obviously couldn't trust Tom anymore, but there was no way out of this warehouse full of vampires. How could I be sure he'd keep his word? I went over to the ladder and looked down at him.

"Come. You don't want me to come up there and get you. There's no escape."

I sighed and turned around. The ladder rungs felt cold on my hands as I eased down them. Tears came to my eyes.

Before I reached the last few rungs an arm wrapped around my waist. It was Tom. I struggled against his hold, but it was no use. His strength was no match for me.

"That wasn't so hard, was it?" he whispered into my ear then set me down.

"Put a wristband on her," he said as he held out my wrist to one of the men. This man—vampire—was different than the others. I saw him in the Herrick-Peyton building before and he wasn't one of the visiting vampires. His eyes were bright green—just like the secretary. I tried to resist him putting on the wristband, but he locked it onto me anyway.

"This device is a handy little thing." Tom said. "Here's the simple version. If you wander too far from me, it will start to beep. If it beeps ten times the device will deliver a dose of my venom into your system and you will be changed whether you want to or not. I prefer you to be compliant because, well, I do still like you, even though you stabbed me. Not to mention, I want to be the one to change you. Your blood taunted me through your wrist and your neck the other night. It's a wonder I didn't change you then."

I cringed at the reminder that I actually made out with this monster. I glanced at his chest where the stab wound should be. There was no blood. Just a hole in his shirt and no wound. The rules were different in real life than they were in the movies. The knife my mother gave me was broken in pieces on the floor. I touched the wristband.

"If you try to tamper with that wristband, it will inject you," Tom said with a smile. I turned my head away and crossed my arms. I couldn't believe what was happening. I didn't know it could be possible. One thing I knew beyond a doubt, I had to get away, and I had less than three days to do so.

CHAPTER FOUR

Tom grabbed my arm and brought me toward the door of the warehouse. The other vampires followed.

"We'll meet here again tomorrow," he said as we stopped at the door and the others filed out. Some of them said good-byes and some did not. I watched them pass by as they looked at me as though I were something to eat.

After they left, Tom turned to me and said, "Don't worry about them. They won't hurt you. I already formally claimed you as my prospect, and vampire law forbids them to bite you or drink your blood. Also, I told them about you and they want you to be one of us almost as badly as I do."

"That's comforting," I said. My voice was thick with sarcasm and hatred. He kept my arm in his grasp and it tightened when the words hit him.

"Don't act this way, my little dove, you are only making things worse with such an attitude," he said as he touched my cheek with his fingertips. I flinched away and he released my arm.

"Forgive me if I don't want to be a blood-sucking monster."

"You're just nervous. Don't worry. Only the initial bite hurts. You'll see soon enough that this life is a grand life.

Now, we are going to your house so you can gather some things and then we'll go to my place. Please, don't fight me on this. What I say goes right now, but once you're one of my equals, you'll be able to make your own decisions and go where you please."

"Why not leave me human? You say you have feelings for me. What if you let me stay human to make me happy?"

"I can't do that. If you stayed human would you stay with me? Even if you did, vampire law forbids a human who knows about us to stay human for long. Eventually, they'd force you to become a vampire or die. I care about you too much to let that happen. I'd much rather have you for an eternity."

I couldn't believe what he just said. He was talking about an eternity and I barely even knew him. I didn't want this. I wanted to go back and decline his offer to take me on a date. I'd let my guard down, and now I couldn't find a way out of this mound of trouble.

A monster named Tom and his pet named Ava. The horrible thought sent shivers down my spine.

"What if I don't want you for an eternity?" I asked. I put my hand over my mouth as soon as the words escaped. I waited for his reaction. He walked toward me but stopped short. An emotion flickered on his face, possibly sadness, but most likely anger.

It was gone as quickly as it had shown, and he simply stared me straight in the eye and said, "Then I guess your life will be shorter than expected."

He grabbed my arm and walked us out of the warehouse. His car waited there. Tom opened the door and put me inside before he slammed the door. The tears were coming on again, and I tried to fight them but I lost before he even got to his door. Tom got in the car then turned his gaze on me at me.

"I didn't mean to frighten you. Please, don't cry. This is how it has to be, we can't risk you running and telling the world what we are planning. It is crucial that our kind remain a secret for now."

"I won't tell anyone, I swear," I said through my sobs, "Just let me go."

"I can't do that, and I will not argue with you over this matter. You will be one of us, or you will die at the hands of my associates."

"But you said that they couldn't hurt me."

"They can if I renounce my claim. I'll be forced to if you chose not to allow me to change you," he said harshly.

"I can't believe you are trying to force me to be with you. Don't you have any respect for my wishes?"

"I know you had feelings for me before I told you my secret, can't you put that aside and let me show you my way of life. Please give me a chance. Vampires starve to keep our existence a secret. We've only been feeding when we need it. Now that we control something that humans want, we can procure enough blood to let us thrive."

"Why not just go out on a killing spree? Why even set up a system like this?" I asked.

"If we are let loose on the population, we will kill every last food source. However, if we work with the humans and get them to donate blood, we will keep ourselves fed and keep the human race alive and subordinate."

"How can you do this? I thought you were someone else."

"Ava, I'm trying to survive. I was changed against my will. They wanted me to be one of them because I have tremendous leadership skills. I want you to survive too, but I don't want your blood being drawn and distributed as if you were a dairy cow. I can't stand the thought of anyone else drinking your blood. I'm trying to protect you. Don't you understand that?"

"Protect me? You want to turn me into a vampire! How is that protecting me?"

"You need to understand. Try to understand, please," he said. His hands gripped the steering wheel and his foot pressed on the gas pedal a little harder.

"All I can think about right now is the way you acted in the warehouse. You seemed evil. That's the only way I can describe it. I will only think of you that way from now on. How can I see you in any other light? You're doing all this against *my* will," I said.

"I was putting on an act, Ava. I had to do that in front of them. The politics in my world are complicated. You'll figure that out soon enough," Tom said as he pulled up to my house.

I didn't want to believe him, but his eyes seemed truthful. I couldn't trust him, not after what I'd been through today.

"Come on," he said, "Let's get your things together. We can discuss this more at my house." He got out of the car and went to the other side to let me out. He grabbed my arm again.

"Why do you keep pulling me around like this? I have this stupid wristband on. I can't do anything," I said, gesturing to his hold on me and down to the wristband.

"I don't want you to do anything stupid, okay? I can tell that you're angry and I want to make sure you don't act on this strong emotion. It would not end well."

"Don't worry, I'll be on my best behavior," I said and suddenly flashed back to the night we went out. The gentleman he pretended to be had disappeared. Part of me

48

longed for that passionate kiss again, but I stopped myself from thinking about it. I couldn't lose focus on my escape or the fact that Tom was a monster masquerading as a gentleman.

Once inside, I gathered my things. I did it slowly, to make sure I got all the necessities.

"I have food for you at my house," Tom said when I went to the kitchen.

"I'm afraid a bag of blood doesn't sound appetizing," I snapped.

"Don't be so cruel. My only wish is to make you as comfortable as possible."

I didn't reply. I simply moved on to the living room and packed a few movies into my bag. I wouldn't use them, but at that point I stuffed more and more things into my bag to further irritate Tom. He grew impatient. After stuffing a few more pointless items into my bag, I mentally prepared myself to be his captive until I figured out what to do.

We rode in silence to his house. The place looked bigger and more intimidating since the night cap after our date. He opened the door for me, yet again. A glimmer of the gentleman he'd been during our date returned. I told myself it was an act. The real Tom was the man I'd seen in the warehouse.

"Alright," he said as he typed in a code on a screen on the wall, "You may go wherever you want to in this house. I switched the signal from my beacon to the home perimeter. If you leave this house, you will be injected with venom. Anything of mine is yours. You can do whatever you want. Go ahead and explore if you wish."

"Okay," I replied. The couch was the only thing familiar to me, so I set up camp there. Tom sat down at the opposite end which gave me the space I needed to process things.

"I'm not evil, Ava. I may have been wrong to drag you into this, but sooner or later a vampire would have found you and made you sign a contract or done something even worse, something unfathomable. I don't want you to live like that. Or die like that."

"Fine, whatever makes you feel better," I said flatly.

Tom changed the subject. "Is there anything I can get you? Are you hungry?"

"No, I'm not hungry. A blanket would be nice. I'm tired."

Tom went to the closet and pulled out a blanket and a pillow. He set down the pillow and gently laid the blanket over me.

"Get some rest," he said. I stared at the blank TV and tried to think of a plan. Nothing came to mind. I suspected it was because I was still trying to process everything. I gave up and fell asleep.

I woke to the sound of Tom's voice. "Ava? Ava? Wake up, my dear."

I opened my eyes. Tom had made me breakfast, which seemed strange to me. I didn't think it could be morning. I thought I'd only taken a short nap. When I checked the clock, however, it read 8:00 a.m.

"You slept for about 14 hours. Are you feeling alright?"

"Yeah, I guess. I'm not sick or anything, just groggy." Shit. I slept away 14 hours of my precious plotting time.

"I made you breakfast. I didn't know what you'd like so I made a little of everything. Toast; white and wheat, four different kinds of eggs, pancakes, bacon, sausage, ham, hash browns, French toast and waffles," he said as he gestured to the coffee table covered with food. I blinked and rubbed my eyes. I thought I was seeing double or triple with the amount of food in front of me.

"I also got you milk, chocolate milk, orange juice, apple juice, coffee and water."

I turned my attention to him then back to the table again. I told myself not to fall for his façade. He was being kind so that I'd warm up to him and allow him to change me into a vampire.

"I'm not hungry," I said.

"Of course you are. You haven't eaten since lunch yesterday. Please, eat something. I wouldn't poison you or anything," he said looking at me with arched brows. "Is there something else you want? I could make you anything. Bagels? I should have gotten bagels. I'll get you some." He stood, seeming to be losing it. He thought that bagels would make me like him and want to be a vampire. Bagels.

"No, I don't want bagels. I'll eat what you prepared," I said then picked up the French toast and he handed me a few different syrups and a fork. I took the maple and poured it over the two slices. He had three types of jelly, peanut butter, powdered sugar, butter, cinnamon sugar, and any breakfast condiment I could imagine and more. After the French toast, I went for the scrambled eggs and bacon then drank the chocolate milk. All the while Tom watched me. Once finished, I pulled the blanket back over me and laid back down.

"Is there anything I can do for you?"

"No," I said, not wanting to be bothered. I wanted to be left alone to my thoughts and figure out a way out of the mess I fell into yesterday. Tom sat with me a few more minutes then cleared the coffee table. After that, running water and clinking echoed from the kitchen. Once silence fell, he came over to me and took my hand. I snatched it away and glared at him. He seemed somewhat irritated for a moment, but the expression quickly faded.

"I want you to think of yourself as more of a guest than a prisoner. I want to remind you that you can go where you please in this house. There is a guest room on the second floor where I put your things. It has a bathroom and everything you may need. Would you like me to show it to you?"

I didn't reply. I simply sat up and looked at him. He pulled me up then led me to the spiral staircase, where he helped me climb the stairs as if I were a child. It annoyed me, but I needed to focus less on my hatred for him and more on how to get away from him. We stopped at the second door on the right. He turned the handle then ushered me in. A king-size bed with luxurious linens sat in the far corner. A large dresser and armoire sat side by side across from it. Tom walked to a door on the far wall and then opened it. A large tub with jets, a separate shower, a large vanity, sink and, of course, a toilet made up the inside.

"This is your room. If you need any further amenities, please tell me and I'll send my assistant out for them."

"Thank you," I said, with little sincerity before I sat on the bed and took in my surroundings.

"I'll leave you to your privacy," Tom said with a little bow of his head. He left the room, and shut the door behind him.

I decided to take a shower. The bathroom was bigger than my bedroom at home. I gave another look at the large bathtub and thought a hot bath would be better. Hot baths helped me think.

Once the water came close to the top of the tub, I sunk into the water. I rested my head on the side and began to think.

Still, nothing came to me. My brain simply didn't want to believe that any of this was happening and therefore refused to find a solution.

When I finished, I got dressed and went to the enormous bed. The hopelessness began to weigh me down and I situated myself in a comfortable position as more tears threatened to come. Moments later, a knock came at the door.

"Yes?" I said.

"We must go to the office earlier than expected, there is an emergency," he said, "NASA is close to finding the virus and we must get a team to create a solution."

"I don't want any part of this," I said firmly.

"That's too bad because you are coming with me whether you like it or not. Have you forgotten about the wristband?" he asked.

I glanced at the thing tightly locked around my wrist. "No."

Tom stepped toward me. "Come along."

He loaded me into the car once more then sped down the roadway. He seemed eager to get to the office. His cell phone rang. It had a device connected to it, like the one in the laptop at the warehouse.

"Walker . . . I know, we need the Texperts and Sarah on this immediately. Find the best and get them into the warehouse, I'll be there in 10 minutes . . . If they figure out how to remove the virus our whole plan is in jeopardy and it will be your head." Tom hung up the phone and sped up.

I grabbed the handle as we raced around the turns in the road. His jaw hardened and his knuckles turned white as he gripped the steering wheel. His attention then focused on me, and his angry expression faded and his speed slowed. I wished he would keep his eyes on the road, but I was glad he slowed down a little.

"When we arrive, I want you to stay close to me. There are going to be a lot of my kind there and they may not be on their best behavior. Just because they can't hurt you doesn't mean they won't try to get you into trouble. They've been known to lure banded prospects away from the vampire wearing the beacon. Once the venom is injected, you are no longer considered a prospect, but your blood will still be desirable for about ten minutes. They will take advantage of that time," he said firmly.

Fear pulsed into my veins.

We pulled up to the gate. The security guard nodded us on. Todd or whatever his name was looked different. More "zombie" like. I wondered if he'd signed a contract, and if so, how many others had done the same.

We pulled up to the warehouse. Tom got out and went around, opened my door, then led me inside. I remained right behind him, afraid to go too far from his side. The second we walked in, all eyes turned to us.

There were a lot of people in the warehouse. I assumed they were all vampires. He quickly announced I was his prospect, and most of them went on with their business. A few, however, peered at me with devious eyes. My heartbeats sped up again, like it had the last time I was in the warehouse.

Tom rushed to an area resembling a command center. In the place of the simple table and laptop was a row of computers with multiple screens. Three Texperts worked frantically to keep their plan from falling apart.

"We've put up more roadblocks," one of them said.

"Good, but we need to get someone in there. We need someone to go to NASA's mainframe and trash it. There shouldn't be a way around this, but we can't be too careful," Tom said. He turned to one of the men I recognized from the last time I was here. He was one of the higher-up authorities. "If we don't get someone into NASA, we're going to be dangerously close to losing all our work here. This has been in the works for years. The Emperor will not be happy."

"Pick someone," the man said assertively. "Get him on a plane by tonight."

"Soon we'll have a more permanent solution and we can pull him out of there," Tom said. "I have men working around the clock."

"Good. It looks like you have things under control here. We will take our leave tonight. See that your man gets into NASA, and be in contact next week. I do need to speak to you alone before we leave," he said. He gestured to me when he said the last sentence.

"Yes, I'll meet you in the control room in a moment," Tom said, then turned to me and took my by the arm again to lead me to a chair.

"Stay right here," he said. "Don't talk to anyone."

He left me there . . . alone . . . in a warehouse full of vampires.

I watched them at work. There were at least fifty running around. Some were on cell phones. Some were on computers. After about five minutes, one approached.

"You're Ava right?" he said. He was the one who put the wristband on me.

I didn't want risk anything, so I nodded and turned so that I could see him out of the corner of my eye. His gaze wandered and then settled back on me.

"Tom sent me. I'm supposed to take you to him."

I looked at the man again. He was thin, with dark blonde hair. I wasn't sure he was telling the truth. Tom told me to wait here. I couldn't tell if he was still in the control room or not. This had to be a trick.

"I'm his assistant, James. I'm the one that brought you your car the other night."

"You're also the one that put this on me yesterday." I gestured to the wristband.

"Boss's orders," James said.

I thought it over some more. It was possible Tom had sent him. If he were going to send anyone it would be his assistant. I tried to get a better read on James, but nothing came. He stood there, staring at me. Then he held out his hand and I stood up, cautiously, but didn't give him my hand. Instead, I crossed my arms and looked around one last time for Tom.

"Right this way," he said. He walked toward the back of the warehouse. Soon we were almost at the back wall and my wristband started beeping, which meant he wasn't taking me to Tom at all. The beeps kept coming, three, four, five six, seven, eight, nine . . . I closed my eyes and counted the beeps that signaled my approaching death. Suddenly, they stopped and I heard Tom's voice.

"I thought I told you to stay put," he growled. Then he turned to James, "What are you doing back here, James?"

"I thought you came back here, I was simply trying to bring her to you," James said with an evil looking smile.

"Did I ask you to bring her to me?"

"No, but a prospect shouldn't be left alone, I thought you'd appreciate it." He still had a smile across his face.

"Well, James, I'm afraid I can't trust you anymore. Find a new Swami. Give me your pendant, now." Tom held out his hand, and the smile disappeared from James' face. James pulled out a necklace from under his shirt and took the pendant off of it and tossed it to Tom. The pendant had a W on it with five rubies. One at each point. James scowled at him as Tom grabbed my arm, yet again. He swiftly took me out of the warehouse and to the car.

"You can't be doing things like that. It will get you killed, Ava," Tom lectured as we sped away. "If I hadn't gotten to you in time he would have drained you. You must understand that even people who work for me are not trustworthy."

"What was that pendant thing all about?" I asked curiously.

"New vampires must study under a Swami Vampire for their first two years. The Swami teaches the new vampire about the laws and ways of a vampire. New vampires must wear a pendant to show who their Swami is. If any new vampire is caught without a pendant, they have three days to find a Swami."

"How can you tell if a vampire is 'new' or not?"

"The bright green eyes are a dead giveaway. After about two years, a vampire's eyes turn dark brown or blue."

"And what happens if you don't find a Swami in the time given?"

"You're killed. It's our way of making sure that we live civilized and not like wild animals. Swamis are important and trustworthy vampires. You don't get the title handed to you. You get it by being on your best behavior. Your record must be clean. When you're changed, I will be your Swami," Tom said. The words had a horrifying finality to them that produced a lump in my throat.

I sat and stared out the window. He said "when" not "if". Another reminder that I had to escape. I'd almost wasted a whole day, and I was no closer to a plan. "How did you know where to find me?"

"I didn't. I thought logically about where someone might take you. Outside is too risky, and I was toward the front of the warehouse, so I assumed you were at the back. All I had to do was get within range of you in ten seconds or less."

"How did you even know that I'd left your range?" I pried.

"My beacon beeps when your wristband beeps," he explained.

So he'd be alerted the second I left. Great. I needed more information in order to get away.

"You got to me quickly."

"Yes, well we're fast and strong. That legend is true."

I pondered this for a while and checked Tom over for the "beacon". He wore no necklace or wristband that I could see.

"It can't be seen by humans," he said bluntly.

"What?" I asked.

"The beacon. You were looking for it right?"

"No, I was just . . . studying you," I said. I needed to throw him off the trail. "I know so little about you, so I'm trying to understand who you are and what you can do."

"I'm surprised that you didn't look for it sooner," he said with a grin. He could see right through me. I needed to build his trust.

"Really, Tom. I only wanted to study you," I said. Warmth washed over my cheeks and neck. I had to manipulate him the way he tried to manipulate me. "Tell me more about the vampire world?"

"Ava, my dear, you will have plenty of time to hear about it after you are changed. Now, how would you like spaghetti for dinner?" he asked.

"Okay," I replied.

CHAPTER FIVE

We arrived at his house, and then he got out and opened my door like always. We both sat on the couch again. After a few moments of silence, Tom started cooking dinner. Scents of vinegar, garlic, and boiled pasta filled the air.

"Time to eat," he called to me after a while.

"I want to know more before you change me. I don't like going into anything blind," I said.

"I had a feeling you'd say something like that. I suppose I telling you some of the simple things and setting you straight on the legends won't hurt. First, we do have reflections. That is a legend made up to give humans a false sense of protection. Second, garlic does not keep us away nor does holy water or crosses," he said as he took a large bite of garlic bread and smiled for my benefit. "They're all lies made up so humans could believe they had defenses against us. And, you already know about the sunlight thing. Also, we can't turn into bats." Tom gave a little chuckle.

"Can anything kill us?" I asked. I thought if I used the word 'us' he would think I'd accepted my fate and would trust me with this information, but he saw through the word as if it were made of glass. To my surprise, he didn't draw attention to my failed attempt to manipulate him.

"That, dear Ava, will wait until after you are changed. It's not that I don't trust you, but it's part of vampire law. Also, vampire law states no vampire may kill another vampire unless a major crime is committed."

"What are the major crimes?"

"Killing a vampire without cause. Killing another vampire's prospect or drinking the blood of another vampire's prospect. Revealing the secrets of killing a vampire to any non-vampire. There are other things, but that's for another day."

We sat in silence for a few minutes. Nothing he said helped me. The desire to kill him didn't exist, but I wanted to get away from all this, and to do that I needed to learn his weaknesses. He took my wrist in his hand. His eyes roamed over it for a while. My wrist began to feel like a prized jewel, but his eyes traveled up to mine and he said, "Why don't you let me change you now?"

His fingers curled and showed off his well-groomed nails on my skin. "Don't worry. I won't change you before the three days are up unless you ask me. Why won't you let me do it now? You sounded like you wanted it a few seconds ago."

"I—I just want to wait. I'm still afraid. Afraid it will hurt. Afraid I won't be myself after," I tried to lie as convincingly as I could, but the words came out forced, like baby birds being pushed by their mother to fly.

"Ava, I will do everything I can to make sure you remain your lovely self. I was still the same man after my transition. My personality remains intact even after two hundred years."

One thought ran across my mind like a stock market ticker: How did he become this? With these thoughts, I realized I needed to beat him psychologically rather than physically to get out of this mess.

My voice took over and I asked, "Would you tell me the story of how you came to be a vampire?"

"If you think it would put you more at ease, I would be happy to. I must warn you, it's not the most interesting story. You may even fall asleep," he said with a smile.

"I want to hear it," I said. My lips trembled as I formed a smile.

"I was born in 1794. What I told you about my parents was true. We lived on the east coast, amongst the historic American roots. After my mother died, I was devastated. I was 20 years old. Then, at 21, my father died. In 1817, just after my 23rd birthday, I met a man named Henry Orris. He offered to take me in. At the time, I was homeless, jobless, and lonely. I accepted his offer. He had me do odd jobs for him, but his plans for me were more sinister. I was with him for almost a year. On my 24th birthday, he changed me. I didn't even see it coming.

"His bite stung. It spread to the rest of my body, and I became weak. He brought me a beggar, a man I'd seen many times on the side of the street. He told me to bite him and feed to regain my strength. At first, I refused. He told me I needed to drink or I would die . . . so, I drank. The decision came down to me or the beggar and I had a feeling that the beggar would die no matter what I did. I experienced hesitation to sink my teeth into him at first, but instinct took over. His skin broke and unleashed just one drop. Suddenly, I grew fangs, and with them came more blood. Soon it ran like a fountain, and I drank him dry."

I put my hand up to my mouth and glanced down at my plate. Spaghetti didn't seem like the right food for this conversation. He'd gone through so much. I realized his thirst wasn't a choice, but a primal instinct. One that took over his body and would take over mine if I didn't get out of here.

"Do you want me to stop? I've upset you."

"No," I said. I cleared my throat. "I want to hear it all."

"Alright. After my transition, Henry taught me about the vampire world. He was my Swami. You might have seen him at the warehouse today. He was the one I went to talk to. Thirty-five years after my transition, I was put into business school after being introduced to the Emperor. The Emperor saw something in me and told me that I must learn everything I could for the greater good of the vampire world. He said that something big was coming and that I would be a big part of it. Psytech was created in 1990 and I was drafted to be a Texpert. And, just like I told you before, I worked my way up. The Emperor expected a lot from me, and I didn't want to let him down. The politics of it are so complicated. If I had not excelled as expected I would have been disposed of. Once the Emperor appoints you as a leader—" He paused. "There is no choice in matters such as this. After I earned my position here, I was named a Swami. My symbol is the ruby-studded 'W' you saw earlier."

I took a deep breath then said, "At least you told me most of the truth before. I'm sorry that I labeled you a liar in my head after yesterday's events. I understand you a little more now," I said. Some of the clouds in my mind dissipated and I understood why he acted like a monster before, but I still couldn't agree with the way he lived.

"I'm glad that you understand now. I hope that you also understand why I must change you."

I remained silent for a moment, then answered, "Yes, I understand why you want to change me. I just wish there were another way."

"I do too. Sometimes I wish I had never been changed. At the same time, I'm glad, because I would have never met you if I hadn't been," he said, looking into my eyes.

"How can you say that? You barely know me."

"I can say that because you are the first woman I've been drawn to since I changed. I have never kissed a woman the way I kissed you the other night. The intense attraction has been there since the first day our eyes met and since then I have done everything in my power to make sure that you were safe."

"What do you mean? I haven't been in any danger until the last couple days."

"There was a night that you left work late and there were muggers stalking you. I put an end to that before they could get anywhere near you. Then, there was the time your house caught fire. If you're still wondering how you got out after you passed out on the floor, I'm the one who pulled you to safety before putting out the fire."

I flashed back to the night of the fire. I remembered someone—a shadow—standing over me and pulling me out. The fire started outside my bedroom door in the hallway. I was trapped. My window wouldn't open and I passed out from smoke inhalation before I could break it. They told me afterward the cause was bad wiring. They weren't sure who put out the fire or how I got out.

"That was you? But, why? Why would you do all that for me?"

"I just didn't want anything to happen to you. You were always so kind and polite to me, no matter what. I wouldn't be able to live with myself if I let anything bad happen to you. Anyone who is as loyal and caring as you should live a long life. There aren't many people like you around today, and if you stuck around, you'd rub off on some other people."

"How do you know all this? How do you know the kind of person I am?"

"I looked into your financial records. I shouldn't have, but I found that all the money in your account at the end of the month goes to a charity. It's always a different charity. You try to help everyone. You're selfless."

I couldn't believe his words. He'd been keeping tabs on me. His secret intrusion into my life made my head spin even more. He wanted to know me, but he was afraid to get too close to me. When he found out I would be asked to sign a contract, he brought me into his life to protect me, or at least that's what he wanted me to think. My thoughts splintered into a million strands. Each leading me to a different conclusion about Tom. One strand stood bright red against the crowd of gray tones. This one formed the shape of a question mark tethered to all the others and made me wonder if he was being genuine with me or not.

"Would you like some wine?" he asked.

"Yes, thank you." The strands dissipated into a smoke.

Tom prepared the glasses. He pulled out a different bottle than the one we drank from the night before. It was a red wine, like the one before but the bottle wore a different label. He poured the wine and brought the glasses and the wine to the coffee table.

One sip washed over my tongue and down my throat. The sweet liquid with a small bite woke my taste buds from a short nap. I took a few more sips. My mind raced with all the new information and my nervous drinking kicked in. Tom got up to find the remote to the stereo and allowed low music to fill the room. A high pitched violin sang a sad tune while a piano chased it with deep sorrowful steps.

I finished my first glass of wine then began to pour another, but Tom grabbed the bottle with such swiftness it disappeared before I grasped it. He smiled his sly grin and filled my glass halfway.

"I'm glad I can be myself around you now," he said.

I took a sip and set my glass down knowing I'd keep drinking if I left it in my hand. I turned to Tom and began to study him again. I could see his dark brown eyes, the way his hair laid across his forehead, and his moist lips that I'd kissed the other night.

"What color were your eyes? Before, I mean."

"They were green. After my change they were brighter, but then they faded and became darker and darker until they landed on the dark brown you see now," he said, looking into my eyes. "They were nowhere near as beautiful as your eyes are."

I tore my gaze from him and picked up my glass as a nervous gesture. I took another sip. As we listened to the music I finished my second glass. I set it back down on the coffee table and mentally cut myself off. The music was so lovely I let myself relax and gaze around the room. Shelves on the south wall housed a vast collection of music, books, and items from cultures around the world.

"You have many interests," I said.

"Yes. It comes with all the free time. Hobbies are a must if you want to stay sane."

I listened to the music more intently. I sensed the emotion in the particular song that was playing. It was much like the man sitting before me—sweet at times and strong tones of passion at others.

Tom was a passionate man. His kiss the other night had been passionate too. I tried to make myself stop thinking about it, but couldn't. That was before he revealed himself as a monster. I had a hard time considering this man a monster. His actions seemed too gentle. He reminded me of a movie I'd watched as a kid: Beauty and the Beast. The only difference is there's no magic spell to break here.

Tom's eyes were kind and gentle, but I'd seen a beast in there somewhere at the warehouse. Yet, as I looked into his eyes, what happened in the warehouse became less important. He said it was an act. The beast hadn't resurfaced since, which led me to believe him, but there was a dangerous part of him. There always had been. He leaned forward and put his hand behind my head and gently pulled me into a kiss.

My heartbeat raced and the butterflies flew into my stomach. I kissed him back on instinct, or perhaps because I simply wanted to. The adrenaline surged as my mind struggled to gain control over my heart.

I realized I was kissing a dangerous creature.

I was kissing a vampire.

The thought made me come up for air with my eyes wide open. I caught my breath as his lips went for my neck again. He kissed it tenderly, careful not to cause me discomfort. For a split second, I wished that he would bite me, so I could be his forever. The thought disturbed me. I closed my eyes and said, "Stop."

Tom stopped in his tracks. "I'm sorry, Ava. I got carried away again. I promise I wasn't going to do it, though. I swear to you I won't take you unexpectedly."

"I know. I'm just getting so confused. My head is spinning." My emotions and thoughts rollercoastered through my head.

"Don't worry, my love, your change will not be as violent as mine. I keep blood on hand so you won't drink from a human if you don't want to. We can even mix the blood in with wine if the taste is too much for you."

"Okay," I heard myself say.

"I was planning on doing it tomorrow at midnight. Midnight is the time we are strongest, and you will need your strength. We could do it here. An intimate affair between the two of us. I'll make sure you get through the change peacefully."

Time had slipped through my fingers. In 24 hours, I would be a vampire if I didn't do anything about it. My head swirled. I slid down to a reclined position on the couch. Tom helped me lie down all the way. Part of me still wanted him. I wanted to know why I craved him so much. The fog of his charm kept me lost in my thoughts.

He saved my life multiple times. Maybe I had damsel-in-distress syndrome. Or Stockholm syndrome.

"Would you like me to lay with you and keep you warm?"

I nodded. An action controlled by my heart and not approved by my brain. He moved me with ease, slid behind me, and then wrapped his arms around me. If he wanted to bite me he could do so easily in this position. I decided to trust in his word for tonight and use it to my advantage tomorrow. After a short while, I drifted to sleep.

CHAPTER SIX

I woke in a big bed. According to the color of the sheets, it wasn't mine. I moved a little and realized Tom's arms encased me. He moved in order to gaze into my eyes.

"Good morning. I wasn't expecting you to wake up for a little while longer or else breakfast would be waiting."

"That's alright. You don't have to go through all that trouble again."

"Well, one advantage is I can ask you what you would like today. So, what would you like for breakfast?"

"Do you keep cereal on hand?"

"Yes, Honey Oats, Frosted Flakes . . ."

"Honey Oats sound great, actually," I stopped him. I didn't need any more choices to make today. The choice of how I'd behave today loomed over me. I considered completely rebelling, but the uselessness of the option turned me away. My only choice was to keep pretending I wanted to be a vampire and that I wanted to be with him. Although, I wondered if I needed to keep pretending to want him or if that part had become true.

"Okay, wait here, I'll go make you a bowl," Tom said. He kissed me on the forehead and left the room.

I smiled at him as guilt crept into my heart. I would not be turned into a vampire the way he planned. I had to figure out how to get out of the house.

First, I'd create a distraction just before he bit me, but after he took the wristband off. My whole plan assumed he wouldn't leave it on until after he changed me. I would have to do everything in my power to make him trust me today.

My guilt and anxiety started to build up. I would write a note, but leave it in my room. The note would serve as the excuse I needed to get out of the room before he bit me. I'd tell him I needed to give him something before the change. Something sentimental.

Tom returned to the room with a tray and a bowl of cereal, he had a glass of chocolate milk on the tray as well. I thanked him and ate my cereal. After I finished, I told him I wanted to clean up for the day and found the way to my room.

Once inside, I found some paper on the desk and began to write a letter. I folded the letter up and put it in an envelope, before hiding it in the back of a drawer. Once I assured myself everything would work out, I took a shower and dressed myself.

I went to the window in the bedroom. The window opened easily, but the jump would be a leg-breaker. I checked the smaller window in the bathroom. It hung over the kitchen and a section of the roof sat just below. My body would fit through the window, but the feat would be tricky. If I took things slow and didn't get panicked I could open the window, push out the screen, and then get out.

I wasn't sure where I'd go, but Tom would start looking for me the second he found out I was missing, so I couldn't stick around. I thought about my friend Alani. Her brother had a boat. Maybe we'd have a chance in a less isolated place. Food seemed to be disappearing fast in Hawaii. At least in California we would have access to food and other supplies. We could get out and find a way to stop the vampires—assuming I could get Alani and Hiu to believe me.

The plan balanced on a tightrope. Alani wouldn't want to leave Hawaii, but maybe with everything going on I could convince her. Which brought about another dilemma: should I tell Alani everything right off the bat or wait until we got to the mainland? Alani might think me crazy, but it may be the only way to get her off the island. Maybe we could get other people to go. We needed protection, and numbers might help. I wished I knew how to kill vampires. The information might come in handy later. Although, I worried I might hesitate if it came down to killing Tom.

A knock came at the door. Tom's voice rang out. "Ava? Are you coming out? I have something to show you."

"I'll be right out, almost finished," I called back.

His footsteps grew distant as he walked away, and I composed myself. I didn't want Tom to think I was plotting something. I checked the clock. It was almost noon.

Twelve hours to go.

Time overcame me like an ocean wave. I hoped I'd be able to withstand the force.

I descended the spiral staircase and walked into the living room where Tom waited. He dressed in a white button-up and dark brown slacks. The shirt hinted at his strong chest beneath it and the urge to undo a few more buttons washed over me.

"There you are! You look lovely today, as usual."

I wore a pair of black slacks and a navy blue shirt that would please Tom by giving him the sense I wanted to look nice, but also wouldn't give me any trouble when I made my escape.

I reminded myself to be enthusiastic today.

"Thank you. So do you. What's the occasion?" I asked.

"Well, today is your last day as a human. I want to make sure it's a joyous occasion, and I thought we'd eat lunch out on the terrace since it's such a beautiful day."

"That sounds pleasant."

Tom led me out to the terrace where he'd already prepared a chicken dish and some other side dishes. Our plates were already made, and he served wine, as usual. In the center of the table, a small black box sat in a prominent spot.

The box seemed ominous for no apparent reason other than the fact that it was there.

"What's that?" I asked gesturing to the box.

"That's a surprise. For after our meal," he said with a grin.

I smiled mischievously and glanced at the box again. Tom gave me a fake disapproving smirk.

"Ava, I'm glad we waited to do this. Today can be a celebration. I would have regretted changing you in the warehouse with all the other witnesses. This is something I wish to do as a gesture of intimacy."

"I'm happy to share this with you, and although I'm still a little scared, I know you can get me through this. I have come to trust you over the last few days. You've saved my life and for that I am grateful. Now, you're saving me from certain danger, and I don't see how I can ever repay you."

"Repay me by picking up your glass. Let us toast to a day of merriment, and to an eternity of bliss," Tom said as he raised his glass of wine.

I did the same and said, "To merriment and bliss."

With a smile from both myself and Tom, we drank our wine.

I would miss Tom's cooking. His hospitality deserved five stars. I would also miss him. Had we met under different circumstances, Tom may have been the one, but I would never find out. After tonight, I hoped we would never cross paths again. I didn't want to break his heart, but I didn't want to give mine up either.

After we finished eating, Tom cleared the table while I enjoyed the sunny day. The overnight rain released the aroma of Hilo and the air gave me a moment of relaxation. After Tom finished clearing the table, he returned to the deck and refilled our wine glasses. He let his fingers trail over to the black box then handed it to me.

"I want you to take this as a symbol of my dedication to your well-being. It's also a symbol of my deep feelings for you."

I opened the box to find a necklace inside. The pendant hanging from it reflected the one I'd seen yesterday, but appeared smaller and more feminine. The "W" was cast in white gold and set inside a circle of 18 rubies. It sparkled in the sun on the spider-web-thin chain that made me nervous.

"Would you give me the honor of being your Swami once you are changed?" he asked, taking my hand into his.

"Yes, Tom, I would be lucky to have you as my Swami," I replied.

"Can I wear it now?" I asked enthusiastically.

"Yes, my dear, of course you can." Tom took the box from my hand and pulled out the necklace, then stood and moved behind me to fasten it around my neck. It hung lightly as I ran my fingers over it and smiled. Tom kissed my cheek from behind me and moved around to see the necklace on me.

"It's perfect for you," he commented.

"Yes, I love it. It's so beautiful."

"As are you, Ava."

Sadness swept across me like a rainstorm as I realized how much I was going to hurt him. The rain turned to tears and a few escaped my eyes. Tom noticed them immediately.

"What's wrong, sweet Ava?"

I tried to compose myself. I failed miserably. More tears came. I quickly tried to come up with a reason for the tears.

"I'm overwhelmed with happiness. You're more than I could ever ask for. You aren't a monster. I'm sorry I ever said that about you. No one has ever treated me so considerately before."

Tom took my hand and pulled me into his lap as he sat in the chair. He held me there for a while as I tried to get the tears under control. He turned me so that I was looking him directly in the face and said, "Don't cry, I know that you may feel bad about calling me a monster, but after what you saw in the warehouse, I don't blame you. I've spent the last two days, and I will spend the rest of eternity, trying to make up for that. I'm so sorry that I scared you that day."

Tom kissed my cheek and I moved so that he would kiss my lips. I pushed my fingers into his thick, gorgeous hair. The butterflies came back. We kissed on the deck for a while longer. In a whoosh, he carried me to the couch where we continued to kiss fervently. He was on top of me and I couldn't stop myself this time. This was our last day together. As his kisses grew more and more passionate I couldn't help but want him to be even closer to me. Somehow this wasn't enough. I wished he would rip off my clothes, but at the same time I was afraid he actually would.

He stopped kissing me and stared into my eyes. He ran his fingers through my long dark hair and then down the side of my face. "Not yet. We must wait until after you're changed. I want it to be special, a symbol of our commitment to each other. I promise you that it will be worth it. When you are a vampire your senses are much more acute. The experience is miraculous."

"Okay," I said quietly with a little relief. I put my hand on his chest. I felt no heartbeat or heavy breathing, but I could feel his radiating warmth. He shifted and was off of me in a flash. He stood at the end of the couch, staring at me with a smile.

"What else would you like to do today?" he asked with a smirk.

"I don't know, I just want to spend the day with you," I replied.

"Alright. How about we go for a drive?"

"That sounds good to me. We could have a picnic at the beach for dinner. How about Punalu'u Beach?"

"Ah, 'Black Sand Beach'. I'll get the food, you get your bathing suit," Tom said with his sly little grin.

I giggled. "I didn't expect to be swimming so I didn't bring one. That's okay though, I want to walk on the beach, no need for swimming."

"I think we'll both have to change. We aren't exactly in beach attire," Tom said looking at me and down at himself.

"Okay, I'll be down in a minute."

I went upstairs to change into something more comfortable. I changed out my slacks for jeans and my dressy shirt for a t-shirt. I slipped on some flip-flops and then went back down stairs. Tom was already changed. He, too, wore jeans. He also wore a plain white t-shirt and some flip-flops. He already had the food packed too. He must have used his lightning speed to get everything done so quickly.

"I figured since we ate a heavy lunch you wouldn't mind sub sandwiches for dinner. I hope you like ham."

"Of course I do. How can you live in Hawaii and not like ham?" I asked. I couldn't take my eyes off Tom. He looked so different without a suit or button up shirt on. The jeans threw me off guard. They fit him well. He seemed so normal . . . if only that were the case.

"Is something wrong?" he asked? He had noticed me staring.

"It's almost a shock to see you dressed so casually," I teased.

Tom laughed. "I think you'd be more shocked if you saw me without the spray on tan."

For a second I thought I saw a flush of embarrassment, but the emotion quickly dissolved.

"Spray on, huh? I wondered what your secret was. All the visiting vampires were pale, so it made me wonder if you were too or if you could get a tan."

"Unfortunately, we are cursed with permanent pale skin. But, since I live in Hawaii—land of the tan people—I figured I better get a light spray on in order to fit in."

"Can I see you without it tonight?"

"If you wish, but I warn you, I'm pale. I might hurt your eyes."

"Well soon I'll be as pale as you, won't I?"

"Yes. Although, it does take a while for your skin color to fade, it will eventually be as light as mine. Most of it goes during the first two years, but as you get older you get paler. No need to worry though, you will be beautiful no matter how light your skin is. It is impossible for you to ever be less than perfect to me."

Tom ran his fingers through my hair and down my arm. He kissed me lightly on the cheek before leading me through a door and into the garage where a black Jeep Wrangler sat without its top on. Tom opened the door for me and helped me up. After he climbed in himself, he opened the garage door, and we began the drive to the beach. It didn't take long to get out of the city. Soon we were driving south on Highway 11 with the preserved rain forest on one side and the ocean on the other. The flowery scenery of Hilo popped against the slightly overcast sky. The rain forest dominated this side of the island even though recent lava flows had destroyed some of it. The flora and fauna always found a way to survive. I would do the same.

"We might be getting some rain tonight," Tom said. "Rain is calming to us vampires, so that will help you with the change."

"Ah, so that's why you chose to live in one of the rainiest cities in the world."

"Yes, the rain helps keep our cravings down. Your throat won't burn so much if you're thirsty. I don't need to feed on blood as often here as I would in the desert. It's the moisture in the air. The beautiful landscape is a bonus."

"Yes, it is. That's one of the reason's my parents loved it so much," I replied. I gazed out the window and remembered taking trips to the beach with my parents. Sometimes they would even let my skip school on beautiful days like this.

Tom pulled off the highway and on to the beach. His Jeep did well in the rocky black sand. He came to a stop near some trees then climbed out of the Jeep without using the door and went around to my side. His charm and thoughtfulness would be deeply missed.

He took a blanket and a cooler out of the back. I helped him lay out the blanket in the sand under the shade of a palm tree. We ate the ham sandwiches that Tom had prepared while watching the waves at the shoreline.

"So, is there anything else that can help with the uh, cravings?" I asked.

"Well, there's wine. Any kind of alcohol really, but red wine is the best. I think it's a psychological thing, but what do I know? Then there's chocolate. Chocolate helps a little, but not as much as wine."

"Hmm, that's weird."

"I brought some chocolate for dessert. It's French. Would you like some?"

"Sounds delicious!" I said. I'd actually been craving chocolate all day.

Tom took out the package and broke the chocolate into pieces. We both ate some while staring and smiling at each other. Together we shifted our focus to the ocean. The calming sound made me feel comfortable and almost like we were a normal couple sitting on the beach. Tom ran his fingers through my hair and locked eyes with me once again. Then he kissed me. His lips moved slowly at first but my excitement grew and I kissed him back with more passion. We leaned back on the blanket and Tom rolled over so that he hovered over me again.

The scene glittered with elements of a romance novel, but reality snapped at me. I realized I wasn't reading about this passionate love scene in a book. I was living it and I was leaving him tonight. The thought forced me to stop kissing Tom. I genuinely wanted to be with him. I wasn't playing along to get out of the situation anymore. As far as I could tell, Tom shared my feelings, and I was about to break his heart. His reaction would be strong. He would be so angry with me for deceiving him. His forgiveness could not even be dreamed of.

"What's wrong?" Tom asked.

"I can't believe what a wonderful day we've had. I don't want it to end," I replied.

"It may end, Ava, but we'll have many more like this. I promise you that. We'll live for an eternity and I will make sure you're happy every day."

I smiled uneasily. I knew we didn't have an eternity. This was our last day together. It was worse than when I knew everything about the sale of Herrick-Peyton and my co-workers didn't. My secrets were killing me.

It was nearing seven o'clock. Soon, the sun would go down and midnight would be near. I decided that the letter I'd written earlier wasn't quite right. The course of the day made me want to convey my feelings for him even more. I wanted him to know how I felt. I wanted him to know that it was real and I wasn't acting.

We laid on the beach until the sky grew dark. Tom packed up the cooler and blanket and then helped me back into the Jeep. We went back to his home. The drive was dark and quiet. We were holding hands and enjoying each other's presence. Every now and then our eyes would meet and we would smile. I wondered what he was thinking, but it was impossible to tell. I wondered if he was suspicious of me. He certainly didn't act like he was. I'd played the part too well.

By the time we got home, it was nine o'clock. Only three hours before my escape. Only three hours for me to spend with Tom. We spent two of those three hours cuddled on the couch like any normal couple watching a movie. When the movie was over, Tom got up to prepare for my changing.

He set the dining room table with two wine glasses, a bottle of wine, and another bottle with what I assumed was blood. Then Tom took out a white box from the pantry and put it on the table. He opened it to reveal a chocolate sculpture of a rose. It was colored chocolate and had deep red petals and a dark green stem. He carefully took the rose out and placed it in the center of the table between the two glasses of wine.

"I'm going to go upstairs and change. You can do the same if you wish, but you're beautiful just the way you are. I'll meet you down here in 30 minutes," Tom said. We shared another deep kiss. I knew this was more than likely the last time we would kiss. We walked up the stairs together and to my door. Then he kissed me again before going to his room.

Once I was in my room I changed back into my black slacks and the dark navy blue shirt I had on earlier. I left my tennis shoes in the bathroom but put on my heels. I also put my black jacket in the bathroom. I refreshed my make-up and hair before I rewrote my letter to Tom. The first one didn't convey my feelings quite right. After I was finished with that, I burnt the old one and left the new one on the desk. It was nearing the time to meet Tom downstairs. I figured it might help my case if I were down stairs early.

I waited a few minutes then heard Tom descending the stairs. He reached the bottom and looked at me standing by the dining room table. I smiled at him as he walked over to me. His strong body always wore his suits well. He was strikingly handsome and his smile sent a beacon to me. His eyes were bright with excitement. I could see his true skin for the first time and it was a lovely shade. It was light, but somehow radiated warmth.

"Hello, Ava," he said in a smooth voice before continuing. "Before we start, I want to assure you that I am committed to you. Both as your soon-to-be Swami and as your companion. I want to be the one you can rely on and I want to make every day with you a special day."

"I would love that, Tom. You're special to me and any time I spend with you is precious," I said sincerely.

Tom hugged me and kissed me softly on the cheek and escorted me to a chair. I sat down and let my eyes find his. They were full of hope and happiness as he prepared everything. Clearly, the events of tonight burned in Tom's mind as they did in mine. Just not in the same way. He arranged to change me while I plotted my escape.

"You're so lovely tonight. There's only one thing that doesn't fit."

My heart skipped a beat.

He took my wrist and unlocked the wristband with his key that came out of nowhere. He took it off and kissed my wrist where there was a light mark from the band.

"I'm deeply sorry I had to put that on you. I promise that nothing of the sort will ever happen again. I want us to go into this with complete trust. I'm glad you came around and that you understand why I wanted to do this in the first place. At first, I wanted to change you to keep you safe, and now I want to change you so that we can spend our lives together, that is, if you'll have me."

I breathed out. The air caught in my trembling throat. I was about to break this man's heart and my own, but I had to force the words to come out.

"I'd love to spend the rest of my life with you, Tom. My desire grows with every moment we are together. Over the last few days, something changed in me and now I want the same things you do. Oh my! I forgot the poem I wrote for you. I wrote a poem for you this morning after breakfast, it's in my room."

"Would you like to go get it?"

"Yes, I wanted to read it to you before I was changed so that you know my true feelings before we do this," I said. Then I held out my wrist to give Tom a chance to put the wristband back on, but I knew he wouldn't. I could tell that he'd come to trust me, which made what I was about to do even more difficult.

He reached out for my wrist and brought it to his lips. "No, dear Ava. I know you will come back to me. I should have taken it off much earlier, but to tell you the truth, I'd forgotten about it," Tom said. Then he helped me out of the chair and kissed me. "Hurry back, my love. I will pour the wine and blood."

I went quickly up the stairs and into my room. I pulled the necklace off my neck and left it with the letter. I quietly kicked off my heels and dashed to the bathroom as I tried to keep my footsteps light. I threw on my jacket and slipped my feet into my tennis shoes, then quickly opened the window and climbed out. I was on the roof of the kitchen so I had to be quiet since it was so close to the dining room. I climbed down the gutter and ran out of the backyard into the alley. My heart was beating so loudly I could hear nothing else. I felt my chest pounding with the sound.

I was free, but I became overwhelmed with sadness when I realized that I could never see him again. I ran a few blocks with my head turning back every few steps. I expected to see him emerge from the shadows and take me down. I reached a busy street. Luckily, a cab stopped for me right away, and I took a deep breath as soon as I was inside. My adrenaline levels dropped back down to normal and I told the cabby where to go, and then silently cried a few tears on the way to Alani's.

CHAPTER SEVEN

TOM

I waited for Ava to return, although I knew she wouldn't. After a few minutes, I went upstairs, just to check. I knocked on the door, but there was no answer. I opened the door to find an empty room. Empty except for the white envelope resting on the desk and the necklace I'd given her. Her heels lay abandoned on the floor. I went to the bathroom with the thought that maybe I'd catch her, but she was long gone. She had probably made it to Banyan Drive and a cab would have picked her up. Unfortunately, cars couldn't be tracked and clever Ava wouldn't risk going home.

No matter. Phase one had failed. One small chance to save it remained, but I'd have to find her first. Of course, it all depended on her true feelings and if she played me or if she genuinely cared.

I went back into the bedroom and walked over to the desk. I picked up the necklace and stared at it for a minute. I should have been more careful. I wondered if she just acted the whole time or if . . . no, surely she couldn't be such a great actress. Something real existed between us.

I thought I had won her over. My efforts had fallen short, and Ava slipped through my fingers. The bosses wouldn't be happy, but I would assure them their mission for me wasn't over and neither was mine. I would have her again and this time she would stay mine.

I put the necklace in my pocket and picked up the envelope. I opened it to find a letter—a Dear John letter. I'd gotten a few of these in my day, but none could be as devastating as this. I unfolded the paper to see Ava's neat handwriting.

Dear Thomas,

I know that no apology could make this up to you. I wish we met under different circumstances. I just can't do it. I can't make the change. Something like this is too big. Living forever sounds so strange to me and I never thought that I would have that chance. But, once you offered it to me, I couldn't go through with it.

I also can't be a part of something that will hurt innocent people. I know that you don't want be a part of it either, deep down you want to be able to say no. I understand why you can't. I also understand why you wanted me to be a part of your world. You wanted to protect me from what will be done to others. I can't abandon humanity. I would never be okay with that.

I want you to know that the last few days were very real. Today was especially real for me. I fell in love with you today, Tom. I've never fallen in love with anyone. I didn't want to hurt you, but it was my only option. I hurt myself too. Choosing to leave was the most difficult thing I've ever had to do and all day the only thing I could think about was how much I will miss you. I will miss you until the end of my days.

Everything I said to you was true. I'll understand if you are angry with me. I'm angry with myself for being the monster I thought you were. If we cross paths again I'm sure that will be the last day I take a breath on this earth as I predict you will renounce your claim of prospect over me and

I will no longer be protected. If you want to kill me yourself I would understand that too. I left the necklace because I didn't want a reminder of what I've done to stay with me.

I love you, Thomas Walker. And, I'm sorry we can't be together. I hope that you may one day understand why, even if you don't forgive me. I know that you would've made the perfect Vampire Swami and I would have been lucky to have you. My heart breaks as I write this letter. I've known all day that today was our last day together while you believed it was the first day of the rest of our lives. It was difficult to endure, knowing that I would break your heart this way. I know that your heart, even though it doesn't beat, is the kindest heart I've ever met.

Goodbye, Tom. I love you and I always will. Don't forget that.

Ava

I sat on the bed as I read the last sentences. I folded the letter up neatly and tucked it back into the envelope, then stuffed it in my suit jacket pocket and went back downstairs to drink some wine and blood.

I took out my cell phone and pressed call on Henry's number. He answered without saying a word.

"It didn't work," I told him.

"And what is your plan moving forward?" he asked.

"There's a chance I could save it, but if it falls through, we'll have to try plan B."

"That's a last resort since we don't know if it would actually work. However, if change under duress doesn't put her under your control, you know what you'll have to do, right?"

"Yes."

"You're prepared to do that?"

I paused. I wasn't, but I'd have to lie to him, "Yes."

"Good. By the way, your former student has been punished for putting the operation in jeopardy."

"I still don't know what got into him. I taught him better than that."

"I suspect it was her blood. You know young vampires. Sometimes they can't control themselves—especially around blood that smells like that."

"Yes. I was looking forward to tasting it tonight. It's quite a disappointment."

"I agree. I've had blood such as hers only once before. A delicacy. Keep me updated. I look forward to seeing if you can salvage this."

"I will. Goodbye." I ended the call and sat on the couch.

A slight sadness crept inside me; a feeling I had not known in a long time. I pushed the emotion out of my head and replaced it with determination. She would be mine. One way or another. The stem of the wine glass in my hand snapped. I threw the remaining piece into the cold fireplace and leaned back to get a handle on my emotions.

CHAPTER EIGHT

My cab arrived at Alani's house after a short drive. I paid the cabby with cash I'd kept in my tennis shoes before quickly going to the front door. It was twelve-thirty, but I had to knock anyway. I had nowhere else to go. After a few seconds, the window illuminated and Alani made it to the door. Relief flooded through me.

"Ava! Oh my gosh!" Alani squealed. She gave me a big hug. "What happened to you? I've been trying to find you for days. I went to your house a few times but you weren't there, and the Herrick-Peyton building is no longer Herrick-Peyton. At least that's what the guy at the gate said."

"It's a long story. Can I come in and explain everything?"

"Of course! Get in here!" Alani pulled the door open wider.

I stepped inside and went to the couch. Alani started boiling water for hot tea and then sat on the couch with me. She was already in her pajamas, which consisted of a bright green tank top and a pair of colorful printed shorts. Alani's black hair hung just below her chin and flared out a little. She was as thin as I was but had much more tone to her build. She played volleyball at the beach every week. Alani's dark eyes hinted at curiosity.

"So, where were you?" Alani asked.

"Well, it all starts the day that the satellites went down. I went to dinner with one of my clients, Tom Walker. He's the head of the Hawaiian branch of Psytech."

"Oh, yeah, I remember him from when I worked at Herrick-Peyton."

"The guy at the gate told you the truth, Herrick-Peyton no longer exists. Psytech bought the building. I knew about it before everyone else because Tom told me at dinner. I went on a date with him."

Alani gasped, "You actually went on a date! I'm so happy for you!"

"Wait 'til you hear the rest of it, you'll wish I hadn't gone on a date. At least not with him. On Wednesday, the owners went to a meeting and that's when Herrick-Peyton sold the building. Tom told me that I could work any position I wanted at Psytech and to meet him at the warehouse when the news broke."

"What about everyone else?"

"Psytech had jobs for them too, but everyone was to be accessed and then place in a position that suited them if they wanted the job. But anyway, I went to the warehouse after a staff meeting with the shareholders, and this is where things get really crazy, Alani."

"Okay, let me get the tea first and then you can finish." Alani got up and poured the hot tea into two cups. She handed a cup to me then sat down again. She turned her attention to me with curiosity. I hesitated, not knowing how much to tell her.

"You can tell me, Ava. I'll believe anything you say," Alani pressed.

I sighed and took a minute to think about how I could tell this part of the story. "Well, I went to the warehouse and there were these corporate men video chatting, Alani. They had a device that made the internet work for them."

"Wow, why haven't they released it to the public?"

"Because, Psytech is responsible for the satellite viruses."

"Oh my gosh! Are you serious?" Alani asked. She set her tea down on the coffee table and brought her legs up to the couch as she turned toward me.

"They asked me to stay and work for them. They wanted me to be like them."

"What do you mean 'be' like them?'"

I took a deep breath and prepared myself to tell the truth. No more secrets. Definitely not secrets I had to keep from Alani. I had to tell her even though she might throw me in the nut house if she didn't believe me, "They are vampires, Alani. The whole Psytech Corporation."

"What? Like figuratively speaking?"

"No, I mean they are vampires. Blood-drinking, fang showing, vampires. They planted the virus in the satellite so that they could control humans and make us give them our blood in return for technology."

"What? You can't be serious. That's impossible," Alani said slowly.

"That's what I thought, until Tom tried to change me. He came at me with fangs. Fangs, Alani!"

I continued. "I tried to get away. I stabbed him with my pocketknife but it only distracted him. I climbed up a ladder in the warehouse and I found these big crates with the all the shareholders in them. They were alive but at the same time, they weren't. The vampires kept them as snacks after they signed over the deed to Psytech."

"This makes no sense. Are you sure you aren't drunk? How did you get away?"

I ignored her first question. "I didn't. Tom convinced me to come down. He said he'd wait three days to change me. He wanted me to see things his way. It bought me time, so I agreed. They put this wristband on me that would inject me with vampire venom if I tried to go too far from Tom."

"I can't believe you got away," Alani said. She stood up quickly and started to pace the room. "Nalani told me. She told me there were vampires. I never believed her, but she was right. You're not making this up, right? She and Hiu didn't put you up to this?"

"No. It's real, Alani, and we have to stop them."

"Okay," she said as she sat back down. "So keep going. How did you finally get away?"

"I spent Thursday and today with him and his plan was to change me at midnight. I earned his trust, so when he took the wristband off, I made up an excuse to go up to my room and I slipped out the back."

"And now you're here. I'm so glad you made it out!" Alani said giving me another hug. Then Alani pulled away and looked at my face. "You seem like something else is bothering you though."

"Well, in the time that we spent together, I came to . . . understand him." I took a strand of my hair and started twirling it between my fingers. "We shared a lot about our lives. He told me his story and he treated me like royalty. I think I actually fell in love with him, and leaving him was . . . hard."

I swallowed a lump in my throat. "Remember the house fire and how we didn't know how I got out? Tom is the one who saved me."

"That was him?" Alani asked as she bobbed her head forward in disbelief.

"It has to be true. How else would he know?"

Alani pulled me into another hug. "Only you would fall in love with a vampire. Are you sure it isn't Stockholm syndrome?"

I forced a little laugh and wiped my tears. "I'm sure. It was real. And his feelings for me were real too. I broke his heart. And mine," I said.

"It will be okay, Ava. What other choice did you have?"

"We need to get out of here, Alani. We can't stay in Hawaii. Food is already getting scarce. This is where Psytech's plan will hit the hardest."

"Can't we get the police?"

"I don't think it's safe. On Thursday we had to go back to the warehouse and there were a lot of vampires running around, one dressed in a police uniform," I said as my memory of the warehouse came back to me. Then I remembered what happened with James. I decided not to tell Alani exactly how close I'd come to death. Or undeath.

"What do we do? I don't want to leave, Ava. This is so crazy."

"It's our best chance. What about your brother's boat? Can it get the four of us to California?" I asked.

"I think so, but it will take four or five days since it's kinda small. If the wind is on our side it may only take three. It might be hard to navigate through without GPS. Convincing Nalani to leave her home will be the hard part."

"We might be able to get one of those devices, but if there is any way we can do without, it would be best to stay away from the warehouse and Psytech."

"We'll talk to Hiu in the morning. You need some rest."

"I don't know if I can sleep. What if he finds me? I'm worried and I don't want you to get hurt," I said as I glanced around the room and expected Tom to burst through the door at any moment.

"I don't think he knows where you are. He'd be here already."

"You're probably right."

"Of course I am," Alani said while she stood up, she smiled and continued to wish me a good night. "Aloha Ahiahi!" she said before heading to her room.

"Aloha Ahiahi," I said back to her with a shaky voice. I worried about Tom coming for me.

After tossing and turning, I fell asleep on Alani's couch and no heartbroken vampire burst through Alani's door that night. Instead, I woke to the smell of ham and eggs, Alani's favorite breakfast.

"Aloha Kakahiaka," Alani said.

I replied to her morning greeting and rested on the couch until breakfast, then moved to the table to sit and eat with Alani.

"So, today we need to get supplies gathered and hopefully leave tonight or tomorrow morning," I said.

"Hiu is on his way over right now. I already told him everything."

"He doesn't think I'm insane?" I asked. I wondered how Alani and Hiu could take the news so well.

"No. Neither of us thinks you are crazy. I told you last night. Kapunawahine told us about vampires for years but we dismissed it as a combination of old age and bedtime stories. I guess we should have listened to her."

"What did Nalani say?"

"I don't know. I kinda just tuned everything out when she talked about vampires," Alani said with a shrug.

"We should go see her and convince her to go with us. She might be able to help."

"I do want to take her with us, but I'm not sure she knows all that much about vampires. I think she just heard stories as a young girl," she shrugged again.

"Well, right now even made up knowledge might help. If they come after us we are going to have to be able to protect ourselves," I replied.

"Yeah, you're right. Well, we'll wait for Hiu to get here then we'll go see her and then gather supplies. If she tells us anything valuable we can try to get one of those do-hickies," Alani said.

She was good at planning stuff out, but I still wasn't sure if we should risk our lives just to have GPS. Soon, Hiu arrived and he gave me a big hug. He'd had a crush on me since I moved to Hawaii but I loved him in a way I'd love a brother. He resembled Alani. His hair was a little shorter, and he wore it wavy. He was much taller too. I had never met Alani and Hiu's father, but I assumed Hiu's height was a result of his genes. Hiu was a surfer, so he had a lean musculature and dark skin. He wore khaki cargo shorts and a light gray wife-beater.

"Howzit, tita," he said to Alani. Then he turned to me, "Aloha, nani! Sorry to hear about your boyfriend turning out to be a vampire. That must really suck!" Hiu said with a silly grin. Alani gave him a disapproving glance and said, "No make ass, kokohe."

Hiu ignored her and asked, "So, woddascoops?"

Alani and Hiu could both speak Hawaiian. They mostly talked English around me, but their second language showed up in conversation. Pidgin, a slang language that came about in the pineapple plantation days, was also something they had picked up. Their grandmother didn't approve of it, but Hiu talked more pidgin than Alani since he was part of the surfing community. *No make ass<* meant don't make a fool of yourself. I wasn't sure what kokohe meant, but *woddascoops* meant what's happening?

"We gotta go see Kupunawahine," Alani replied.

Hiu was the older sibling, but Alani was more mature. They were the first people to welcome me and my parents to the island and their grandmother, Nalani, was always generous and welcoming. Their father had run off and their mother was currently in California pursuing an acting career.

I smiled to be a good sport, but deep down, I was still hurting over what I had to do the night before. I tried not to think about it. We had to get to Nalani's house, so we all piled into Hiu's white Range Rover. I sat in the back and hid from the eyes of any vampires on the lookout for me. I peered out to make sure I didn't see anything out of the ordinary.

"You act like you're runnin' from the law," Hiu said as he eyed my through the rearview mirror.

We arrived at Nalani's place. Nalani was the organic type. She liked to be outdoors so her house resembled a little shack on the beach. When the weather got bad she would go to Alani or Hiu's house, but she was pretty stubborn and only left for extremely violent storms.

Nalani was already outside sipping on sun tea. She stood at about the same height as Alani and I. Her hair was a dark gray—she wasn't the type to dye it—and it was pulled back into a loose bun. She wore a white sundress with light blue flowers that hung loosely on her average body. Nalani wasn't thin or thick. She was healthy. When she saw me, she stood up with a big smile on her face and came to greet her "adopted" grandchild and her two biological grandchildren.

"Aloha, keiki!" she said.

"Aloha," we all replied.

"What brings you out on this beautiful day?"

"Kapunawahine, we wanted to talk to you about something," Alani said.

"Sounds serious. Come inside and we will get everything straightened out," she said. She was also intuitive.

Inside, I retold my story that I'd already relayed to Alani. Nalani listened with intent and did not interrupt once. When I was finished telling my story, Nalani sighed and looked at all three of us with some despair in her eyes.

"I knew that one day they would come up with a plan like this. My mother told me many stories of vampires. They have been passed down since ancient times. The vampires came here with the Polynesian settlers. They followed them here all the way from East Asia. Vampires have been around since the beginning of civilized man. Their origins are unknown. Our ancestors fought them frequently. At first, they could not kill them because they were so strong. No spear could pierce their skin. Soon, the discovery and widespread use of obsidian became a blessing.

"When our ancestors started using obsidian as tools they also became weapons against the vampires. If a vampire is stabbed in the heart with an obsidian stone they will die. This is the only way to be sure they are truly dead. There are other ways, but this is the most effective.

"Also, there are ways to ward them off. Our ancestors found that if they killed a vampire with an obsidian blade and then used that blade to carve a ring or bracelet from a single seashell that it would protect whoever wore it from the charm of a vampire and also keep vampires from getting too close. It was said that the vampire's spirit was trapped inside the obsidian when it was killed. Carving a shell with the same blade moved the spirit into a more permanent home.

"Once trapped inside the carved shell, the vampire's spirit would warn other vampires of the danger. Any vampires that got close enough to someone wearing one of these rings or bracelets would feel the effect and be overcome with the sensation of being ensnared. The vampire would be warned that if they harmed the human anyway, they too would become trapped for eternity.

"Vampires are also fast swimmers, and would often follow the great navigators on their journeys to new lands, but soon our ancestors put a stop to that as well. Pennants made of feathers hanging from the top of their sails would protect the entire vessels' occupants as long as they were at sea. It is important to remember that this only works on water vessels. It will not work on a home or building."

We were astonished that Nalani knew so much about the vampires. When she had finished her story none of us said a word. Then, Nalani got up and went to a small chest near her bed. She opened it to reveal three obsidian daggers and a small jewelry box. She took out the jewelry box and opened it as well. Inside, were two rings and one bracelet all carved from seashells. Nalani was already wearing a bracelet and wondered if it, as well as the others in the jewelry box, contained the spirit of a vampire.

"I want you to pick one of these out, Ava," Nalani said as she motioned to the jewelry box.

"Are you sure? What about Alani and Hiu?" I asked, but my question was answered when she gestured at them. They both wore rings carved from seashell.

"Of course I'm sure. I've saved these for an occasion such as this and they already have theirs," Nalani said as she nodded towards Hiu and Alani.

"Okay, I like that ring," I said as I pointed to a light pink ring.

"Can we borrow those daggers too?" Hiu asked.

"I hope you aren't planning anything that will get you into trouble," Nalani replied.

"We need GPS, if I don't have da kine it may take forever to get there. Time is important, right?" Hiu reasoned.

"I suppose you are protected with those rings and you'll go even if I say no, right?"

"Yes, I will," Hiu said.

Nalani took the daggers and handed one to each of us. I put mine in my jacket pocket. Hiu put his in the pocket of his cargo shorts. Alani wasn't sure what to do with hers. She was a non-violent person.

"Alani, maybe you should stay with Nalani, you guys can gather the supplies while we get the equipment. I don't think it's wise for all of us to go, sneaking in will be hard, but it will be easier if it's just Hiu and I. We'll be okay. We have the rings," I said.

"Are you sure? It sounds too dangerous for just two people," Alani protested.

"Don't worry, Tita, we cockaroach da kine wikiwiki!" Hiu said enthusiastically.

I giggled and rolled my eyes, "It will be fine. Besides, someone armed needs to watch the boat. Make sure you guys get that feather pennant up right away."

"Okay, I guess I can miss out on the fun."

Everything was decided. Alani and Nalani would gather the supplies and guard the boat while Hiu and I went into the vampire's den. My heart jumped when I thought about whether or not Tom would be there. I couldn't imagine the look on his face if he were to see me again. I couldn't imagine my reaction either.

CHAPTER NINE

Hiu and I took his Range Rover and headed to what used to be Herrick-Peyton. We told the others we were going to wait until dark to sneak onto company grounds and would be scouting the area until then. When we neared the building, we observed a bunch of people—or vampires—going in and out of the gate that I used to drive through. The security guards ID'd them before allowing entrance. We would have to sneak in another way.

We got some fast food from one of the adjacent buildings and sat in the car eating and watching. I saw Tom's car pull through the gate at one point. I wanted to see the expression on his face and possibly get a clue about what kind of mood he was in, but the tinted windows made that impossible.

"There's a service gate around back, we'll have to use that, but we'll need bolt cutters," I said.

"I saw a hardware store down the street, I get da kine, you stay. Scope it out," Hiu said.

"Okay, hurry back though, it will be getting dark soon and I want to get this over with before my nerves explode."

Hiu smiled and then shut the car door. He headed south on Aneko Road then disappeared. Alone, my thoughts started to compete for attention. I hoped Tom would be in the office and not in the warehouse. In fact, it would be nice if no one was in the warehouse or, at the very least, only a few vampires. We may have a problem if it was anything like the scene it had been last time I was in the warehouse.

Soon, the sun sank lower and lower. Shadows took over the concrete.

Hiu returned with the bolt cutters and slipped back into the vehicle. Once the level of darkness brought comfort, I told him to pull into the alley behind the warehouses.

The alley was wide, and cars lined it on one side, so we wouldn't stand out. A few nearby businesses used it as an overflow parking lot. We found a spot near the gate, which would make our getaway fast. We got out of the car with the bolt cutters in Hiu's hand. I wrapped one of Hiu's shirts around the lock to muffle the sound and he snapped the padlock with ease. Luckily, we didn't make enough noise to be heard. Hiu quickly put the bolt cutters and his shirt back in his car and then we slipped through the gate.

We walked behind the warehouses to avoid being seen. Finally, we came to the back of the warehouse as I hoped the vampires hadn't moved the devices to another warehouse yet. We snuck up the side of the building closest to the small entrance. Hiu gestured to me to take out my dagger. Just in case.

We could hear people scuffling around inside the warehouse. It didn't sound as busy as the day I almost lost my life to James as there weren't as many voices. We stood around the corner from the entrance as my heart pounded. Hiu seemed to control his adrenaline rush easily. As a surfer, he lived off the stuff.

Hiu motioned for me. It was time.

We rounded the corner and entered the building. About ten vampires worked inside, and they all stopped and stared at us. A few of them showed their fangs and others flashed an evil smile. Until Hiu brandished his obsidian dagger. The smiles faded.

Tom and I locked eyes. A gravitational pull existed between us, and I could tell I hurt him by the way his emotions flickered and disappeared. He fought to control them.

"We want da kine that block the virus. Geev 'um to us and I won't have beef," Hiu shouted.

One of the vampires ran toward Hiu. It was a younger one with bright green eyes, but before he could get to Hiu he hit an invisible wall and bounced backward landing hard on a table that collapsed with his weight.

"You can't attack them, Jovan, they wear protective rings from the ancient Polynesians," Tom said. His eyes found the one on my finger. His expression was calm. Too calm for a man who'd been dumped.

"Ava, I'm disappointed that you chose this path. I'm afraid I have no choice but to release my claim of prospect now. Not that you're in danger with that ring, but if you take it off, you will be."

"We want those things, now," Hiu said firmly.

"They're right over there," Tom said calmly as he pointed at a box near the ladder that I used to get away from Tom before. Hiu strolled to the box while I stayed at the door and guarded our way out. Hiu pulled out a handful of the devices and stuffed them in his pocket. The one called Jovan tried to attack me, this time he hit the invisible wall, slammed backward into the wall of the warehouse and dented the aluminum.

I let out a scream and flinched away from him, my reaction was a little delayed since the attack happened so fast. The whole thing was over before I understood what happened. The act of violence against me angered Hiu because he charged Jovan and stabbed him in the heart with his obsidian dagger.

Almost instantly, Jovan's body shriveled up, as if his soul had been sucked out of him. The dagger glowed in Hiu's hand and then settled. The dagger sucked the soul out of the vampire's body and left it a crumpled mess. I had wondered how the dagger worked, and now I knew.

I also knew I could never do that to Tom.

I turned to the rest of the room. Seven vampires stared at Jovan's deformed body in shock. One snarled at Hiu while being held back by Tom.

Tom's eyes captured mine. I couldn't move. Hiu came to me and pulled me back toward the door. I snapped out of my daze and started running with him. We quickly got outside and went back to the gate the same way we came. The Range Rover remained. No vampires waited for us, although I had expected it.

We quickly got in the rover then headed for the dock where Hiu's boat was. I kept an eye behind us for followers, but none showed up. I took a deep breath and turned around as we pulled up to the dock.

"Wikiwiki! To the boat!" Hiu said as he grabbed his dagger.

I opened the door and rushed to the boat with Hiu at my side. We arrived at the dock with no attempted attacks. Inside, Alani and Nalani were waiting. Alani's dagger sat within her reach.

"I'm so glad you guys are back! I was starting to worry," Alani said, giving them both a hug. "Did you get one of those thingies?"

"Yeah, I cockaroach a choke ov da kine," Hiu said excitedly.

"That's good! That means we can get to California with no problem!" she said.

"Did something happen at the warehouse? Ava, you're white as a sheet," Nalani said.

"I killed a vampire. He make-die-dead. He try to attack me, then he try to attack Ava. I show 'em I got beef. I wen bus him up. That oughtta send a message not to mess wit' us," Hiu said, setting his dagger on the table.

"I will use it to carve a ring or bracelet then, but I need a good shell," Nalani said. She examined the dagger. "You can kill more than one vampire at a time with these, but it's best to get the souls out right away. Will one of you go fetch me a shell?"

"I'll go. Ava, can I cockaroach your dagger, just in case?" Hiu asked.

"Of course, here," I said as I handed him my dagger.

Hiu took it and then headed out to find a "good shell." I sat at the table with Alani and Nalani then looked around. It had been a while since I had been on Hiu's boat. Technically, Hiu's yacht.

He used it to give people mini-cruises around the islands. He made pretty good money doing it too. Tourists loved the mini-cruise. Some would rent out the whole boat for their family. With six bedrooms, four bathrooms, a good sized galley, a dining and entertaining area that opened up to the deck, and a lounge area that opened up to the deck as well. His business was a popular attraction.

Hiu returned shortly with the shell and gave it to Nalani who then said her good nights then retreated to her room. Hiu showed me where my room would be and gave me back my dagger. My room was large for a boat cabin and I had my own bathroom. Alani must have picked up some of my clothes because a bag was on the bed with a few changes of clothes and some bathroom necessities in it. After getting settled in, I decided a hot shower was in order. Everyone had gone to bed except Hiu who piloted the boat. He said that once we got out far enough he'd put it on auto and then rest. His room sat adjoined to the pilothouse.

I put my dagger on the dresser then decided that since the feather pennant was up, I could take off my ring to shower. I didn't want it going down the drain. Still shaken from the whole warehouse scene, a shower was exactly what I needed to relax. The movement of the boat helped a little too. I never got seasickness. I figured it was part of living on an island, and when I was young my parents would always take a ship to get from California to Hawaii. My mother liked the feeling of the ocean too. She'd always said that flying didn't allow you to get to know the ocean. I never knew what it meant, but I did have an immunity to seasickness.

After feeling much more at ease, I shut off the water then threw on a bathrobe. I hated going to bed with wet hair, so I dried it. I knew I'd wake up with some serious bed head if I didn't. Because of the long length of my hair, it took some time to dry, but eventually I finished and left the bathroom.

A dark figure waited for me. I jumped back and peered at the man.

Tom.

A scream welled up inside me, but didn't release. My eyes darted toward my ring, which was too far away to dive for, so they darted back to Tom.

CHAPTER TEN

"I suppose I should be glad your eyes went to the ring on the night stand and not the dagger on the dresser," he said. He practically spat the word dagger at me.

"I don't want to kill you, Tom," I said, backing away toward the bathroom.

"I don't want to kill you either, Ava."

"No, you want to change me, which is pretty much the same thing."

"I only wanted to protect you."

"Well, I can protect myself. Your protection is not what I would consider convenient. Becoming a vampire is not in my five year plan."

"And becoming a fugitive is?" Tom raised his voice a little. I backed up another step. "I'm sorry, I didn't mean to startle you. Go ahead and put your ring on if it will make you feel better. I'm only here to talk. I wouldn't try to change you on the boat. I didn't bring any blood with me and I'm sure you wouldn't want your friends as a snack. Oh, and you guys should tie your feather pennant a little tighter next time," he said.

I went for my ring. I thought it would push him away from me, but it didn't. He still stood only a few feet away. I assessed his body language He seemed to be calming down.

"Why isn't this ring pushing you away?" I asked.

"I have to mean you harm or you have to be afraid of me. I mean you no harm and you are a little afraid of me. I can feel its force, but you must trust me a little because it's not pushing me through the window or anything."

"What did you come to talk about? I'm not coming with you. You can't change my mind."

"I came to tell you that Hiu has been branded a slayer and as his accomplice you are in danger. The other two are in danger as well. I can protect you if you let me change you, Ava."

"We're fine, we have rings and daggers."

"You don't understand. They will send the drudges after you. Those rings only protect you from vampires, not humans," Tom said, raising his voice again.

"We can handle humans. I can't leave them, Tom. They're my friends. They're my family," I corrected, "And I'm staying with them. I will not abandon them and if you succeed in changing me someday, I will not drink one drop of human blood. I refuse to cause my kind harm."

"If I change you, and you do not drink blood, you will die. You will need to drink human blood at first in order to stay alive."

"Then I guess I'll die if you change me. That's all there is to it," I said as I crossed my arms.

"You will drink. After a while you'll get so weak that you won't be able to think straight, you'll drink blood thinking it's water. I've seen it happen."

"No, I won't do it. I'm strong willed and I'll make sure of it. I'll drive an obsidian blade through my own heart before I drink human blood."

"I'm not going to argue with you right now, Ava. I just wanted to tell you that they have yours and Hiu's picture and they've already sent it out to all Psytech employees. I don't know if the loners are aware of you yet, but they will be soon enough. Even the rogues might want to kill you to get on the Emperor's good side."

"This is all gibberish to me."

"All you need to know is that all vampires and their drudges are going to be after you. You must especially avoid all Psytech buildings," Tom warned.

"Vampires can't hurt us. Not with these," Ava said, gesturing to her ring.

"The human drudges can, and they will. This is the sort of thing that could get them accepted into the guardianship."

"What is that?"

"Drudges are humans that seek out vampires to become one. The vampires see them as brave and put them through a training period. If they pass the training period, they become our guardians."

"Oh, so, killing one of us would be like an initiation test."

"Yes, I guess you could put it that way," Tom replied.

"Well, I'm still not worried. We can take care of ourselves."

"Ava, I just want you to be safe. Please, come with me," his eyes were pleading and he was leaning toward me. My ring kept him from closing the short distance between us. I ached for his touch, but I pushed past the feeling. I broke my gaze from him.

"Why don't you come with us? Leave the other vampires. Be with me." My ring let up on Tom a little. He stepped closer.

"I wish I could, but that would make things even more dangerous for you and I would be hunted as well. We can't be together as long as you are human, Ava," Tom's voice was quiet.

My heart sunk. Our forbidden love was too much for my emotions. I let down my guard completely, and so did the ring. I trusted him. I trusted him more than I probably should, but I didn't care, I wanted to touch him. I wanted to be in his arms.

Tom opened his arms and I hugged him. I started to cry and he held me tighter. I gazed at him. He was sad too. He was hurting. I wanted to take away his pain. I kissed his lips. First I kissed them tentatively. I had to make sure that he wanted my kisses. After I decided that he did, I kissed him more passionately. He kissed me back and his hands moved down my body. They went down to my lower back.

"This is our only night," I said between kisses then looked at his eyes, staring right back. He wanted me, and I wanted him. He pushed me down on the bed, gently but playfully aggressive at the same time. My ring put out a short burst of force field, but it ended and Tom kissed me again with a little chuckle. I pulled off Tom's shirt with a little help from him. My robe opened with a little more help from him. I hadn't put anything on underneath and Tom's excitement grew. His kisses were more and more urgent and one of his hands ran down my ribcage.

I unbuttoned Tom's wet slacks. Wet from the swim, I assumed. His shirt was damp too, now that I thought of it. My thoughts snapped back to the passion when Tom yanked off his pants with lightning speed. He wasn't wearing shoes, which made things even easier. Then, we were making love. It was different with him than it had been with anyone else.

He obviously knew what he was doing. His strength carried me through a whirlwind of skin and sensations. No other man had ever pushed me to such incredible limits. I felt a sense of euphoria and was in a daze from all the adrenaline.

I fell into Tom's arms as our lovemaking came to an end. We laid in the bed while I drifted off to sleep in his arms. The night was full of dreams for me. I dreamed of Tom and what it would be like if he wasn't a vampire. I dreamed of us being together like a normal couple with nothing to worry about except figuring out what to eat for dinner. I woke wishing my dreams could come true, but reality set in when I realized Tom was gone. He left a letter on the dresser beside the obsidian dagger. It was my turn to read a paper made of heartbreak.

My Dear Ava,

I'm sorry for leaving you like this. A one-night stand is not what I had in mind when I pictured our first passionate night together, but unfortunately it is not safe for us to be together right now. I gave you a kiss before I left. I hope that means something. I will miss you so much.

Please reconsider my offer. I don't want to live without you, especially after last night. If you decide to let me change you, then I will see what I can do about your friends. I can't make any promises, but I can try to save them from death or from becoming blood slaves. I realize it doesn't sound very promising, so I don't blame you if you decide not to go through with it.

Wherever you go from here, please know that I will always love you, and I will never hold anything against you. You can always come to me and trust me. I promise not to change you unless you want it. I see my mistake now.

Forcing you into changing pushed you away and I won't ever try that again. I only want you to be happy and I wish I could do more to make you happy. If you ever need anything please don't hesitate to ask.

I hope that someday we can be together, I have a very long life ahead of me and I will be heartbroken if you are not in it.

Until we meet again, my Sweet Ava, I love you and farewell.

Tom

CHAPTER ELEVEN

I wiped away a tear as I folded the letter back up. I noticed Tom had left one of his shirts. I wasn't sure if he did it on purpose or not but the soft white fabric brought me a little comfort.

Echoes of my friends' voices reached me. They came from the galley. I gathered myself, taking hold of my emotions, then got dressed and went to say good morning to everyone.

"Aloha, Kakahiaka!" Alani sang as I walked into the galley.

"Mornin' everyone," I said as I forced a smile. Hiu and Nalani looked up from the breakfast table and bid me good morning in their Hawaiian language.

"Are you okay?" Alani asked, "You look . . . tired."

"Yeah, I'll be okay, I didn't get a lot of sleep last night," I said with a yawn. Then I sat down at the table. It wasn't really a lie, I just didn't say why I didn't get enough sleep last night.

"Well, I guess seeing Tom again couldn't be easy," Alani said.

My heart jumped. "What?" I hoped Alani hadn't seen Tom sneaking out.

"Last night, at the warehouse, you saw Tom right?"

"Yeah, it was weird," I said with relief.

"I'll say. That buggah was like their kahuna or something. He the only one who talk. Definitely not da kine you want to hang with, Ava. Good thing you got away from him," Hiu said before he shoved a spoonful of cereal in his mouth.

I forced a smile and gave a little hooray gesture with my arms. Alani plopped down a plate in front of me. It had bacon, eggs and toast on it. She poured me some chocolate milk as I stared out the window at the ocean. Nalani left the galley to finish carving the shell into another ring.

"I'm glad we got all the supplies we needed. I thought it would be more difficult to get food and stuff. Did you guys get all the food from my house?" I asked.

"Yeah, we had to gather all the food from everyone's house. The supermarkets were all pretty much empty. People were going lolo. We need to figure out how to get the ships going again, I don't feel right leaving all those people on the islands with such limited food," Alani said.

"I hope we can do that. I think the vampires want everyone off the islands. They want to be isolated. Anyone left when the vampires reveal themselves will likely become a meal. If people find out about the vampires and how to kill them, all Hawaiians will be in major danger. I don't think the vampires will think twice about killing anyone who stands in their way," I replied.

"You're right, we can't let word get out. A war between humans and vampires on the islands would end with a lot of human blood spilled," Alani said.

Hiu, who had moved on from his bowl of cereal to sharpen his obsidian dagger, spoke up, "I think it would end in a lot of vampire deaths, not human."

Alani and I both gave him a disapproving smirk.

"You aren't thinking about starting a war are you?" Alani asked.

"If it's gotta be done, it's gotta be done. Hey, Ava, you still throw knives?"

"Not for a long time, but I'm sure that I can still stick one or two. I might be rusty, but I could pick it up fast. Why?" Another skill passed down from my mother. I had left it behind after she died.

"Well, I thought about making some obsidian throwing spikes once we get to the mainland. That way you can protect yourself from a distance."

"Are we even going to be able to find obsidian in California?" I asked.

"I think we can find some in northern California. If not, I'll figure out how to track it down. I'll start looking in L.A. We're gonna need it. I'm sure I pissed them off when I killed that Jovan guy," Hiu replied.

"Yeah, which reminds me, we need to steer clear of any Psytech buildings. When I was with Tom he told me something about vampires having humans as guards."

"So?" Hiu said with a shrug.

"So, this shell jewelry only protects us from vampires. If word gets to other vampires with human guards they will send them to kill us. We need to lay low. The first thing we do when we get to L.A. is find Moana and set up a safe house," I explained.

Alani and Hiu displayed reluctant faces. They dreaded showing up on her doorstep, especially with their grandmother. Moana, their mother, went to L.A. to become a movie star. Moana may be selfish, but she would also protect her own to the death. She was our only contact in L.A. so we needed her. Alani and Hiu loved their mother, but sometimes being around her magnified the drama of any situation. We weren't sure how she would react to vampires trying to kill her children, but she would likely make a big scene.

We would tell her the truth, of course. If we made her house a safe house she would need to be aware of the lurking danger. Another issue was the small detail that Moana and Nalani didn't quite coincide. In fact, they would have been enemies if their mutual love for Alani and Hiu wasn't common ground. Nalani thought Moana shouldn't put her career before her children, and Moana resented Nalani for allowing her son, Alani and Hiu's father to abandon them. Of course, Nalani had no knowledge of what Kaholo was planning to do, but nevertheless, Moana still blamed Nalani. Alani had once explained to Ava that her father's name was ironic to her. Apparently, Kaholo means runner in Hawaiian.

The next few days went by slowly. Tom and the night we spent together clouded my thoughts. My heart ached. The more I thought about him, the more I hurt. Eventually, Alani had to try to get my mind off of things, so she tried distractions like card games and board games and even talking me to death. At times, I let my mind focus on the activities and conversations that Alani planned for us, but I couldn't forget about him completely. Everything reminded me of him, even though we had only spent a short time together.

Nalani made French toast for breakfast one morning, and that was all it took to get me thinking about Tom. Even the chocolate bar that Alani shared with me took my memory back to the day on the beach.

Finally, on the fourth day we reached the mainland and docked at Marina del Rey. When we arrived, it was about 9:30 at night. We couldn't call Moana because she only had a cell, so we called a cab to take us to her house. Moana lived in Santa Monica, which was only about 5 miles away. The cab took a long time to get to us since the city's cab numbers had been cut in half by the virus and there was more demand for them now that most cars didn't work. Soon after the cab arrived we were dropped off at Moana's house.

Alani knocked on the door and after a short wait, Moana answered. "Alani! Hiu! Oh! And Ava! Hello, Nalani, what are you guys doing here?" Moana asked excitedly. She proceeded to give us all hugs except for Nalani, but she didn't seem to mind.

Alani answered for us all, "Makuahine, we're here because we ran into some trouble back on the islands. We took Hiu's boat here. If you let us come in we'll explain everything."

"Of course!" she answered, "Come in, you must have had a long trip."

The inside of Moana's house was clean and upscale. Designer furniture, a modern kitchen, an open floor plan that reminded me of Tom's house all told us that Moana was doing well. Moana led us into the living area where there were plenty of luxurious seating.

Moana was decked out in designer clothing. A silky blouse flowed behind her as she walked and a tight pencil skirt hugged her carefully crafted figure. Moana took pride in her body. She was always on a diet and worked out every day. Her long hair was neatly curled. It was almost as long as mine and went a few inches below her shoulders. After everyone found a seat, Alani motioned to me to explain my part of it.

"Well, Moana, we came here for a few reasons. As you know, the satellite virus has made it difficult to get any supplies on the islands. But the more pressing reason is because the people responsible for the virus were my clients at Herrick-Peyton, the Psytech Company. Psytech bought the Herrick-Peyton building and . . ."

"The people who run Psytech are actually vampires," Alani finished for me. "They tried to make Ava turn into a vampire, and so we're kinda on the run from them."

Moana glanced at Nalani, then back at Alani and I. "Well, I'm glad you are all safe, I trust Nalani has told you the stories. I suppose I better find my ring."

Alani looked at Hiu. We were all shocked that Moana was being so calm about the matter. Hiu shrugged and announced, "I killed one of them."

Apparently, he thought he should slip that in there while she was being calm. Moana stared at him for a second, an emotion flickered, and then she calmed herself and said, "That was brave of you Hiu, you've become quite the kane. Thank you for protecting your ohana and getting everyone here safely."

Moana went up the stairs to her bedroom. Everyone exchanged glances. Nalani was sitting quietly on a chair. Soon Moana came back down with a ring on her finger.

"Makuahine, are you okay?" Alani asked.

"Yes, keiki, just a little shocked. I think the best thing for us to do would be to settle in for the night and we can talk more in the morning. Nalani, you can take the guest room by my room. Girls you can stay in the other guest room. Hiu,

I'm afraid you may have to sleep on the couch," Moana said apologetically.

"Minors, I don't mind," Hiu said with a smile.

Alani and I went up to the second guest room and settled in. There was only one bed but it was king sized so we would have enough room to sleep comfortably. We took turns in the bathroom and then settled in. It was getting late so we weren't saying much. When we crawled into bed Alani asked, "I can't believe this is all happening, what are we going to do?"

"We'll figure it out. We need to lay low for now. We need a safe house, but I'm not sure this house is going to work. It's not hard to find. I bet they could track us here if they tried."

"You're probably right, and we'll bring that up tomorrow morning, maybe my mom knows somewhere else we can go," Alani added.

"Yeah, we'll get it all figured out," I said. I was still thinking about Tom. I wouldn't get much sleep if I kept it up.

"Are you okay?" Alani asked, "You seem a little depressed."

"I'm fine. I'm just stressed out."

"So, you're not thinking about you know who?"

"Yeah, I am, but that's going to take time. I'll get over it, eventually. I mean, it's probably just infatuation, I mean being in love with a vampire is crazy."

I said the words, but I didn't mean them. Not from my heart. I knew it was love and I probably wouldn't get over it anytime soon. I didn't want Alani to worry and this meant I'd have to start acting more like myself. I didn't want anyone to worry about me when there was so much more going on that we needed to keep on top of.

"You're right, I'm just worried. You are my best friend. I don't like to see you heart broken."

"That's not why I've been so distant, it's the stress. I mean our lives have changed so much in the last week. I can't believe that life is ever going to be the same."

"Yeah, it is crazy to think about. Maybe someday things will go back to normal. You never know," Alani shrugged.

"I don't think it will be the same, now that those creatures are out in the open. I don't think I will ever be the same," I explained.

Alani nodded in agreement and gave me a hug.

After that we said goodnight. Alani fell asleep fairly quickly, but I couldn't sleep. Again. I laid there with thoughts running through my head. I kept looking at the clock until the last numbers I remembered were 3:23.

Alani woke me up the next morning around eight. She was moving about the room after her shower and so I woke gently.

"Sorry, I didn't mean to wake you," she said.

"That's okay. I need to get up any way."

I got out of bed and went to take my shower. I took my time. My thoughts kept me in a daze. When the water started getting cold I snapped out of it. I got dressed and went downstairs to see everyone gathered around a table full of waffles.

Moana was the first to see me. "Hello, Ava! Good morning!" she said.

Everyone turned to greet me and I replied with a, "Good morning." I sat at the empty seat next to Alani. Moana gave me a plate of waffles and some syrup.

"Well," Moana began, "I think we need to talk about exactly what's going on and what we should do about it."

"Yes, well, I feel like I'm responsible for all of this," I said. "I'm the one that dragged you all into this. I'm the one that ran away from a powerful vampire and showed up on Alani's doorstep."

"It's not your fault, Ava," Moana said. "Alani filled me in on that whole situation and you did the right thing. I'm glad that you went to Alani and that all of us are together. I would rather us all know what they're planning than find out when the rest of the world does. We can be better prepared this way and maybe even stop them."

"Shouldn't we tell a radio station or something to get the word out?" Hiu asked.

"No, that would cause mass panic," Nalani said. "We must continue to keep this a secret unless it becomes a last resort when attempts to stop them fail. We can only tell a select few. Only people we trust."

"Yes, for once Nalani, I agree," said Moana. "It is imperative that we keep a small circle, but we do need more allies. I know some people. I'm sure they'll open their home to us."

"Who are these people?" Nalani asked. "Can we trust them?"

"I met them when I moved here. Trust me, they are exactly who we need in a matter like this," Moana replied. "I do need to tell you one of them is a vampire, but he is a rogue vampire with no connection to the Emperor or any other vampire for that matter."

"You know a vampire!" Alani burst out. "What is wrong with you? If Ava's experience is any indication, it's extremely dangerous to hang out with vampires!"

"I no hang with vamps!" Hiu added.

"Now, calm down. His name is Perry Eberly. He was changed against his will and he does not feed from humans anymore. He only drinks animal blood, which is something that only old vampires can do. I trust him. He lives with my other friends Latoria Gray and Jesse Sutton. Then there's Edison and Kassidy Marsdon who live across the street from them. They all live in Malibu and I think it would be a good place to go."

I was astonished at the way Moana was behaving. She was friends with a vampire. She had a possible plan. This was not the Moana we were all used to.

"I'm not sure I want to trust a vampire right now," I said.

"I swear he is a pure gentleman. He won't hurt any of us, I've known him for a long time now," Moana replied.

"So was the one that I met," I said blankly as I stared down at my waffles.

"Why don't we go meet them? Then we can take a vote, alright?"

Everyone but me said, "Okay," and after a few seconds of thought, I agreed with a nod of my head.

Moana used one of the stolen devices on her cell phone and called her friends to tell them we would be over in a couple hours. Meanwhile, everyone gathered supplies. We all knew our time at Moana's house was running out.

The frantic packing and running around to get everything ready was interrupted by a knock at the door. Everyone turned to Moana in hopes of seeing her expectant face, but hers seemed just as clueless as the rest of ours.

CHAPTER TWELVE

Moana quietly told us all to go upstairs, but Hiu refused to leave her alone. She looked through the peephole as we watched from the hallway upstairs. She kept the chain on the door and opened it a little.

"Can I help you?" she asked.

A man's voice intruded. Something about it sent chills up my spine as I listened from atop the stairs.

"Hello, I'm Mike from Scrapton Security, I'm here because there has been a surplus of breaking and entering in this neighborhood since the satellite virus and we at Scrapton would like to let you know our security systems still work without satellite technology. Here are some pamphlets I'd like to show you," he said.

Moana wasn't buying it.

"Well, I'm on my way out, you can hand them to me through the door and I'll check them out later," Moana said politely.

Then the man pushed the barrel of a gun through the crack in the door and threatened Moana, "Open the door or someone will get hurt," he said.

Moana froze.

I froze.

"Open the door," he said again.

Not seeing another option, she did what he asked. He walked in and grabbed her by the arm while pointing the gun at Hiu.

"Everyone get in the kitchen. That means you ladies upstairs, too," he called out. I peered down at the man. His platinum hair shone brighter than the sun and he was thin in an almost deathly way. The condition of his teeth led me to believe he had drug problems. He wore a crooked smile and evil eyes.

We slowly and cautiously descended the stairs. I saw the fear in Moana's eyes and the fire in Hiu's. When we got to the bottom, the man motioned with the gun for us to get moving into the kitchen. Once everyone gathered, he made us sit at the table.

"Hands on the table. I want to see ten hands," he said as he waved the gun around.

We followed the orders of the man waving the gun.

"Here's what's going to happen. You're all going to give me your rings or bracelets or whatever it is that protect you from the vampires. The Drudge General is coming here in a few hours and I can't have those things stopping him from serving justice."

We all took off our rings and put them on the table. He collected them into a plastic bag and put them in his jacket pocket. Then he started pacing back and forth, watching us with his gun pointed in our direction.

"Where are all the obsidian daggers? I'll need to confiscate those as well."

None of us spoke. I quickly thought about the location of the daggers. One in my bag, one in Hiu's and one in Alani's. I thought Moana probably had one or two in her possession but wasn't positive. I did know of one thing in Moana's bag. I just needed to get to it. The man moved toward Moana with the gun.

"We only have the one we killed Jovan with, it's in my bag," I said. The man turned his attention to me with crazy eyes.

"You. You're the one I'm not allowed to kill," he said after assessing me with his eyes.

"No matter. I've got plenty of people here that you care about. One wrong move and I'll start shooting them. Now. Where's your bag?" he asked.

I wondered why he wasn't allowed to kill me. I couldn't think about it too much at the moment. The shot of courage the words gave me would wear off soon.

"Over there on the floor," I motioned toward the door.

"Go get it. Don't open it, just get it and bring it here," he replied as he brought the gun to Hiu's temple. The fire in Hui's eyes burned hotter.

I got up and walked to the bags. I picked mine up but also grabbed the gun in the side pocket of Moana's bag. I'd shot a gun many times before and I prepared to do it again. I'd seen Moana load it earlier, so all I had to do was take the safety off and pull the trigger. I hid the gun behind the bag as I walked back to the table. As soon as the man took the gun away from Hiu's head, I decided to give him one last chance before I put a bullet in him.

"You don't have to do this. You're human just like us. Just tell them you got here too late. We'll even let you keep the dagger," I tried to sway him.

"Don't play games with me. I may be human, but that doesn't mean I want to be," he spat.

"We are all born as humans. You can't do this to your own kind, it's not right," I said loudly as I clicked the safety off at the word "right" so as not to be heard.

"I don't consider humans my kind. I was meant to be more. Stronger, faster, and a true machine that lives off blood. Now, drop the bag and sit down."

I dropped the bag, but I wasn't planning on sitting down. As the bag dropped, my hand came back up with the gun and I shot him in the chest. The power of the .45 caliber bullet jolted him back and an astonished look briefly entered his face, but a blank expression replaced it as he exhaled his last breath and fell. I shot him right in the heart. A quick death. After the surprise on everyone's face wore off, Hiu opened the dead guys' jacket and went looking for the protection jewelry. Moana approached and slipped the gun out of my hand.

"Mahalo," she whispered.

"Anybody else would have done the same," I replied as I stared down at the body.

"Did you know it was there before you went to the bags?" Moana asked.

I snapped out of my daze and faced Moana, "Yeah, I did. I remember you loading it and putting it in the side pocket. I figured it would be easy to get to."

"She's one akamai wahine!" Hiu said. I mentally translated Hiu's phrase as 'she's is one smart woman.'

"Well, you did good," Moana said as she gave me a side hug with one arm. Hiu redistributed the protection jewelry.

"Alright, let's get out of here before another one of those things shows up," Alani said. Everyone gathered up their stuff and went to the garage to load up into Moana's old Nissan Xterra. Moana got into the driver's seat and Hiu took the passenger's seat. Nalani, Alani, and I piled into the back.

"I'm going to need you all to keep an eye out for anyone following us. Let me know if you see anything suspicious, we don't want to lead anyone to the possible safe house," Moana announced.

Alani and I watched out the back window while Nalani and Hiu checked the side streets. The coast was clear.

It took a while to get there since we took a round-a-bout way to be sure no one followed us. Moana took twists and turns and finally, about an hour later, we made it. Moana first pulled into a driveway that was a block away to check for anyone smart enough to stay on our tail after the twists and turns. After a while, she decided that no one followed us and drove to the real house.

Someone waited near the garage door. The woman motioned for Moana to pull into the garage, and as soon as we pulled in all the way she pushed a button and closed the door behind us. Moana turned off the engine then we all got out of the car.

"Where have you guys been? I was worried," the woman said.

"A drudge tried to hold us hostage, but Ava shot him," Moana replied. Pride and jealousy mingled with each other in her voice. Moana always wanted to be the center of attention and I assumed she wanted to be the one to take the drudge out.

"Oh," the woman said. She seemed surprised at the blunt comment. "Well, I'm glad you got away. I'm Latoria. You must be Ava," she said before shaking my hand.

"How did you know?"

"Well, you are the only non-Hawaiian of the bunch."

"Of course," I said with a smile.

"And you must be the brave Hiu, the intelligent Alani and the great and wise Nalani," Latoria said as she shook each of their hands, "I've heard so much about you all. I'm honored to be your host. Everyone else is inside."

Latoria lead us into the immense house. The inside was open, yet cozy. It brandished an old Victorian style. It would be big enough for all of us. The light allowed me to see Latoria a little better. She had light blonde hair about the same length of Moana's and curled in the same way. She had an hourglass figure accented by the tight red pencil skirt and the white short sleeved button-up blouse she wore. Now I knew where Moana got her style from. Her black heels clattered on the dark wood floor in the hallway.

We all entered the lounge where four others sat on the high-end furnishings. I spotted the vampire right away. His pale skin gave him away. His light brown hair had subtle, blonde highlights.

Latoria made all the introductions. Kassidy and Edison Marsdon were a married couple that lived across the street but moved in because of the recent events and a break in. Kassidy was a little thicker than the other women in the house, but she had a gorgeous curvy figure. Her red hair came down to just above her shoulders. Her kind, green eyes focused on us as newcomers. Edison was also thicker than the other men and had average height and features. His hair was brown and his eyes were blue. Last to be introduced was Jesse Sutton, the owner of the house.

Something about him caught my attention. My gaze lingered on him a little too long. His eyes were dark green and deeply set, framed by eyelashes that no man should ever be allowed to flaunt. They were partially hidden by his almost black hair which fell freely around his face. His hand swept some of it back as his eyes connected with mine. I smiled and turned my attention to Moana as she began to tell them about our situation. Latoria suggested we all move to the living room.

Moana updated them with the info we had as I sat quietly. I measured their reactions. Perry the vampire seemed upset that the other vampires plotted such an evil plan. Kassidy and Edison reacted like most humans would, however, Latoria didn't seem quite as shaken.

After a while, I noticed Jesse Sutton again, sitting with one elbow propped on the back of the chaise lounge in the corner. He looked statuesque. His eyes were the only part of him that moved. He had no nervous ticks, no itches, no moments of repositioning and he only said a few words— none of which were directed at me, although, I did feel his stare every once in a while. When I would glance over, his eyes would dart elsewhere.

He seemed bored with the conversation. His arrogance troubled me. I couldn't see how he could be so nonchalant about the subjects we were discussing. Soon he stood and announced he was going to "retire" even though the sun still illuminated the sky. It was only about eight o'clock. I thought it was an early bedtime for someone who didn't even have to work a day in his life according to Moana.

My eyes trailed Jesse as he left the room. The rest of us continued to talk and make some plans but nothing concrete. We would have to wait until morning to finalize anything because Jesse was part of our group, and since this was his house, we needed his input.

It was strange to me that he didn't seem to care about anything that was going on, yet he was to make the decisions. I pushed the thoughts out of my mind. I had more to worry about than the business of a complete stranger. Maybe he'd understand the gravity of the situation once a bunch of vampires came knocking on his door.

The conversation turned to lighter subjects, and everyone became more comfortable with each other. Perry wouldn't be a problem.

Nalani was the first to leave the conversation for bed. I would follow soon. I forced myself to talk and it was getting tiresome. I tried to present the façade that I was okay, but my week couldn't have gone worse.

I went on a date with a vampire, who took me captive and made me fall in love with him. Then I left him and left me. Then there was the fact that I had killed a man less than six hours ago. As if I didn't have enough to worry about, I had to add a splash of guilt to my soul. I tried convincing myself that he was no better than an evil vampire, but the fact that he was still human made my gut lurch.

I excused myself, but didn't want to go to bed just yet. I needed to get my mind off of things first. Latoria told us to explore the house, except for the doors with names on them. The house had a large courtyard behind it with flowers and plants everywhere and a small pond with fish. It reminded me a little of Hilo so I decided to explore it. Winding pathways led to a gazebo. Tall hedges made it seem like a maze. I walked around smelling the wonderful aroma of the plants and flowers. The calm and beautiful night showcased the stars full moon.

As I walked, I came upon a statue of a man, who stood plainly, facing west. He was dressed in modern clothes and was not in a pose. He just stood there. The statue resembled Jesse Sutton, the owner of the house, in some ways.

If it was a statue of himself, that may explain why he seemed disinterested in the events of the past days. Perhaps he was just a rich narcissist. I worked with many men like him in the past. Egotistical, arrogant, and stubborn. I suspected I wouldn't get along with him. Of course, I'd be polite. We had just taken over his house and doubled the occupancy. I was never the kind of person to be rude.

I walked around a little more before bedtime snuck up on me and went inside to find my room. It was even nicer than the one on the boat. Again, I had my own bathroom, furnished with all the best amenities. I ran a bath to help me relax. I found some bubble bath and scented bath salt and added them to the warm water. Thoughts of my own home teemed in my head. I missed my house and my bed, and most of all, I missed feeling close to my parents.

CHAPTER THIRTEEN

In the morning, I woke feeling rested. I looked out my window. The bright and beautiful day contrasted my current outlook on life. The view overlooked the courtyard, where birds and bugs flew. Then I noticed something odd. The statue of Jesse was missing. I thought back to the night before, wondering if I had imagined the statue. I may be going crazy, but rationalized it may be hidden from view or possibly that it wasn't in the place I thought. The courtyard was practically a maze, so I couldn't be sure.

I dressed for the day then went downstairs to the dining room. The main tables overflowed with fresh fruit, muffins, toast and bagels, along with orange juice, coffee, and milk. I helped myself. It seemed I was one of the first to wake up. Kassidy and Edison were the only others in the dining room. We said good morning to each other. There was still a new acquaintance feel between us.

I sat in one of the chairs across from the couple. Jesse came in soon after. He spotted me right away and brandished a debonair smile. I smiled back but mentally rolled my eyes. He was probably just being polite.

Unexpectedly, he sat directly next to me instead of taking the head of the table as I assumed he would. He looked at me with his piercing gaze again.

"Good morning," he said while maintaining eye contact. "I'm Jesse Sutton. I'm sorry we didn't get a chance to talk last night. I wake up rather early so I'm forced to retire earlier than I would like."

"It's okay, I understand," I replied. Then I took a bite out of my bagel.

"Good, I don't want you or your friends to think I'm rude. I was a little distracted and I'm simply reserved when meeting a group of people. I prefer to meet new people one on one," Jesse explained.

"Yes, I agree. It's uncomfortable when there are so many new people to meet at once. You never know what they're thinking or how they will react to what you say. Talking one on one is easier because you only have to gauge one person's reactions," I said.

For the first time an emotion swept Jesse's face, he smiled and said, "Exactly."

Then he turned to Kassidy and Edison and asked them what they had planned for the day. They replied saying they were going with Perry and Hiu to find some obsidian, and as if on cue, Hiu and Perry, who seemed quite friendly for a vampire and a marked "slayer," came into the dining room. Hiu greeted me in his Hawaiian language, and stuffed some food into his arms before his expedition. Perry went for some chocolate and wine; a classic vampire breakfast. Soon the four of them headed out, and I was left alone with Jesse. I wondered what happened to Alani, Nalani, Moana and Latoria, but didn't ask.

I glanced at Jesse who quietly ate next to me. I was sure he could see me out of the corner of his eye. The uncomfortable silence formed a cloud above us. I didn't know what to say to him and wasn't sure if I should bring up the statue mystery because I could just be crazy or blind, one of the two.

I finished my food and was about to leave the table when Jesse spoke up.

"So, you are the one who saved the other's lives with your quick thinking?" Jesse asked.

I resettled in my seat before answering, "Yes, I suppose I did. But killing another human being is not something I'll soon be able to forgive myself for."

"You gave him a chance. He chose the side of evil, Ava. You must not hate yourself for protecting those you love from evil."

I was surprised he even cared. "You might be right, but I still feel guilty. I wish I would have just wounded him or something. Maybe that would have opened his eyes."

"He was a drudge. He would be killed anyway if he had decided to try to get out of that crowd. The vampires don't like humans knowing their secrets, but you've experienced that first-hand."

"Yes, I do now. Two weeks ago I didn't know they existed. Now I'm all too familiar with them and I'm caught in the middle of this big mess. Sometimes I wish I could be one of the people still oblivious to the vampires and their plans of world domination. I want to be one of the people thinking the satellite problems are the only major issue in the world at the moment," I explained.

"If it wasn't for you, we wouldn't be aware of the situation. Now that I think about it, it does make sense they would be the ones behind the virus. I should have made the connection right away, but I've been preoccupied with other ventures. Those will have to be put on hold until we find out how to stop the vampires."

"Life won't return to normal until we get this cleared up. But what are we going to do?" I asked. I'd been wrong about Jesse not caring about the situation. He might actually be able to help.

"Well, you were with that one for three days, did you hear anything or see anything that may be of some use?" he prodded.

"I don't know. I'm still kinda processing it all," I said. I left out that Tom seemed to be the only thing on my mind lately.

"Well, if you'd like to tell me about those days it's possible my perspective can help you sift through it all. If you are comfortable with that, I mean."

"Actually, I think it might help. Where should I start?"

"Wherever you are comfortable," he said. He repositioned himself and turned more toward me.

I felt like I was in an interview.

"Okay, well, I guess it all started the day the virus hit. I went into work and I received a call from Tom, he was my client and he needed passes for some corporate executives coming to town. I now know they were members of the vampire council—whatever that means. So, after I made the passes, I went to see Tom to give him further instructions and he asked me out to dinner.

"I said yes against my better judgment, and we met at the restaurant. That's when he told me about the possible buy out of my company. The news angered me, but he calmed me down. The next day, I saw him with the council members in the lobby and we made a lunch date, he told me he wanted to offer me a job at Psytech and I could take any position I wanted."

"Wait," Jesse cut in, "Why did he do that? You aren't a vampire."

"Well, he said I had a good work ethic. He'd been trying to get me to work for him ever since I signed him on as a client. Not to mention he wanted me to become a vampire, but that's later on in the story," I explained.

"Right, please continue. Sorry for the interruption."

I smiled. "No problem. So, anyway, I told him I needed to think about it, and he told me I should meet him after the meeting on Wednesday in his company's warehouse and give him my answer. After I thought about it, I decided I'd be a fool to turn down the offer, so I decided to accept the job. On Wednesday, Tom told me the news before I heard it in the staff meeting; Psytech bought Herrick-Peyton. I went to the meeting anyway and acted surprised when they told my co-workers the news. After the meeting, I went to the warehouse where I met Tom and the entire vampire council. This is where I figured out Tom and his corporate executives were actually vampires and they were behind the virus.

"Tom tried to turn me, but I stabbed him with a pocketknife and tried to run away. I couldn't get out of the warehouse, so Tom made a deal with me that I could wait three days. They put a wristband on me that would inject me with venom if I got too far away from Tom. So then he took me to his house. The next day we returned to the warehouse. There was some sort of crisis so he drove fast on the way there."

"What was the crisis?"

"NASA was getting close to disabling the virus. They had computers set up and two Texperts working on them trying to put up more firewalls or something. They avoided the crisis, but ultimately they decided they needed to send someone into NASA to keep them from finding the virus. They wanted someone in place within 48 hours."

"So they infiltrated NASA?" Jesse interrupted again.

"I think so, they seemed fairly confident it would be easy to do," I replied.

"A friend of mine works for NASA, I'm going to give him a heads up. Maybe he can find the mole. What happened after that?" Jesse asked as he leaned a little closer.

"Well, one of the council members—Tom's creator, I later found out—asked Tom away and I was left alone where Tom's assistant nearly got me killed or changed. Tom intervened and stopped him from draining my blood. Apparently, there are some loopholes in vampire law. Oh, I didn't tell anyone else that part. I don't want to worry Alani. Could you keep that between us?" I asked. I'd said too much, but Jesse's expression was kind and understanding.

"Of course, I won't. I understand you don't want Alani to worry more than she already does," he replied.

"Thanks. After that we spent the rest of the time alone. I made him trust me, and he took off my wristband just before he was going to change me. That's when I made my escape," I finished my story with a shrug.

Jesse nodded his head, "I see. Well, that NASA bit is helpful. Although, I am wondering why Tom wanted you to become a vampire so badly. It's uncommon and quite a mystery to me. Even if he did have true feelings for you, the vampire council would never allow it. The risk of a human knowing the information exposed to you is too large to justify. The feelings of a vampire with a crush are insignificant to the council," Jesse explained.

"He said it was because he couldn't bear to see me become a blood slave. He cared for me. I think he's a pretty powerful vampire, he is head of the Hawaii branch."

An emotion flickered on Jesse's face. I couldn't quite tell what it was. "You care for him too, don't you?"

Heat washed over me from my face down to my neck. I paused before answering. I didn't want to expose my feelings for Tom. "Maybe it was Stockholm syndrome. I don't know, but I did develop feelings for him. Reality slapped me in the face, and I knew we couldn't be together when Hiu and I stole those devices. His world is too different and I'm not willing to give up my humanity and my life for that world."

"Is there anything you're leaving out?"

"No. I told you and everyone else all the important stuff. I'm not going to go into all the little moments Tom and I spent together," I replied.

"Okay," Jesse said.

"Why would I intentionally leave out anything important?" I asked.

"Sounds like you were in love with the guy. Or still are. I just want to be sure you're on our side. This might end in his death," Jesse said.

I crossed my arms. "I'm on your side. I'm on the same side as my family. That's why I escaped. If I hadn't, I'd be a vampire right now and no one would know about any of this. I want to stop this just as much as you do."

"But if the situation calls for it, will you be okay with killing Tom?" he asked.

I didn't answer, but the question hit me like a brick.

"I'm sorry. Obviously that's a conversation you're not ready for. I do believe you're on our side. I just don't think you'll kill him if you need to and that worries me a little."

I was about to tell him I needed time to think everything over when he changed the subject.

"I wonder, why did the council decide to give you three days? Why not just change you?"

"Tom declared me a prospect. He didn't want to force me."

"Oh, trust me. It must have been sanctioned by the council, but I still don't understand. You do realize he's wanted to change you since the two of you met, right? Possibly even before you met."

"What do you mean?"

"Well, they only let vampires work for Psytech, if he wanted you to work for him before all of this, then he wanted to change you back then."

My thoughts started going back to the first day I met Tom. Tom had responded to an ad I put out and set up a meeting to look at the office spaces and warehouses. After Tom finished signing the papers, he asked me to come and work for him for the first time. I declined, of course, passing it off as a come-on. Throughout the three years I worked with Tom he never relented. Now I questioned his motives.

"I . . . I think you are right. What if he was motivated to change me before we even met face to face?"

"I'm 99 percent sure he was, but the question is why?"

We sat in silence for a while. I thought back, trying to recall everything Tom had ever said to me. I could find no hint of why he wanted to change me so badly. He could have easily done it the other night in the boat, but he didn't. I wondered, why it had to be on my terms and why me?

"I suppose we will figure it out, soon enough. Motives always come out eventually," Jesse said. "Perhaps we should talk about something else. Stress builds if you don't forget about your problems every once in a while."

"That's true. So, how did you come into owning this beautiful house?" I asked, trying to stay with the spirit of keeping subjects light.

"Well, I inherited a lot of money from a rich uncle who died some time ago. It happens to be more than I can spend in a lifetime, so I try been trying to keep busy with hobbies and such. Traveling is also one of my passions," he replied.

"That must be wonderful; seeing the world."

"Yes, but seeing the world doesn't always lead to finding what you're looking for."

"And what is it you're looking for?" I asked.

"What I'm looking for can't be found. Unfortunately for me, I will be wandering the earth until the end of my days," Jesse replied.

"Haven't you found something to give you a reason to call this your home? What about all these romantically styled furnishings? There must be a reason your home is so beautifully decorated," I said as I motioned at the room around us. There was a lot of red and a lot of dark wood. Furnishings you would imagine as the background of a romance story.

"You mean love? No. I am not destined for love," Jesse chuckled.

"Everyone is destined to be loved at one point or another. It's whether or not you can return the favor that determines how you spend the rest of your life," I countered, "You can either end up alone or with your soul mate."

"I don't know if I believe in true love. Love is for two people. Unfortunately, most of the time, only one person is truly in love with the other."

"I'd rather try to find love than die alone," I said.

"And how many times have you been in love?" he asked with clear disgust and sarcasm at the last two words.

I dodged the question, not wanting to reveal my feelings for Tom to a complete stranger. "Have you ever fallen in love?"

"No. Most of the women I meet want my money, not my love."

"That's unfortunate. It's too bad you've had so much time to travel the world but have yet to meet a woman that meets your standards. I imagine you must have high standards considering you won't even give it a chance," I said as Jesse's expression turn to anguish.

"I prefer not to casually date. Especially the dull-witted women of this town," Jesse gestured out the window.

I smiled, "You should move. This is possibly the worst city to live in if you want to find a meaningful relationship."

Jesse smiled and sent me an intense gaze, "You are both stubborn and clever."

"And you're both mysterious and pessimistic," I responded.

Jesse smiled again. I was surprised a man I deemed egotistical would take part in such a strange conversation. We barely knew each other yet felt comfortable enough to talk about love.

He was witty and quick to respond to my prying questions without actually answering them. This frustrated me, but also made me want to learn more. The two of us sat in silence for a few minutes, measuring the other for reactions. The mystery about his past stirred my thoughts. I wondered if he'd had his heart broken.

Hiu and the rest of the roommates coming back from weapon hunting interrupted the silence. They had obsidian, and a lot of it. Perry stayed away from it for the most part. He said he'd take one blade just in case one of his own kind turned on him but he wouldn't carry anything else. I could tell that just being around the obsidian made him wary.

"Hey, where dem girls?" Hiu asked.

"They're out trying to get guns for protection against drudges. I doubt they'll find any. The virus has made everyone want to keep and buy all the guns they can," Jesse answered. "The whole world is starting to go into panic mode. I'd be willing to bet people are trying to link the virus to the end of the world, using the fact that it was implanted on 2/2/2020 as some sort of code."

"Nalani went too?" I asked.

"I asked her to go along for the ride so that I could have a conversation with you and she graciously obliged," Jesse answered.

It was helpful to talk about everything going on, but I wasn't sure the way he'd manipulated the situation was a good sign. I was surprised at how much I had opened up to a stranger. The end of our conversation veered in a strange direction, but my first impressions of him from the night before were obviously inaccurate. Something about him hinted at deeply hidden secret. Something I wanted to uncover. It was possible Jesse wasn't the conceited man I had thought he was the night before. The thought reminded me that I had to go try to find the statue again to ease my troubled mind.

"Well, I'm going to get some fresh air," I said as I excused myself.

Jesse nodded at me with his eyes locked on mine. I turned, and Hiu gave me a strange expression I couldn't quite read. Everyone else just waved.

I went out the back door and started to explore the courtyard again. The maze of tall bushes made finding my way back to the place I saw the statue a little difficult. I remembered it faced west, and that it was west of the gazebo. I started making my way over there.

The courtyard was even more beautiful during the day. I noticed there weren't any other statues. Most courtyards had statues of lions or dogs or some kind of animal, but I didn't even see so much as a concrete squirrel. Soon I started to think I had hallucinated the statue because I couldn't find it anywhere.

After about thirty minutes, I gave up on my search. I drew the conclusion that Jesse must have seen it, decided to give it a chance in the courtyard and then eventually sent it back. I was under a lot of stress, but hallucinating statues that looked like Jesse seemed impossible.

I pushed it out of my mind. My thoughts needed to be controlled. They grew wild and I needed to cage them like the little beasts they were. Stress swelled up like a balloon in my head.

I started walking back into the house. Now all I could think about was the stress and how much I wanted a little wine. My mind cautioned me about my nervous drinking. I didn't want the new roommates to think I was a drunk. After giving it more thought, I decided I should indulge a little and try to relax. After all, the stress of the last week weighed on me. It was making me worry about silly things that were irrelevant to the issues at hand.

CHAPTER FOURTEEN

I went to the kitchen to find a bottle of wine and came up with one-year old cheap, but good, brand. As I poured myself a glass, Alani came into the kitchen.

"Hey! Pour me some too?" she asked.

"Okay, let me get a glass."

I got out another glass and poured Alani some wine. We both sat at the bar-height counter top. I hadn't talked to Alani much since the shooting incident.

"How are you doing?" I asked her.

"I'm good. The hunt went well. We got some guns and ammo. But, I'm stressed like everyone else," she answered.

"Yeah, me too. With everything that has happened it's a wonder I'm not going insane."

Alani looked at me with a little envy in her eyes, "You are so strong, Ava. I've been thinking about that guy; the drudge. I don't know if I would have been able to do what you did. I think I might freeze in a situation like that and get someone hurt, and I've really been worrying about it."

I sighed, "Alani, that's normal. Most people don't react like that. It's hard for one human being to kill another human being. Even an evil human being."

"But Hiu did it too. He killed the vampire when you guys went to the warehouse," Alani countered.

"Yes, but that was a vampire. Plus he's a guy. Guys go to war and stuff. It's in their nature to have the ability to kill another human. I'm not saying Hiu is a monster, I'm just saying it comes easier to men."

"Maybe you are right, but how did you get up the courage?" Alani asked.

"I just did. Our lives were in danger. It was either us or him, and that motivated me enough to pull the trigger."

"I get it. I just don't know if I could do the same. I'm still not sure I can protect my friends; my ohana."

"Well, if the time comes, I think you'll do fine. Just follow your heart," I said.

Alani gave a nervous smile. I could see she wasn't quite convinced but knew she would be okay. I changed the subject and the two of us talked for a while. We tried to stay off the darker subjects running through both our minds.

"So, how about that Jesse Sutton?" Alani said with a silly grin. She was always a little boy crazy. Ever since I met her, Alani had loved chatting about hot guys. Jesse was apparently her new eye candy. I could see why. With his boyish good looks and eyes that could stop a woman in her tracks, who wouldn't target him for girl talk?

"He's good looking, but a little eccentric, I think," I said, remembering my conversation about love with him.

"Yeah, I think you might be right. He's really quiet and he keeps to himself," Alani mused. After that, the conversation changed to the subject of the weather and more mundane subjects.

Eventually, we drank most of the bottle of wine. We were both feeling buzzed but not drunk, which was good because Latoria made arrangements for all of the house-mates to meet for dinner and discuss everything. Alani and I ate sandwiches together before I slipped away to my room. I rested on the bed until dinner time came around then checked myself in the mirror before joining the rest of my house-mates in the dining room.

Jesse sat at the head of the table, Latoria sat at his left and I was at his right. Next to me sat Alani, then Nalani, Hiu, and Moana. Next to Latoria sat Perry, then Kassidy and Edison. The ten of us were quiet at first. Kassidy had set the table. She'd prepared a spaghetti dish. The memory of Tom making me spaghetti bombarded my mind as Kassidy served. I tried to put it behind me so I could concentrate on the conversation.

Jesse started. He seemed to take the lead easily. His confidence made him a good leader. His demeanor contrasted heavily from the night before.

"So, where do we sit as far as obtaining obsidian?" he asked. I assumed the question was meant to get everyone on the same page since he had greeted them after the weapon hunt.

Hiu answered, "We got plenty. We bought four daggers, two spears, and about eight pounds of raw obsidian that I'll be making into daggers and throwing spikes. Add that to the three daggers we had before and we coasting."

"That's great. What about guns?" Jesse asked as he turned his gaze to Moana.

"We weren't able to get as many as I would have liked, but we did get a shot gun, two rifles and two pistols. Plus we have my pistol. So, there are six guns total. I made sure all the pistols use the same bullets and the two rifles use the same bullets. We've got about 600 rounds of ammo, roughly 100 rounds for each gun. I'm hoping to find more tomorrow or the next day, but ammo is even harder to find than guns right now," she answered.

"I see. Who knows how to handle a gun besides Moana, Ava, Hiu and myself?" Jesse asked, his gaze lingered on me. I turned my gaze to the strangers across the table.

"I do," Latoria said.

"So do I," said Edison.

"I would like to learn," Alani said out of the blue. I had no idea Alani wanted anything to do with guns. Our conversation earlier must have made her interest in protection grow.

"Alright, I can teach you," Jesse said. "When I feel you're confident with yourself, you'll have my gun. Moana you keep yours. Hiu, which one do you want?"

"I'll take the shot gun."

"Ava?" Jesse turned to me and stared into my eyes again.

I felt a rush of warmth on my face, "Uh, one of the pistols would be fine."

"Same for me," said Latoria.

"Alright, that leaves the rifles to Alani and I, and Edison."

"My security system is up and running, I used one of those devices to turn it on, then I disconnected any communication to the satellites and unhooked the device. I did it quickly, so I don't think they can track it, but we do need to be on high alert. We need someone watching at all times. There are six of us with guns so we can run in four-hour shifts. Perry will be on the lookout whenever he can since he doesn't sleep and doesn't necessarily need a gun to defend himself. Who wants mid-night to 4 a.m.?" Jesse asked.

"I'll take it," Moana said.

"Okay, 4 a.m. to 8 a.m.?"

"I'll do that one," I said.

After a short hesitation, and a strange glance toward Latoria, Jesse said, "I'll take 8 a.m. to noon. Who wants 12 p.m. to 4 p.m.?"

"I take that one," Hiu said.

"Alright, 4 p.m. to 8 p.m.?"

"That's me," said Latoria.

"I guess you have 8 p.m. to mid-night Edison," Jesse said.

Edison just nodded. He didn't seem to care.

"If anyone wants to trade, that's fine, but we'll post the shifts on the white board in the kitchen, both parties must agree to switch, of course."

Jesse paused to take a couple bites of his spaghetti. The rest of us took the opportunity to do the same. I watched him out of the corner of my eye. I got the feeling he was doing the same to me. The strange air between us since the earlier conversation became more difficult for me to ignore.

"Now," Jesse began again, "In the event that we unexpectedly become host to some unwelcome visitors, we need an escape plan. Any ideas?"

"We will need a meeting place, just in case we all get split up," Nalani said.

"Yes, I was thinking about Hiu's boat. There is a marina a few blocks away. We could move your boat there and use that as a getaway. Can you do that Hiu?" Jesse asked.

"Yeah, but I need some money to dock it, I'm broke from buying the obsidian."

"That's not a problem. I will pay for it. What's the name of your boat?"

"It's Palila."

"Alright, everyone memorize that. Hiu, when you get a boathouse tell us the number. I'll call the marina tomorrow to set up a spot for you. We'll need a code of some sort that will get the message to all of us without alerting visitors to where we're going, any ideas?"

"Well," Hiu said, "Palila, means bird. So if we say, 'find the bird,' that should get the message out and make the eke futless. They think we mean plane or helicopter, no one thinks 'bird' means boat."

"Okay, not sure what eke futless means, but that's a good plan. Everyone must memorize this along with the name and boathouse number. Do not write it down, we can't risk the potential intruders finding any clues. The fastest way to get to the marina is by car. But, there is a tunnel in the courtyard that was built before I acquired this property. It leads toward the marina but it's only about a football field long. It's tight and you'll have to run the rest of the way, but if you can't get to a car it is a good way to get out unseen. After dinner I'll show you all where the entrance is," Jesse told them.

The rest of dinner was rather quiet. We ate and talked quietly. I caught Jesse's glance a few times. I started to wonder if I had something in my teeth. Sitting so close to him made me nervous, for some reason. The energy between us made me tense and left me second-guessing everything I did. I couldn't shake the almost intimate fog between us, but I pushed it out of my mind. I started telling myself he couldn't be watching me. Not for the reason my body seemed to suspect. After all, he was the man who didn't believe in love. Although, who could say what he thought about lust?

After dinner, Jesse took us all outside to the entrance of the tunnel. The tunnel itself was extremely small. I couldn't believe anyone could even fit through it. No one claustrophobic would be able to handle it. The entrance was behind a bush on the west side of the courtyard, somewhat near the spot I had seen the statue, but again it was nowhere to be seen.

The tunnel was completely concealed. Anyone oblivious to its existence would never notice it, and it provided an advantage for us. I knew if anything ever happened, this was indeed a good plan.

We all stood around the tunnel entrance and finalized our plans. Hiu volunteered to take some supplies to his boat in the morning. He was also going to try track down another gun to leave on the boat. His plan was to be back in time for his shift.

A chilly wind came up and everyone headed inside. I was at the back of the group, and Jesse stayed behind.

"See you at eight tomorrow morning," Jesse called to me.

I turned and smiled back at him before waving. I decided I'd better get some sleep before my shift. I wanted to be at my best while I was keeping watch for vampires and drudges. The sun was about to go down, and the western part of the sky was turning a beautiful orange color. It seemed it was going to be a clear night with not a cloud to be seen.

Everyone went inside the house, except for Latoria who was on watch duty, and Jesse who was still out in the courtyard. Latoria would have a short shift tonight. Edison would be taking over in about an hour, and then Moana at midnight, and then it would be my turn.

I went directly to my room, and set the alarm clock for 3:15. I she wanted to take a quick shower in the morning to help wake me up a little. Aside from a few thoughts about Jesse and the safe house, I fell asleep quickly, and didn't wake until my alarm went off.

CHAPTER FIFTEEN

I felt well-rested for the first time in days and the shower rejuvenated me. After looking out my window into the dark courtyard, I grabbed the gun I'd been assigned and went to find Moana. The breeze chilled the night air and the temperature had cooled considerably since sundown. I remembered my jacket, but I glanced down at it with a pang of anguish. It was the same one I wore when I escaped Tom's house. That memory would forever be attached to it; like a patch sewn on that only I could see. I ran my fingers down to the place I imagined the patch would be. The image of a heart broken in two came to mind. Moana's call startled me.

"Hey! You've come to relieve me?"

"Yeah, I'm here," I said, "Anything happen on your shift that I should know?"

"Nope. It was pretty quiet. I saw a jogger come around, but they never came back around, so I'm pretty sure it was just someone from the neighborhood. Keep your eye out for things like the same car driving by more than once, or the same person walking by more than once. Monitor everything, and if you need to review something, the video surveillance equipment is pretty easy to use."

"Alright, I think I can handle it," I said with a smile.

"Basically just make your rounds every so often, but you can spend most of your time in the video surveillance room. I went on my rounds whenever my eyes tried to shut, so maybe that will help you too."

"Thanks, Moana. Go get some rest, alright?"

Moana waved and went inside to catch some more sleep. I decided to make my rounds first and then go to the room. The grounds were serene. I walked out to the front to see if there were any cars or people around. Nothing. I went to the courtyard and walked along the fence line to find any possible weak spots. Once I entered the area where the tunnel began, I found the statue again. I looked up at it, bewildered.

I stared at it, afraid that if I blinked it would disappear. I walked around to the front while I wondered what was wrong with me. It stood in the same position as the first time I'd seen it, and also facing west. It resembled Jesse . . . I was sure. He was just standing there. The empty expression showed no sadness or happiness or even anger on the statue's face. I was certain it was Jesse; the likeness was uncanny. The only other possibility was that it was someone genetically close in his family like a brother or father.

I wondered if Jesse had the statue put away during the day but then realized that was a ridiculous thing to do. Why would he be so protective over something so plain? It could be considered art simply because it was a statue, but there seemed to be nothing interesting about it. It may hold sentimental value for him, which is really the only person the statue had to please. The mystery surrounding the statue confounded me. I tried to stop thinking about it and decided if I ever got up the courage, I'd ask him about the silly thing. Maybe he was messing with me.

I finished up my rounds and went back inside to the control room. The cameras were placed strategically on the property. They focused all the weak spots and the entry points. The street had sufficient lighting and passing cars were easy to identify.

Minutes turned into hours. I had gone out every half hour to check the grounds. The sun's rays started to peak over the horizon when I went out around 7 a.m. I started in the front again. I developed a routine of sorts to make sure I checked everything I needed to.

Toward the end of my routine, I came upon the statue again. I'd never seen it in the light so I decided to take another look since the sun started to rise. I turned east, and as soon as the first sliver of the sun peeked over the horizon I turned back to the statue. I was surprised to see the statue taking on color. And life.

The statue was coming to life.

Jesse was coming to life.

Jesse blinked and his eyes were no longer granite, but real human eyes. I was standing so still that I could have been a statue. My thoughts came up with only one conclusion. I'd fallen asleep in the control room and I was dreaming. But as I took in the morning air, I realized I still had my sense of smell, which was the one sense that never worked when I dreamed. Fear crept into my bones. I didn't know whether I should run away or start questioning him or possibly even scream.

One thing was for sure, my legs definitely weren't moving. As for my voice, it had done the running away for me. Jesse's expression was steady for what seemed like an eternity. Then, he took a tentative step toward me and outstretched his hand. He approached me like one would approach a frightened rabbit caught in a trap. I remained frozen to the ground.

Jesse hung his head. "I was afraid of this. I didn't want you to find out before I could tell you, but I suppose that's out the window now," he paused and brought his head back up. "Won't you say something?"

My mind raced. Flashbacks of Tom's big reveal in the warehouse hit me. I half expected to see the vampire council lurking in the courtyard.

A big secret about Jesse had just been revealed to me. I wasn't sure exactly what the secret was, but my past experience with vampires told me he probably didn't want it out in the open, and that scared the hell out of me. What would he do to me?

I asked the only thing that popped into my mind, "What are you?"

"I'm human, Ava. I've just been . . . enchanted."

"What does that mean? How do you turn into stone? I've never even heard of any such being that can do that."

"It's not a choice. I'm cursed, Ava," Jesse said taking another step toward me.

Reflexes finally kicked in and I took a step back. Jesse stopped moving again. He held out his hands in a position meant to calm me down.

"A witch did this to me. I turn to stone from sunset to sunrise, and I will do it for an eternity. I wanted to tell you. I wanted to tell all of your friends, but I had to know I could trust you first. I was going to tell you tonight, and everyone else tomorrow morning. You've been through so much and I didn't want to shock you like this."

I didn't realize witches were real. I hadn't thought of the fact that if vampires existed, other strange things creeped around the earth too.

"For an eternity? You mean you have eternal life?"

"Yes, and eternal youth," he replied.

"Why would a witch curse you with that?"

"Because I broke her heart. We were to be married. Her name was Sarah and I had no idea she was a witch. I didn't love her. It was an arranged marriage. Set up by my parents. So, I snuck around with another woman at night and during the day I chaperoned Sarah around town to make wedding plans. She found out through her magic that I was unfaithful. The day before our wedding she confronted me. She was livid. Before she cursed me, she said since I had snuck around like a creature of the night, that I should never be able to roam in the night again, and then she sentenced me to be imprisoned in my own body every night for the rest of eternity."

"Imprisoned? Do you mean you can see and hear everything but you just can't move?" I asked.

"Yes. It's more agonizing than you may think. I've watched many horrible things happen in front of me without being able to do anything about it," Jesse said. He was looking into the distance, but I could tell he saw remnants of his past.

"I can't imagine what that must be like," I replied.

"Trust me, you don't want to know. The night you all first arrived, I saw you looking at me. I've seen people look at me before, but the way you looked at me was different, almost as if you knew already. I questioned if you were Sarah re-incarnated, but once I spoke to you the next day I knew it was impossible. You and she are nothing alike."

Words refused to form in my throat, so I studied him. I felt he would return to his stony condition at any moment. I wondered how long he had walked the earth. He said "arranged marriage," which was a custom from many years ago. I hesitated to ask. I was still uneasy about the situation.

"Who else knows?" I asked.

"Latoria and Perry. They're helping me with something related to my situation so I had to tell them. They make sure nothing happens to me while I'm in statue form."

"What does that mean?" I asked.

Jesse broke eye contact with me and stared out at the distance, before saying, "I've met a lot of people who view my curse a little differently than I do." He looked back at me, "I hope you aren't frightened."

"Well, I just found out you're a gargoyle," I said before I could stop myself. I wasn't sure he'd like the term, but he chuckled and showed me a genuine smile.

"Gargoyles are rumored to come to life at night, my curse is the other way around," he said with a chuckle still in his voice.

I was glad he didn't take offense, but I couldn't help feeling awkward. "Right, well I better go and check the monitors." I said abruptly, "I'm still on duty."

Jesse's face seemed confused at first, but he regained his former smiling expression, "Yes, of course, I will see you again at eight. I still hope I didn't scare you. I have no control over when I change from stone back to living human being. If you want to talk more about it, let me know. I'm going to go clean up before my shift."

I nodded and returned to my surveillance. I checked the front before going back to the control room. Once inside I let out a breath that had been stuck in my chest since I witnessed Jesse's transformation. I thought I might hyperventilate.

I had to catch my breath and get a grip on what had happened. I sat in the chair to calm myself. Soon, Jesse came to replace me. I relayed the info I had. There was nothing exciting happening yet. Jesse told me he was going to hold a house meeting and asked if he could talk to me afterward. I agreed and also told him I'd keep his secret until the meeting. I thought that would give me enough time to process.

Later, at the meeting, Jesse told everyone what had happened to him all those years ago. My mind was the same as it had been at the staff meeting the day everyone else had found out Psytech was buying Herrick-Peyton. I was one chapter ahead of everyone, and my mind didn't want to review that last chapter, so I let my mind wander. Everyone had questions for Jesse, and I left the room early. I wasn't entirely sure I was ready to talk to Jesse quite yet.

I was in the other room when I heard Jesse cut the questioning short because it was starting to get dark. He invited everyone to come see for themselves what happened to him at night. A few people followed Jesse. Latoria and Perry stayed behind.

Hiu was curious and joined the inquisitive group, but he had been the only one to notice my absence and asked, "Hey, where'd Ava go?" on his way out.

His question went unanswered. Everyone was too preoccupied with the excitement at hand to track me down. And that was fine with me.

CHAPTER SIXTEEN

The next day, I steered clear of Jesse's spot when the sun started to rise. I avoided it all together, actually. His statue occasionally entered the corners of my vision, but didn't I get close enough for him to see me.

When the shift change came up, Jesse found me in the control room. I gave the report on my shift and made up an excuse to leave. I dodged him and everyone else by staying in my room that night. My next shift began and I repeated the routine of evading Jesse's spot once again.

I made up another excuse when Jesse came to replace me for the third time since I'd found out what he was. I felt guilty for not talking to him about what happened, but I appreciated that he gave me space and didn't push the issue. I ventured an uneasy wave as I exited the control room, he smiled but it didn't reach his eyes. I could tell Jesse was distressed over the animosity between us, but I wasn't ready to let him in again.

I felt tired as I walked back to the house, so I decided to take a nap. I woke up after almost four hours of sleep. I couldn't believe I had slept so long, and went to get some of my energy out by taking a walk in the garden. It was there that I ran into Jesse. It was a little after noon, so he must have been ending his shift. I was still uncomfortable around him even after he told everyone his secret. I didn't understand why I felt this way, but it was something I couldn't shake.

"Ava! I've been wanting to speak with you, would you mind if I joined you?" Jesse said as he switched to a jog to catch up to me on the path leading into the courtyard.

"Um, sure that would be fine. I was just going for a little walk around the courtyard. It's a lovely place. I've been using it to get my mind off of things."

"I use it for the same reason," he said, "I haven't gotten the chance to talk to you since the other day. I should say I haven't gotten up the courage. I could see you needed some space. Is everything all right? You seem distant the last couple days. Alani is worried, which makes me worry."

"Yes, I'm okay. I guess I just needed to clear my head. Everything keeps changing around me and sometimes I just want things to . . . settle down."

"I'm so sorry you found out this way, Ava. It was sprung on you too soon," Jesse said as he gazed into my eyes.

My mind ran like a city hit by a tornado. All my thoughts were mixed up and chaotic. I couldn't understand why my emotions about Jesse's secret were so much different than everyone else's. Why wasn't I excited to have another immortal on our side? Then I realized, his immortality may be the reason I was so reluctant to be as welcoming. He was immortal like Tom had been.

I hadn't thought about him in days because I turned it all off after Jesse's reveal. I wondered if I subconsciously thought Jesse could be the cure for my heartbreak. My contempt for his curse could be a result of me developing feelings for him. The idea snuck up on me. I knew I was attracted to him, but to develop feelings for him so early?

My depression and the original dislike I had for him when we first met had masked my attraction, and I now realized Jesse would have been someone I'd like to date had I not been preoccupied with my romance with Tom or the delicate state the world was in as vampires rose to power. I started to get dizzy. Jesse must have noticed because he began to lead me to a bench.

"Are you feeling all right Ava?" he asked holding my arm to give me support.

"I don't know. Everything is spinning in my head, but I think I know why I avoided you," I said with a guilty bob of my head. I was reluctant to reveal what I'd just uncovered in my subconscious.

"Why is that? Are you afraid you'll turn into a gargoyle?" Jesse asked me jokingly.

I giggled a little. Then, I took a deep breath as I sorted out my feelings by saying them out loud. "I think it's because I started to have feelings for you before I found out about your curse. Ever since our conversation on my first morning here, I felt electrically charged around you. I think after I found out what you were, I was scared because you were now another immortal being to me. My head thinks, 'You can't be with him, Ava. Remember what happened last time, it's not going to work.' But my heart still wants to try. Of course, I don't even know if you feel the same way about me, but even if you did, I'm terrified it will end before it even begins."

"Ava, you're over thinking this. My situation has changed the way I think about love. I never wanted it, even before I was cursed I only cared about myself. I often wondered what it would be like to stop being so selfish and give in. But I knew my curse would prevent it from even happening, so I put it out of my head and resorted back to my old ways. I didn't want anyone to know what I was, so I kept the opposite sex at a distance. But, our conversation the other day made me reconsider what I want out of life. I've never desired a relationship, but there's something about you that makes me want to try. I do have feelings for you Ava, but it's not the end of the world. The difference between 'last time' and me is I'm on your side. Not to mention I don't drink blood and I don't want to change you. I want to know you, Ava, not my own personalized version of you."

"But, you don't age. I'll grow old while you stay perfectly frozen in time."

"Perfect is not exactly what I would call it, but there may be a way to change that Ava, if we can find another witch. One powerful enough to break the curse, then I can have a normal life. Of course, we have to save the world from vampire domination first, but eventually I'm hoping to get the curse removed. That's what Latoria and Perry are helping me with."

I smiled a little. "How can you give up an eternity?"

"I never wanted an eternity to live. I've spent a lot of time in this world. When I met you and talked to you, I knew there was something different about you. I want to see if love exists for someone as cynical as me," Jesse said as he moved closer to me on the bench.

"Hasn't there been anyone else?" I asked.

"Well, as I said before, I had a few flings, but no woman has ever been able to hold my attention. I always wondered if part of my curse was not being able to fall in love. Latoria tries to make me happy, she wants to change my mind about the idea of us, but I just don't feel connected to her. There is no chemistry. I felt instantly drawn to you, as if you were the earth and I was the moon. Like gravity," Jesse said as his intense gaze sharpened.

This came as a little surprise to me. I didn't know how to react and where my feelings stood so I changed the subject. "What about this curse breaking thing? How do we find a witch that can break it?"

Jesse snapped out of his intense stare and turned his attention to the horizon, "We have a few leads. I think we should wait until this vampire business is over. I might need my immortality if I'm going to be battling vampires. I just want to take things one step at a time. I don't want to push you into this. If you want to move on, I will understand. I know it's a long shot that I'll be normal again. It's going to be a long road. So if you would rather just forget about this whole conversation, I will understand."

"I think taking things slow is a good idea. I don't think we should make any rash decisions right now. We should concentrate on the vampires for now," I said.

Jesse nodded in agreement.

The awkward energy that surrounded me, when I was near Jesse, dissipated into the air around us. I took a deep breath. We had both laid it all out on the line. I was completely at ease now that we had talked. I was surprised my feelings came out so quickly. I was barely aware of them before I started talking about it. I suppose when it's possible the world as we know it will end. There's no time to lose.

Tom popped into my head. I wasn't prepared for the assault on my thoughts. I questioned whether or not I still had feelings for him. The love we had shared was so strange, I couldn't be sure it was real. And if it was, I couldn't be sure it mattered anymore. Part of me still loved him in some way, but the fact that we could never be together had sunk in. There was nowhere for our relationship to go, and there was a strong possibility that he had deceived me from the moment we met.

I thought all this over and then looked at Jesse. His eyes made me forget everything I had going on in my brain. Our eyes locked on each other. He flashed a brilliant smile, and I returned it. I took a deep breath to keep myself from jumping into his lap and beginning a make-out session.

I'd never met anyone as rare as Jesse. He had the face and style of someone who had lived in another time; most likely because he was from another time. His brown hair swayed in the breeze, his brown eyes astonished me, and his smile was kind. There was nothing evil about his smile, unlike what I'd seen of Tom.

He put his hand on the middle of my back and pulled me closer to him. He stared into my eyes as if to make sure I approved of his intentions. When he determined I was, he kissed me gently. His hand moved up toward my neck and his other arm wrapped around my lower back.

Then, without warning, it started pouring rain.

We stopped kissing for a moment. I looked through squinted eyes at the cloudy sky that had snuck up on us.

"I wonder if this is some sort of sign?" Jesse asked.

I laughed and shrugged then cuddled back up to him and we stood up and ran through the maze-like courtyard to get inside.

Most of our roommates held a conversation in the dining room, so we snuck through the kitchen and went upstairs. We were soaking wet, so I was going to head to my room but Jesse caught my hand and led me to his room.

"I'd like to show you something," he said.

I went along with him. I didn't care how wet I was as long as he didn't either. He opened the door to his room and made a "ladies first" gesture. I obliged and stepped inside.

The room contrasted starkly with the rest of the house, which was decorated in shades of red, dark brown and gold. The bedding, the walls, the curtains—everything—was white. The dresser, nightstand, and bookshelf were stained so dark they were almost black. It reminded me a modern hotel room. The modern décor of his room clashed with the more traditional and romantic themes in the rest of the house.

Balcony doors swung in the breeze and rain trickled in. Jesse rushed to close them.

I looked around a little more to see if I could find something that would give me a clue about Jesse's personality. He was so mysterious. The dresser had a few books on it, and the bookcase was stocked with more. Another book rested on the bedside stand. I was trying to peek at the title but was interrupted.

He had emerged from the closet with a small box. He handed it to me and said, "Open it. I want you to see what I looked like back in the day. I haven't changed much, except my clothing, but that's what happens when you don't age I suppose," Jesse said as he took off his wet shirt. I was too busy looking at the body before me to open the box he handed me. He flaunted muscles chiseled into his form; an association that truly fit someone who turned into a statue at night. I snapped out of my daze and turned my attention back to the box.

I opened it then lifted out the few photographs inside. There were five in all. They all dated back to 1922. There was a picture of him with two other men, who he pointed out to be his father and brother. I thought it was ironic that I'd thought his statue could have been his father or brother and was now finding out he actually did have a father and brother who resembled Jesse.

166

Next, there were two pictures of him alone, a picture with a woman standing next to him, who he pointed out to be his mother, and a picture of him with a dog.

"These are wonderful," I said before I put them back in the box for him. "That is a beautiful dog. I'm not sure I would have ever placed you as a dog person."

"Yeah, I have a soft spot for all animals. My family took him in when I was pretty young. He was my best friend as a kid."

"That's sweet. He must have lived a long time," I said.

"Yes, he lived to be an old dog. He died of old age not long after this picture was taken. Sometimes I wish I had that luxury, but now that I've met you I'm grateful I don't," Jesse said before his eyes caught mine and he kissed me. We were still standing, but Jesse slowly and gently migrated towards the bed. When we were close enough, he put his arm around my back and gently laid me down, all the time still kissing me.

I stopped him, "We're soaking wet," I said.

"I have extra bedding, I'm not worried about that," he said. Then he looked at me again, this time he studied my face. I was an open book. "But, if we're moving too fast, I understand."

I didn't want to hurt him. I did have feelings for him, but I was still confused about the whole Tom situation. I couldn't help feeling guilty since I'd been with Tom only a few days ago. "I just need a little break, you know. Everything is changing so fast, I want at least one thing that will blossom in time. I want this to be right for both of us and I don't want to rush."

"I have plenty of time and patience for you, and I would never want to push you into anything you aren't ready for," he said as he straightened up to a sitting position on the bed.

"Thank you," I whispered before I stood up and leaned over to give him a kiss on the cheek. "I'm going to go take a nap."

It was a white lie. I really needed time to clear my head.

"Alright, will I see you at dinner? There are some things we all need to discuss."

"Yes, I will be there," I said with a smile. Jesse smiled back and then walked me to the door. I went down the hall to my room and tried to wrap my head around everything.

After an hour of laying in complete silence, except for in my mind, I gave up on all notions of sanity and went to find Alani. I needed my best friend right now. I found her and Nalani in the kitchen preparing dinner. They were making a traditional Hawaiian dish, usually served at luaus. They had to improvise a little, but it looked like they were cooking a ham, poi, breadfruit and pineapple. Hiu must have brought the supplies off of the boat at some point. It smelled delicious.

I would get the benefit of talking to both of them. Nalani was great with advice. Both of them were. Alani tended to give me her point of view. Nothing was kept to herself. Nalani used her experience and good moral sense to solve problems wisely.

"Aloha, ladies!" I said as cheery as possible. They both greeted me just as enthusiastically.

"Where have you been?" Alani asked. "I haven't seen much of you the last couple days," she added with a slight worry line crossing her forehead.

"I've been around. Thinking a lot. You know, trying to figure out what I'm going to do," I replied.

"What do you mean?" Alani asked.

"Well, I just can't get Tom out of my head. It's like I'm stuck on him. I want to move on, but my brain won't let me." I took my time to reveal each word as I measured what Alani's reaction was.

"Your brain? Or your heart?" Nalani asked.

"My heart, I suppose. But I'm also being pulled in another direction, which is good since Tom and I can't be together anyway, but I still feel bad leaving him in the dust."

"What direction are you being pulled in?" Alani asked, with one brow lifted.

"Well, Jesse has made it apparent he has feelings for me, and I think I feel the same for him," I said slowly. I was careful not to give away that I'd just been with him this afternoon . . . in his bedroom . . . kissing.

"Well, dear," Nalani began, "I believe Tom's idea of what your life could be is not the right path for you, but you need more closure. Your heart will ache for him, but your head will never let you be with him. As for Jesse, I think you should be patient. You don't want a repeat of what happened with Tom. In order to move on you need to somehow put Tom in the past, and you must do this before moving forward with Jesse if you chose to do so."

"I think you are absolutely right," I replied. "I can't move forward with Jesse until I put Tom behind me, and I can't put Tom behind me without closure. I don't know how I'm going to do that, but I have to figure it out."

I let the silence settle for a moment.

"Do you think Jesse is a good match for me? Or am I just wasting my time? He is another immortal. It's hard to say what our future would be like or if we could even have a future. He did say there might be a way to get a witch to reverse his curse, and make him mortal again, but there are no promises."

"I believe Jesse is a good man, and I hope he can get the curse lifted because he does seem very unhappy in his current state. I also believe it's too soon to tell if he's a good match for you, but there is no harm in trying once you get your business in order and your heart and your head are free to choose him," Nalani said.

"I think he's totally hot," Alani said excitedly.

I giggled.

"Oh, would you guys keep this to yourselves? I don't want the house knowing anything about mine and Jesse's 'might-have-been, but still-could-be-thing.' Not until it's official anyway."

"No problem!" Alani said while Nalani made a locking motion to her lips and threw away the invisible key.

"Well, I'm going to go get cleaned up for this wonderful dinner you guys are preparing for us, I'll see you in a few," I said.

CHAPTER SEVENTEEN

At dinner, only the clanking of silverware filled the air. We all anticipated Jesse's words. Hiu was late and Jesse didn't want to start until Hiu returned. He'd gone to his boat to load some supplies. I started to worry about possible lurking drudges when Hiu walked through the door. Anger painted his face red.

He looked around the room and said, "You never believe what I found on the boat today."

Everyone waited for him to continue. Jesse spoke up, "What did you find Hiu?"

"A tracking device!" he shouted. The contempt in his expression was clear.

"What?" a few people asked, clearly astonished.

"Those leeches put a tracking device on my boat. Ass why they found us at Moana's wikiwiki. They track us there and follow us to her house." Hiu's voice grew louder.

"This is not good Hiu. What did you do with it?" Jesse asked.

"I left it. I figure I bettah let you guys know first. They must know where we are. We need to move. I didn't disconnect the da kine cuz I didn't want them to know we found it. It might make them move on us. I've had-it with those bloodsuckers!" Hiu's fist formed into tight balls. It's a good thing there weren't any vampires in the room aside from Perry, and even now I feared a little for his safety.

"Good thinking, Hiu," Latoria said. Jesse nodded in agreement—too busy thinking to say actual words. His eyes seemed to move across images in his mind I couldn't see. He was formulating a plan.

Jesse's face snapped up. He took a deep breath. "Well, the reason I wanted us to eat dinner together tonight is because I've been in contact with a friend of mine. He lives in Las Vegas and he told me things are getting bad there. He needs a way out. There is no public transportation and working cars are becoming scarce. I told him I would come get him out of there," Jesse announced.

"Are we all going?" Edison asked.

"I think it would be too dangerous," Jesse said, "So, I will go while the rest of you go to the boat. Once you get off-shore, disable the tracking device and I will meet up with you at another location, preferably south, as close to Vegas as you can get."

Hiu nodded then went to the side table covered with maps and began consulting them to find a good location.

"You shouldn't go alone," I said to Jesse.

He looked up at me and shook his head. "I don't want to put anyone else at risk," he replied.

"I want to go with you," I said firmly. Latoria turned her attention to me.

"No, it's not safe," Jesse replied.

"It's not safe anywhere I go," I argued, "I'm the target and they could be watching this house already. It's better that I stay clear from the boat, and safer for everyone else."

"Shit. It's too late now, but we should be discussing this on paper," he said, completely ignoring my argument.

Jesse gestured to Latoria for a piece of paper and began writing. When he finished he passed it to me.

Everyone is leaving at noon tomorrow. Pack only the necessities tonight and make sure your windows and blinds are closed. We do not want them to know we are leaving. We will all take the secret passage, so pack light. We will meet in the garden at 11:15. Do not speak out loud about our plans. We don't know if they're listening, if they are, we already gave ourselves away, but we still need to be cautious just in case.

I passed it to the rest and one by one everyone nodded at Jesse as they read the note. We resumed dinner and tried for normal conversations. I tried to figure out how I could get Jesse to let me go with him. Jesse left the table to go to his spot in the garden, and I followed him once I thought no one would catch on to what I was doing. I caught up to him near his spot.

"I want to come with you. You might need some help out there. You may be immortal, but you can't be in two places at once," I said.

Unaware of my presence before I spoke up, Jesse snapped his head to the side at the sound of my voice.

He stopped just short of his spot and turned to me. "Ava, it's too dangerous and it's my car. I decide who goes."

"You can leave me behind, but you can't make me get on Hiu's boat."

"Technically, I'm stronger than you. So yes, I can," Jesse argued with a coy grin. His expression became more serious and his tone matched it. "I don't want to put you in any more danger than you're already in."

"You may be able to force me on the boat, but you can't keep me there. I can swim."

"So stubborn," Jesse said with a sigh and a slight smile that only touched the corners of his mouth.

"Yes, I am." I smiled, as I realized he was about to give in. "So, I'll meet you tomorrow morning."

"Well, I don't really have a choice. I don't want to take the chance of you not forgiving me for handcuffing you to the boat," he said with a chuckle as he turned and took the few steps toward his spot.

The last ray of sun disappeared from the sky at that moment, and Jesse turned to stone with a smile still on his face.

I grinned and said, "Good-night" before going back inside. I went to my room to pack the necessities. Everything I needed fit in my backpack. I hoped I'd fit through the small tunnel with it on. If not, I would need to push it through and that would be more work than I wanted.

I went to sleep soon after I finished packing, and then took my shift at four.

The morning air betrayed no sounds except for the distant yet steady beat of the waves crashing on the beach. Nothing out of the ordinary.

Dark thoughts crept into my mind, but I told myself we were only being monitored for boat movement. I prayed that the vamps and drudges were miles away, watching a blip on a screen. I wondered how the device ended up on the boat.

Tom came to my mind as the only reasonable suspect. The only time the feather pennant came down would've been the night he'd come to me. A drudge could have done it since feather pennants are useless against them, but Tom had the most motive to track the boat. I considered he wanted to keep tabs on me, in case he needed to contact me. He'd done the same thing since we'd met, always watching without my knowledge. A drudge would have already found Jesse's house and there would have been a confrontation. After all, the first drudge didn't waste any time. I struggled to control my thoughts and forced myself to settle on the theory that Tom planted the tracker.

This potentially meant I had nothing to worry about. To my knowledge, Tom was only interested in my where-a-bout's. He wanted me to be safe. I reassured myself that Hiu would disconnect the device once they got going anyway and they would all be safe.

I reminded myself of the plan we'd all whispered to each other in the den to ease my troubled mind.

Hiu had a virus-blocking device, and he would use it to call Jesse's friend once he got to the rendezvous. Once Jesse and I arrived to pick up his friend, he'd let us know that our friends were safe. After that, we'd simply find the boat and go . . . somewhere. I wasn't sure about the plan after that.

***

Once eleven o'clock came around, tension filled the house. Every little noise sent the hairs on my neck into an upright position. Hiu went through the passage first around 11:30, so he could ready his boat. At 11:45 Moana, Alani, and Nalani took Moana's Xterra to the marina. They were to take a detour to make sure no one tailed them. They carried a lot of the heavy supplies like food and water and weapons. Then Latoria, Perry, Kassidy, and Edison went through the passage at 11:50. Jesse and I were last to go.

Jesse went ahead of me to light the way. He had less to carry, so he held the flashlight. The tunnel was tight, especially with my backpack on. The knees on my jeans became moist as I moved through the damp dirt of the tunnel. Occasionally, I brushed off my hands to keep the slightly muddy build up from making me slip. My hands and knees began to hurt about half way through; at least around the time Jesse said, "Half way there."

Finally, we reached the end. He crawled out and then turned to help me out. I rubbed my knees knowing they were going to be sore for a few days. We crossed the street and hopped on his waiting motorcycle. He drove past the spot where Hiu and the rest waited on the boat. Jesse gestured to Hiu, signaling that everyone was out and Hiu returned the signal, showing they all made it to the boat.

Jesse sped off. We drove around LA for a while until Jesse was sure no one followed. Then he made his way toward his private warehouse where he kept his cars. I studied the storefronts and houses. Fresh damage to the buildings indicated panic and chaos had started. Glass glistened on the ground and ripped packages piled up in parking lots from all the looting. Almost every building showed scars made of shattered windows and broken doors. Spray paint tattooed the sides of the buildings with religious messages and warnings.

People with weary eyes watched as we drove past. Most stores were either cleaned out from looting or had bars installed across windows and doors. Men with guns guarded homes while others had been abandoned. Jesse pulled over his bike near the entrance of a warehouse. Surprisingly, the warehouse was still intact and none of the cars had been tampered with, unlike the cars we saw on the street. We got into a black Hummer and left town for Las Vegas.

We rode in silence for the first half hour. Jesse seemed to be in a determined mood. I knew he worried about what the city would be like and was likely worried about me and the people on the boat as well. My churning mind got the best of me. I had to tell Jesse what I thought about the tracking device.

"I think it was Tom," I said.

Jesse glanced at me with a questioning in his expression.

"I think he planted the tracking device on Hiu's boat," I added.

"Why do you think that?" he asked.

"He was on the boat. On our first night at sea. Our feather pennant fell down, and he got onto the boat. He came into my cabin to talk to me. He tried to convince me to go back with him, but I refused. I think he's trying to keep tabs on me. I don't think he'd hurt anyone . . . I just wanted you to know."

"Well, thank you for telling me. I'm sure that was difficult. I assume no one else knows about his visit?" Jesse said as more of a statement than a question.

I answered anyway. "No. I just thought it was important for you to know."

"I'm still wondering why he is so insistent on you becoming a vampire, and why he wants you to be willing to do it," Jesse said. His eyes shifted as if the answer sat right in front of him. "It doesn't make sense that he would put the wristband on and try to win you over instead of just changing you on day one."

I shrugged, "Maybe he really did like me and he didn't want to force me into it because I would resent him for it."

"Vampires always have an ulterior motive," he replied.

Our conversation came to a halt. I stared out the window as the foliage changed from dark green to tan. The Mojave Desert opened to us.

I began to feel weak and sick to my stomach. I wondered if it were carsickness or something I ate. More likely, something I didn't eat. After all, I'd barely eaten since the night before at dinner. Breakfast had eluded me because of my crowded mind.

"Is there anything to eat?" I asked.

"I don't think so. Are you hungry?" Jesse looked over, and his expression changed a bit when he saw my face.

"Well, kinda. I'm not feeling well. I think I need to eat something. Just feeling weak and nauseous is all," I replied. I tried to keep him from worrying, but my shaky voice betrayed me.

"We'll pull into the next open gas station and get you something to get your blood sugar levels up, okay?"

"Sounds good," I said as I leaned on the door.

"You're under a lot of stress. I'm sure a snack would help."

We were on the outskirts of Victorville, and emptiness surrounded us. No other cars traveled alongside us and no gas station seemed to be open.

I became weaker and weaker with every mile. Finally, a gas station with a bright "Open" sign appeared and Jesse pulled in and went inside. He came back out with a sandwich and some chips along with a soda.

"I hope this helps," he said.

I tried to eat them as Jesse continued driving, but after few bites into the sandwich, I had to make Jesse stop the car so I could throw up on the side of the road. Jesse offered to come with me, but I told him I didn't want him to see me like that.

After the coast was clear, I got back in.

"Are you all right?" Jesse asked.

"I don't know what's wrong. I haven't been this sick in a long time," I said.

"Do you normally get carsick?"

"No, never been carsick. My parents and I used to go places all the time. We'd go up and down the west coast in our family car."

"Did your parents ever take you inland?" Jesse asked. The question seemed odd, but I could tell his wheels were turning. He must know something I didn't because I couldn't connect the dots.

"You mean, away from the coast? No, we usually just stuck to the coast on our drives when we lived in California, and well, there really isn't any inland on the islands, why?"

"Well, it's something I was wondering. Maybe it's the different climate. It's drier around this area and we're about to enter the desert. Have you ever been out of California or Hawaii?"

"No, not that I can remember anyway," I replied. We kept driving in silence.

I felt worse and worse. Eventually, we had to pull over again. Worry lines formed on Jesse's face as I opened the door and rushed out to the side of the road.

When I got back in the car the second time, I caught my reflection in the mirror.

Big mistake.

My skin faded to a sickly pale color, my hair tangled in a mess and my eyes seemed duller than normal.

"Ava, I think I put it together, but I need you to answer a few more questions," Jesse said in a rushed voice.

"Okay," I answered, almost in a whisper. My vomiting had diminished my voice to almost nothing.

"Did your mother sing a lot?"

"What does that have to do with anything?" I asked faintly.

"Just trust me."

"Yes, we used to sing together all the time. When she died I stopped singing," I explained, still not understanding what was going on in Jesse's head.

"When you were between 18 and 23 did you ever lose your voice?"

I failed to see the connection between my bout with tonsillitis and the sickness that had overtaken me now, but I answered anyway, "Yeah, I got tonsillitis a few months after my parents died. I lost my voice for four days."

The engine revved as something clicked in Jesse's mind. Whatever had set him off eluded me.

"Ava, I think you're a siren. I need to get you closer to the ocean. We aren't going to make it to Las Vegas."

I must have been delirious. I thought I heard him say I was a siren, but I didn't have the strength to argue at that moment. I wasn't sure exactly what a siren was. I vaguely remembered learning about them in Greek mythology class in high school. All I remembered about them came to the surface of my mind. They were women that lured sailors to their deaths on rocky shores. I had certainly never done such a thing. Jesse pulled off on an exit and turned around to head back toward LA with more speed than he'd used on the way out. The noise of the engine and the movement of the Hummer pushed me into a deep sleep.

CHAPTER EIGHTEEN

Jesse woke me as we entered LA to tell me he needed to make a few calls at the phone booth just outside the vehicle. I gathered myself and completely sat up in the leather seat.

I felt much better. Symptoms dissipated as I stretched my limbs. I tried to remember what Jesse was talking about earlier. He'd told me he thought I was a siren. I wondered if I dreamt it, but we were indeed back in LA.

After a few minutes, and a quick drink from the soda Jesse had bought me earlier, my groggy-ness wore off. Jesse came back to the car and looked me over. His face still showed signs of worry lines.

"How are you doing?" he asked. His voice showed a morsel of anxiousness.

"Much better," I replied. "I'm still confused, though. What happened?"

"Ava, I believe you're a siren. Siren's get sick if they travel too far from the ocean. I think that's what happened to you. It's genetically passed from mother to daughter. I'd briefly considered it before when you told me about how Tom wanted you to change willingly, but I dismissed it because sirens are extremely rare. I've only met one in all my years. I know there are more, but most of them hide out. And all of them are aware of their supernatural status."

"My mother was not a siren," I insisted. "She would have told me. There's no way she could have been one of those things that lure sailors to their death on rocky shores. There's no way. It's something else, you have to be wrong."

"It's the only thing that makes sense, Ava. Sirens aren't what you think, most of them are kindest women you'll ever meet and do not use their powers for evil things such as luring sailors to their death. That's just an old myth created by jealous women who hated sirens because they could have any man they wanted. It was created so men would stay away from them," he explained.

"That still doesn't explain my mother never telling me anything about us being sirens," I retaliated as I glared slightly at Jesse.

"It's possible she didn't know but more possible she did and she was waiting to tell you until you got the siren fever," he reasoned.

I fell silent. Words tried to form but died before I could get them out. I was confused. Even more confused than I had been in the last month after everything I've been through. I stared downward, trying not to make eye contact with Jesse.

"I know it's hard to accept," Jesse said apologetically, "I think your mother was going to tell you the day she died. Are you sure she died in a car crash?"

"Yes, she was flung from the vehicle. They say the rock she landed on killed her. It smashed her heart and she died instantly."

"What kind of rock?" Jesse asked.

"It was olivine. It's common on Hawaii."

Jesse's expression turned grave as he tried to explain the rest of his theory to me, "Olivine is one of the only things that can kill a siren. I think your mother was murdered before she could tell you what you are, and I think the vampires did it. They didn't want her to warn you not to join them. A vampire siren is potentially the most powerful magical being that could ever exist. If you were ever changed, you would become an important weapon or an incredible threat to the vampires. You see, if a siren is changed against her will, then the vampire who changed her has no control of her. However, if you are changed voluntarily, the vampire who bit you will have a certain degree of control over you."

A weapon or a threat? Of course they wanted me under their control, then. One other fact bothered me.

"What about my dad? He was killed that day too," I countered.

"He must have known too. Or he was just in the wrong place at the wrong time; a casualty," Jesse tried to say gently, but I still took it harshly.

"So, Tom wanted me to change voluntarily so he could control me as a vampire siren?" When I said it out loud, it made sense. Everything made sense.

"That's what I think is going on," Jesse assured me. His hand tentatively rested on my shoulder. I allowed it. Deep down I knew he was right. Jesse had been walking the earth for so long, I had to believe his knowledge of the supernatural world.

I tried to take it all in, but I still wasn't convinced I was a siren. Wouldn't I have known something like that? Wouldn't I have felt it?

"Is there any way to know for sure if I'm a siren or not?"

"You have to use your voice. Different sirens have varying powers, but all of them can control a man with their ancient songs. They can make men come to them, make them leave and never return. They can make them forget about everything else but the siren herself. There are many ways a siren can control a man. It won't work on me, or on vampires, but I believe you can also call to animals in the sea. I do know that when you're close to the ocean you'll be at your strongest. You will be even stronger if you touch the waters."

"So what do we do?"

"I can take you to a beach and you can try out your powers. Try singing some of the songs your mother used to sing," Jesse said. "I know a secluded place."

I nodded.

Jesse drove with determination. He wanted to know the truth as badly as I did. I wondered if he was right about me, and about the vampire's intentions with me. I wondered what part Tom had played in the whole situation. I needed to find out the truth about everything; my heritage, my parents' deaths, and Tom's true intentions.

Finally, we reached the beach. The digital clock in the car read 5:03. No one walked the beach. No one swam the waters.

I got out of the car and made my way toward the beach, Jesse got out too, but he didn't follow. I turned to see if he was coming.

"I think this is something you may want to do on your own. I'll be right here if you need me," he said as he leaned against the side of the Hummer.

I nodded and turned back toward the beach. The sun warmed my face. I walked until I stood just a few feet from the water, then took off my shoes and stepped in. It felt cold at first, but the familiar feeling of the sand under my feet and the waves crashing against my legs calmed me. I tried to remember one of the songs my mother sang with me so long ago. Finally, one came to me and I began to sing.

Oh sacred sea, now hear this call,

Oh swells that rise and tides that fall,

You know not seasons, years nor time,

You know not conscience, reason nor rhyme

Obey me now, for we are one

I am your moon, I am your sun

Obey me now for we are one,

Heed my words, my ancient song

Now stay so calm that ships lie still,

Please bring no vessel or sailor ill,

Hold your power, dampen your pride,

Let all your swirling torrents subside

Obey me now, for we are one

I am your moon, I am your sun

Obey me now for we are one,

Heed my words, my ancient song

Do know that soon you'll rise once more,

You'll grow again, the moon will call,

Your currents will push and pull anew

Your undertows, eternal blue

The waves stopped, and the sea fell quiet. The water lay placid as far as I could see. My heart soared and the air in my lungs swelled. I'd done this. I calmed the sea. I felt a strange, almost electric, reaction pass through my body as I sang. I decided to try another one.

Oh creatures who swim amongst the deep,

Please come to me, please hear me speak,

Wind your way towards the shore,

Rise from the bed, towards my call

Animals of the ocean, I summon you here

Animals of the ocean, do not worry nor fear

Dear whales and dolphins, come as one

Bring your old and bring your young,

Oh porpoise, crab, and manatee,

Please make your way so rapidly

Animals of the ocean, I summon you here

Animals of the ocean, do not worry nor fear

Ride across the waves to silver sand,

Aim for the shore, this golden land,

Push your majestic forms through the shimmering brine,

This is your moment, this is your time

I caught sight of the fins of dolphins racing toward me. I waded out to them. The water pushed and pulled against my hips and the dolphins circled me. There must have been about ten of them, but it was hard to keep track of the racing creatures. I called to Jesse. I wanted him to see this.

He quickly approached the shore, and peered out at me. I laughed and played with the dolphins and motioned for him to come out to me. He nodded before shedding his shoes and wading out.

"This is amazing!" I said to him. "I called them to me, and before that I calmed the waters. You were right," I said and I gave him a big hug that pushed him back into the water. We fell in and resurfaced together.

"Of course I was. I'm always right," he teased after he caught his breath. He shook the excess water out of his hair and smiled. Our eyes connected for a moment. We now shared a secret. It amazed me that he figured mine out even before I did.

We stood in the water with the dolphins for another 20 minutes. Then Jesse told me we would have to find somewhere to stay for the night and Hiu would pick us up here in the morning.

I dismissed the dolphins by saying "Goodbye, my friends," in a singsong voice.

The walk back to the Hummer was short, but I packed twice as many words into the stroll as I normally would. I couldn't stop talking about what I'd done with my voice and the magical sensation I had while I sang. Jesse seemed happy for me. Although, he looked at me differently than before; almost as if we'd just met for the first time.

Surprisingly, we easily found a motel in Long Beach near the beach we were on and made it to our room with time to spare before sundown. Jesse rented a room with two beds, and I sighed in relief for the "no pressure" situation.

"What's going to happen to your friend?" I asked.

"I talked to him on the phone, he said he might be able to get something else lined up, I will keep in contact with him to be sure. I'll call him before Hiu gets here tomorrow, and if he hasn't found transportation, I may have to go alone," Jesse said.

I glanced at him. I had so many questions running through my head.

I wanted to know everything he kept in his mind about sirens. The questions started flowing out of me like I was an investigator on the old show, CSI. "You said the only thing that can kill a siren is olivine to the heart, right?"

"That and being kept away from the ocean too long can weaken you to a point where you could die from just about anything else," Jesse warned.

"What about old age? How does that work?"

"Ava, you won't be aging, you're immortal." He shrugged. "Once a siren reaches the age of 25 or 30 they stop aging. They become frozen in time, I suppose."

"I always wondered how my mother kept looking so young. I always thought it was her carefree lifestyle."

This entire time, I had the gift of immortality and I didn't even realize it. I had fought with Tom about not wanting to be immortal, but as it turned out I already was. The thought scared me. I could potentially live forever.

"So, I'm going to stay like this for the rest of my life?" I gestured to myself.

"Well, you're almost 25, right?"

I nodded. Mixed feelings crowded my head. Forever was such a strange concept.

"Jesse, I don't know if I want to live forever. Immortality is not something I've ever wanted."

"It's not something I ever wanted either, but I've come to terms with it I suppose."

"How have you endured all these years? How can you be happy knowing there is no end for you?" I asked.

"Well, after a while, years seem like months, then weeks. I imagine, after an extended period of time, they may even fade into days. I can tell you, though, the last few days have slowed down. Meeting you has stopped time for me. It's given me a break from the monotony of my life."

"So what did you do to stay busy all these years?"

"I've increased my knowledge by reading and traveling the world. I've had many careers. Most were years and years ago. My savings is what I live off of now. If we ever find a witch powerful enough to take away my curse, maybe she can take away your immortality too . . . if you decide."

"I suppose that's something to think about. If we do find a powerful enough witch, do you think removing the curse will also take away your immortality or do you still want that?" I asked.

"I might consider keeping it, but I might give it up. It might be a decision we possibly make together if things progress in that direction, I imagine," he said as he stared into my eyes.

I smiled and turned away. The thought of spending an eternity with Jesse, or giving up immortality for a normal life with Jesse was pleasant and frightening at the same time. In one case, forever really meant forever. And in the other case, the possibility of a normal life sounded ideal since my life had been turned upside down in the last few weeks.

"How do you know about sirens?" I asked, unsure about whether I wanted to be enlightened or not. I watched as Jesse's expression changed from happy to troubled.

"The siren I met was a woman I came across while traveling in Northern Ireland many years ago, around the time of World War II. Ireland was neutral in the war, so I had ended up there as a safe haven. I was afraid to be in a war zone in my statue form. She was kind to me. I stayed with her and we revealed to each other our secrets. The whole time I spent with her I watched as she helped the people in her village with everything from catching fish to keeping storms away. She had a talent for controlling the weather. Most sirens can control the weather to a certain degree, but she was more extensive in her abilities.

"One night, an outsider came to the village. He was some sort of religious or political figure. He had been informed of her abilities and considered her a witch. I was in statue form when they took her and loaded her into a police truck. When I came back to human form I asked the villagers where they took her and I borrowed a horse to get to her before they could make her weak enough to kill. I was too late. When I arrived in the small town they took her to, she'd already been burned at the stake. I'd thought practices such as that were outdated, but I was obviously wrong. The war surrounding the area at the time turned people into barbarians. Anything perceived as a threat was taken out."

I was silent. I never met the woman, but somehow the story had gotten to me. My heart sank for both the siren and Jesse.

"Did you love her?" I asked without thinking.

"I loved her as I would a family member. I saw her more as a mother or an aunt than anything else. The whole village did. The tragedy is she did nothing wrong. She was the kindest and most generous person in the whole village," Jesse said. I caught his eyes with mine. They were years away. He was remembering every detail as if it happened yesterday.

"Why didn't she use her voice to control the men that took her?" I asked.

Jesse blinked for the first time in a short while. He hung his head. "They were prepared, and they gagged her," he finally replied.

I took in a deep breath. "I'm sorry you had to lose someone so close to you," I said as I put my arm around him and rested my head on his shoulder.

"I only hope I never have to endure that again," he said. He put his hand on my cheek and wiped away the tear forming under my eye.

"You and she would have gotten along well. She would have gladly mentored you in the ways of the siren," he said. A slight smile crossed his face.

"What was her name?" I asked.

"Tullia," he replied.

I sat with Jesse until the sun sank deep in the sky. He stared out the window as the sun disappeared over the horizon and he turned to stone with sorrowful eyes and his mouth set in a hard line. I kissed his marble forehead and after a few more moments of silence, I went to my bed and watched TV until I fell asleep.

That night I dreamed of my mother. I dreamed we were singing to sailors, to lure them away from rocky shores to the safety of Hilo Bay. One of the sailors seemed to resemble Jesse and he waved to me from the ship as it sailed to safety.

CHAPTER NINETEEN

Bang!

My eyes flew open as adrenaline surged into my chest and I sat up in bed. The door to our hotel room was wide open and Tom walked through the doorway with two other men. It took me a moment to realize I wasn't dreaming before I reached for my dagger and gun. Two inches away from grabbing protection, one of the drudges grabbed me by the wrists. I struggled and pushed him back. My voice would only let out grunts and useless words like "stop" and "let me go."

The drudge took out some handcuffs and the other one helped flip me over to my stomach so they could cuff my hands behind my back. I started to yell, but they gagged me.

"Take off her ring," Tom instructed.

I closed my fist, but my ring finger was no match for the strong hands of two drudges. The ring slipped off and the drudges let go of me. I rolled back over onto my back so I could see Tom and the drudges. I glared at them and wished the hate in my eyes could stop them dead in their tracks. Tom stared back at me with a grin one-thousand times more evil than any other I'd seen him wear before.

"Sorry, Ava. I wanted to do this the easy way, but you've forced me to take this route." I glanced over at Jesse. He was still in statue form and watching helplessly while I was being kidnapped.

"Interesting, isn't he? Such a weakness is most definitely a curse," he said as he turned his attention to Jesse. "What a gentleman to give you your own bed. Let's move on, boys."

One of the drudges grabbed me and lifted me off the bed. I got a glimpse of the clock before they rushed me out the door and into a waiting limo. It was only 4:30 a.m. Jesse wouldn't return to his normal state for at least two hours. The adrenaline still coursed through my body, but had diluted itself so that my mind became calm enough for me to form clear thoughts. I would not allow myself to cry or show weakness of any kind.

In the limo, I tried to sit far away from Tom, but the drudges kept me sandwiched between them. After about ten minutes of driving, Tom made his move. He slid toward me and relieved the drudge on my right.

"I'm going to take this gag off. Don't scream. It's not going to do you any good. Oh, and don't sing either, it won't work on me and the boys here have pearls in their ears. You figured out that you're a siren, or Jesse figured out you're a siren. Either way, I watched your little show at the beach yesterday."

I nodded with a glare directed at him. Once it was off, we drove in silence for a minute or two.

"Where are you taking me?" I demanded.

Tom didn't answer.

"I know your plan," I said to taunt him. The story that Jesse had told me the night before was fresh in my mind. They were taking me away from the ocean.

He was still silent.

"Even now you still won't get what you want. You can't change me unless I agree or I'm worthless to you," I said, keeping an eye on his expression.

An emotion flickered. Then he turned to me and said, "The rules say nothing about you agreeing under duress. It's never been attempted, but I guess we are willing to take the chance since all other plans failed. Tell me. How did you figure it out? You must have gotten sick on your way to Las Vegas."

I ignored him.

"I'll bet Jesse Sutton figured it out. He's been on this earth for much too long. Almost as long as I have, but not quite. Long enough to build quite the reputation, though. He hates most supernatural creatures, but I guess he has a weak spot for sirens," Tom retorted. He had his evil grin across his face.

They were going to make me sick, so sick that I might die. My heart raced at the thought, but I knew I could get through this. Emotions spiraled inside my head and anger took over. I wanted to hurt Tom.

"You were so stupid to believe me," I spat at him.

"You thought you were playing me, but I was the one playing you. Nothing we had was real. It was all a result of double manipulation. I won that round, and I'll win this one too," I said.

Tom looked at me with his poker face. "We'll see. You're stubborn, but so am I. I hope you like the desert. It isn't so bad once you get past the dry air. Although, it may be a bit more difficult for you, siren," he said, spitting the word 'siren' at me.

"Unfortunately, I don't plan on staying long," I said firmly. Although I could feel myself starting to get sick, I was determined to show that I was still strong. He wouldn't break me. The urge to vomit started to overwhelm me, but I tried to keep my mind on other things.

Tom chuckled a little, and we drove in silence for a while longer. The sun started to come up when we pulled into an abandoned gas station. By the time we pulled over, sickness tried to push me over the edge and I drifted in and out of consciousness. Delirium started to set in and my vision doubled.

The drudges brought me inside the gas station and into the backroom. They sat me down on the floor and handcuffed me to a cold metal pipe. Tom emerged after a few minutes. Two versions of him walked into the room and stared down at me. I was having a hard time steadying my gaze, but my eyes finally found his blurry face.

"Are you ready to give in?" he asked.

"Sorry to disappoint," I paused to gain my composure, "but it won't happen."

I tried to control the words as they fell off my lips. I felt like I'd been drugged. The spinning room made my head feel light and heavy at the same time.

"A few more hours of this and you'll beg me to change you. Did you know, vampire sirens don't get sick from leaving the coast? You'd instantly feel better and you could travel anywhere you wanted," he said as if it would sway me. He reached for a strand of my hair and tucked it behind my ear. I flinched away from him and scowled, although I wasn't sure if I scowled at him or his slightly ghost-like twin.

"You would be an exquisitely evocative being," he continued. He kneeled beside me and came too close for comfort. "You could control anyone you want. Of course, I would have certain authority over you, but don't worry, I would only call on you for important tasks."

"I'll die before I let you control me," I said. I paused for his response, but he said nothing. Adrenaline built up inside me again and allowed me to see through the fog just enough to say, "Tell me something: what do you really know about my parents' deaths? You know who did it, don't you?"

"I'm not going to get into all the details, Ava. They are gone, why dwell on the past?" his voice started to sound like an echo to me, but I wanted answers, and I was unwavering in my interrogations.

"Was it you who killed them?"

He didn't answer.

"You've been planning this for longer than I thought," I said.

"Does it really matter who did it? Soon enough you'll be one of us. You'll be part of the group that was responsible. After you've changed, what happened in the past won't matter. Your hunger for blood and power will take over. You'll see that when you're one of us, you'll do anything to get what you want."

"I'll consider your lack of denial as a confession. I will kill you someday, Tom Walker. I know in my gut, that it was you and I will drive an obsidian dagger into your heart like you drove that olivine stone into my mother's. Your soul will be trapped in a ring upon my finger. For an eternity."

Tom laughed. "I think it is your soul that will belong to me. You grow weaker and weaker with every breath of this dry air. You will give in, it may take hours, or days if you can last that long, but it will happen." He turned and went through the door.

I struggled to hang onto my consciousness. The last thing I wanted to do was pass out, but I'd used up too much energy talking to Tom.

CHAPTER TWENTY

JESSE

My stone prison dissolved and a shout escaped my lungs. I jumped out of the bed and grabbed the landline phone connected to the wall. I struggled to keep myself from ripping it out of the socket. My fingers quickly tapped Hiu's number.

No signal.

He didn't have the virus blocker plugged in yet. I paced the room from one end to the other. Emotions fluttered through me without warning or control.

I had to find her. I couldn't let what happened to Tullia happen again. I tried to get the emotions out so I could think logically about where they would take Ava. I knew Tom was at his last resort. He must be attempting to get her to change under duress which would entail either taking a friend or family member close to her hostage, or making her so sick she would beg them to change her to stay alive.

Since it was likely everyone was safe on Hiu's boat, I assumed Tom chose the second option. The only way to do that quickly was to take her somewhere with dry air, and the Mojave Desert was only miles away. I tried to think it through. Psytech didn't keep a lot of property in the desert since vampires didn't particularly like dry air either. It made their thirst grow considerably.

The most direct way to the desert from the hotel was Interstate 15. I'd start there and search every abandoned place along the Interstate until I found her. I had to contact Hiu to tell him what happened.

I decided to try again in an hour. I used that time to gather up any weapons I could. Ava's dagger and handgun were still in the room. I took all of our belongings and checked out.

I hopped in my Hummer and sped back to the beach where I arranged to meet Hiu. He wasn't there yet, but I thought I could see the boat on the horizon. I tried to call him again. This time he answered.

"Howzit?" Hiu said on the other end of the line.

"Something's happened. Tom and two drudges took Ava while I was still in statue form. At least I think it was Tom. He fits the description, and he seemed to know about me."

"What?" Hiu asked. The hard "t" conveyed his anger.

"We have to find her. I think they took her to the desert. Remember yesterday when I told you about her being a siren?"

"Yeah, so they trying to make her sick so she agrees to change?"

"Exactly. So get here fast. I'm gonna need you, Perry and Edison to help me search. It's only logical that they took Interstate 15."

"I be there wikiwiki. I meet you at the beach."

"I'm already here. I can see your boat. I'm going to try to find another transportation vehicle. Bring some weapons but make sure the others can defend themselves too," I replied.

"When we find that bloodsucker, I gonna kill him," Hiu said with determination soaking his voice.

I hung up and went to find a car or motorcycle to buy off of a local or hot wire if necessary.

Soon I found the perfect motorcycle a few blocks from the beach. I looked around for the owner and found no one. It had GPS so I reasoned that it had been abandoned. I hooked up a virus blocker, then hotwired the machine and disabled the GPS. I knew that Tom or another vampire could be monitoring the devices. After the job was done, I sped off to the beach. Hiu was coming ashore on a life raft with Perry and Edison. I filled a large water bottle with ocean water as they anchored the boat in the bay.

Once their feet hit the sand, I gave Hiu the keys to my Hummer and told them to follow me.

"Look for 'Closed' signs. I'll bet they're in an abandoned gas station or diner. This road is seeing less and less traffic since the virus. No one wants to brave the desert without a cell phone," I said. I filled a large water bottle with ocean water.

It wasn't long before we were on the Interstate. About 20 miles in, we found the first abandoned gas station. After a good search, we moved on to a diner at the same exit. This happened for five more stops. Soon we were at Barstow with no luck. We continued on, and after two more stops we found a gas station with a 'Closed' sign, but a dead giveaway sent adrenaline through me. A limo sticking out from the side of the building. I thought vampires were supposed to be smart.

I motioned to the others behind me to keep going. We drove until we found a secluded area to park.

"That has to be it," I announced.

Hiu nodded in agreement and asked, "So, what the plan?"

"We're going to leave the vehicles here, we want to take them by surprise," I replied. I got off the bike and grabbed all my gear. I took out my dagger, my handgun and enough ammo to make sure the odds of all of us getting out of there alive were good. Hiu had his shotgun and two daggers. Perry had a rifle, He'd decided he didn't want a dagger anywhere near him. Edison grabbed Ava's dagger and handgun.

We hiked until we came within eyeshot of the building. After watching a few minutes, we didn't see anyone come out of the building, so we moved forward. We watched for any drudges or vampires and soon found ourselves right outside. All four of us tried to be quiet. We made sure the back entrance was blocked before moving to the front. I motioned for Perry to go in first since he had vampire speed. The rest of us followed quickly like a well-trained SWAT team.

Inside, Perry caught two drudges off-guard. When we came in they were even more surprised. Four guns pointed at the two drudges. They were outnumbered and out gunned.

"Where's Ava?" I asked.

"And where is that bloodsucker, Tom?" Hiu added.

Neither of the drudges answered. Then, a door opened and two more drudges walked into the gas station lobby with guns drawn. Hiu chambered his shotgun with a series of clicks and the sound of sliding metal.

I stepped out front. "I realize you're all humans. What you don't realize, is that there are two immortals amongst us. We'll eventually win."

One of the drudges chambered a bullet in his gun. The two that we caught off guard had now pulled out their guns and pointed them at us.

A gunshot rang out in the confined space.

Hiu fired first. He injured two of them with his spread of bb's. The other two ducked behind a counter at the sound. I jumped on the counter and one of the drudges tried to shoot me. The bullet ricocheted off of my granite hard skin and hit a window. A stinging pain made me wince but didn't take me down.

By this time, Perry was already behind the counter and we each shot the drudges down.

Tom came out of the back room with a vengeance on his face. "I must admit, I hoped they would take at least one of you out. You two humans will be easy, but I didn't want to be so outnumbered. Oh well, once I get it down to the two immortals, my job will be a little easier."

He seemed to be stalling. He couldn't beat us all.

"Where's Ava?" I asked again.

Tom just laughed and looked at Hiu, whose eyes filled with fire.

"You know, I might have to keep you alive for a little while," Tom said to Hiu, "You might come in handy with my negotiations."

"You like beef?" Hiu said, lifting his hand to show his ring. "Try something, go ahead. We both wearing rings and dem guys are just like you," Hiu said gesturing to me and Perry.

Tom kept his poker face, but I knew he must have been thinking of an escape route. Suddenly, Tom disappeared into the back room with vampire speed. We ran after him and found him next to Ava with a knife.

"She's weak enough. Her immortality will be useless against a blade across her neck," Tom slithered.

I looked at Ava. Her dulled eyes had just a little spark behind them. She was in bad shape, but she still had some fight in her. I just prayed that something would distract Tom so that I could get the ocean water on her. Even a few drops would give her a few minutes of strength. My prayers were soon answered.

CHAPTER TWENTY-ONE

Gunshots from another room woke me. At least I thought it was from another room. Shouts and crashes reverberated off the walls. My head throbbed at each loud noise.

I blacked out again and came to with an ice-cold blade on my neck and Tom's voice slithering into my ear. Dark figures stood across the room. Two seemed familiar. When one of them spoke, relief washed over me.

"If you even try anything, I'll do to you what I did to that other vampire, that's a promise," Hiu said. I noticed he talked so that Tom would be able to understand exactly what he was saying. Hiu didn't want any misconceptions about what he would do if Tom tried to hurt me.

I'd known deep down they would come for me. I hoped it wasn't too late. The little energy I had left struggled against Tom's hold.

Tom turned his head to Hiu. "Don't underestimate me. I have bloodstone, and I'll kill you before you can get in another blow."

"Bloodstone will only protect you from the first dagger and there are three here, I'd say our chances are pretty good," Jesse countered.

"I will be the one to kill you, and nothing can save you from my rage," Hiu said. His voice grew loud.

My head pounded. Tom was now fully occupied with taunting Hiu. I started to worry that someone would get hurt. Then I saw Jesse make a move. He threw a bottle of water into the air and shot it over mine and Tom's heads.

Water rained down on me and revived me instantly. Tom jumped up and flew toward Jesse at high speed. He crashed into him and knocked the obsidian dagger away from Jesse. Both of them fell to the floor in a punching, rolling fight. Edison took out his dagger and tried to stab Tom, but before he could, Tom knocked him out of the way and into a wall where he collapsed. The ring had no effect once the wearer launched an attack. Perry came to me and broke my handcuffs off. Hiu waited for his chance. Jesse had the strength of a vampire. He tried to hold Tom down so that Hiu could stab him. Hiu lunged and hit him right in the heart, but the bloodstone allowed the dagger to melt right off him and the wound healed before our eyes. Hiu turned to find another dagger, but I had already found it.

Tom wriggled free before I could get to him with it. He headed for the door at high speed, as I hurled the dagger at him. I caught a glimpse of it sticking in his shoulder. He was gone before the rest of us could try to stop him. My throw was a little off, no doubt a side effect of my weakened state. I wished it had landed just a few inches to the right.

"I'm going after him," Perry said.

"No, Perry! He still has the dagger. I don't want to put you at risk. We won't be able to keep up with you," Jesse said.

"I can handle it. He's injured," Perry countered.

"We're all alive and safe, let's regroup and get back to the boat. Ava needs to get back to the coast. That ocean water will wear off quickly in this heat," Jesse said as he turned to me. I could see the relief on his face.

He was right. The effects of the ocean water began to wear off, and my muscles began to shake and fault. Hiu and Jesse both came to my side. I was glad to see them all, but I didn't want them to fuss over me.

"Are you okay, Ava?" Hiu asked.

"Yeah, I'm fine," I replied.

"You're pale. Let's get you into the car," Jesse said.

Jesse and Hiu both helped me outside. The hot desert air hit me like an open oven door. I thought it might knock me out. Suddenly, the urge to vomit overcame me. I pulled free from the guys and collapsed in the searing sand. After getting sick a few times, I motioned for them to help me. Perry had run to the Hummer and brought it around. I climbed in and Jesse gave me some water.

"This should help a little, but it's not ocean water, so it's not going to push you to one hundred percent. It should help with your nausea until we can get you to the ocean," Jesse said.

Everyone else piled in. Jesse took the driver seat while Perry moved to the passenger side. Hiu and Edison were in the back with me. I drifted in and out of sleep like I had when Jesse and I tried to go to Las Vegas.

Finally, I woke when we were back in L.A. It was a short drive to the beach where Hiu had left his boat. It was still there, along with the life raft that they'd apparently hidden behind some trees. The beach we were on wasn't a very busy one, which was good luck for the five of us.

Once we were all out of the car, I felt much better, but the desire to jump into the water shifted my legs into autopilot. I ran, without warning anyone about what I was doing, and dove into the ocean. The cool water splashed, and I came up for air with a smile on my face. It felt so wonderful to be alive. The ocean water rejuvenated every cell in my body.

I turned to see the rest of them watching me.

"Come on!" I yelled.

Hiu and Jesse looked at each other then made a run for it. They both joined me in the water within seconds. Edison and Perry laughed, but neither of them followed. Instead, they got the life raft into the water and started paddling toward us.

"Let's go," Edison said, "I'm sure the others are worried about us."

I smiled. "Don't you wanna have a little fun? Get rid of the some built up stress?"

"Yeah, but I don't want to keep Kassidy waiting," he replied.

I splashed at them, but instead of just getting them wet, the wave I created grew and tipped the life raft over. Both Perry and Edison fell into the water and surfaced. Hiu and Jesse laughed, but I treaded the water with my mouth wide open.

"Hey, no fair!" Perry said. "Playing the siren card is against the rules!" he said with a chuckle.

"I'm sorry! I didn't realize I could do that!" I exclaimed.

"Some sirens can, others can't. It's a rare power to be able to control the ocean with thought and motion," Jesse explained.

"That's amazing. I guess I'll need to be more careful," I said, "I suppose you guys are right, though. We better get back."

We all climbed into the raft after Jesse and Perry turned it back over. They went for the paddles, but I stopped them.

"Hang on guys. Save your energy. Let me try something," I said. My intuition told me that my ability to tip the life raft could double as an ability to move the life raft.

I closed my eyes and tried to concentrate on the sound of the ocean and the movement of the raft. I lifted my hands from my knees and pushed my palms forward. With that motion, the raft moved forward. The guys all gasped as the boat lunged then gently glided out to sea. I opened my eyes and used my hands to persuade the ocean to guide our raft swiftly to the side of the boat. I turned my palms up to the sky and the ocean swelled under us . . . and lifted the raft to the deck.

"All aboard!" I shouted.

Everyone climbed onto the deck. Alani, Nalani, Moana, Kassidy, and Latoria all came up from down below to see what was happening. Jesse helped me off the raft, and Hiu and Edison pulled the raft all the way onto the boat. I lowered my arms and the ocean receded.

"That was amazing!" Alani said, "Did you do that Ava?"

"Yeah, I guess it comes with the siren package," I said as I gave Alani a big hug.

"We're so glad you're back. When Hiu told us what was going on we were so worried!" Alani said.

We came out of the hug and she looked at me as if we had been apart for years.

"I still can't believe you're a siren!" Alani continued, "I asked Nalani to fill me in, she thought they were extinct, but she told me about what you can do and how you can't get too far away from the ocean. It's incredible. I always knew there was something different about you!"

"Yeah, she's a funny kine alright," Hiu jumped in. He gave me the hundredth hug since the guys had come to rescue me. I smiled and hugged him back. Alani smacked him on the back of the head.

"You be good to her, kokohe!" she said.

"What? She's 'ohana, she knows I'm just messing around!" he answered. Then he left us so he could prepare the boat to set sail.

"What's kokohe, again?" I asked.

"It means rascal," Alani replied.

"Oh, that's Hiu alright," I said.

"So, are you ready for some grinds?"

"Yeah, I'm starving! I haven't eaten since last night in the motel room."

"Good, we've been working on dinner. We're having fish . . . that we caught ourselves . . . with no help from the guys!"

I giggled, "Awesome!"

Everyone sat out on the deck. Food and conversation floated around us. We celebrated my return. It was almost a normal dinner; friends and family gathering together for a good meal. Although, I felt bombarded with questions and comments. It was comparable to the reaction Jesse had when he told his secret.

Jesse quieted everyone down.

"We must decide what to do next. Should we stay in California? Or possibly go to Hawaii? We need a plan," he said.

"Yeah, right now we just cruising up the coast," Hiu said.

"Well, our goal is to stop Psytech from taking humans as blood slaves," I said. "We need to get the virus removed from the satellites. Have you talked to your friend from NASA?"

"I haven't been able to contact him. I called the NASA office, but they say he hasn't been coming into work. I left a message. I hope he receives it soon."

"Okay, so what should we do in the mean time?" I asked.

"Well, I think we should go to Hawaii and see if we can find out more about Psytech and the virus they planted. There has to be some sort of code or anti-virus," Moana said.

"Maybe, but what about all the vampires and drudges? They'll be after us. Along with Tom," I said.

"Good!" Hiu replied. "Any of them mosquitoes like beef, they can see what happens when they boddah us."

"Hiu, we must not start a war. There are many innocent lives on the islands, we can't risk the vampires' retaliation," Nalani scolded.

"We should still go back to Hawaii," Alani replied. "Hawaii is the center of operations right now, and we have to protect our home land."

"I think Alani is right," Jesse said, "Hawaii is ground zero. Does anyone want to stay and track the situation here?"

Edison stood up, "Kassidy and I will stay."

"I will too," Perry said, "They may need my help."

"We can figure out a safe house. Once we get settled, we will contact you," Kassidy said, "We will call Hiu's cell at noon, Hawaiian time, so plug in your virus blocker for a minute at noon every day. If we don't get an answer, we'll send a text and it should go through next time you turn it on."

"Okay, that sounds good. So, everyone else is alright with going to Hawaii?" I asked. Everyone nodded.

"Okay, where do you want me to drop you guys off?" Hiu asked.

"Marina Del Rey or Santa Monica is fine, whichever we are closest to," Edison replied.

"We are about to come up on Marina Del Rey, so I'll dock there. Should be about 20 minutes."

Jesse kept his eyes on me throughout the rest of dinner. He was being very attentive. He asked a few times if I needed anything and I declined. I didn't want Jesse to beat himself up over what had happened and I didn't want him to feel like he owed me anything. I sent quite a few smiles his way to show that I was just happy to be back.

CHAPTER TWENTY-TWO

About 20 minutes later, we said our goodbyes to Kassidy, Edison, and Perry. Then the rest of us shoved off for Hawaii. It would be another four-day journey. We all decided Hiu would use the virus blocker, but only to double-check his own navigation and only for a moment to keep the vampires from tracing us. I was waving to Kassidy, Edison, and Perry when Jesse came up behind me.

"How are you doing?" he asked.

I turned around to face him. "I'm doing well. Especially since I got some closure today. Tom's a monster. I should have paid more attention to my initial reaction to the news that was a vampire. He was so manipulative, I guess I manipulated him too, but what he did was much worse. I made the right decision."

Jesse's eyes met mine, but sadness tainted them.

"I'm glad you're alright. I hated my curse more than ever when Tom and the drudges came crashing in. I came back to human form in a panic. I'm so sorry I couldn't stop them," Jesse said with his head hung.

"Don't worry about it, Jesse. The important thing is that you found me, and everyone is alive and well," I said as I brought my hand to his shoulder.

"With the exception of those four drudges," he added.

Jesse put his arm around the small of my back and pulled me a little closer. We both peered out at the shrinking marina as Hiu piloted Palila out to sea. The sun painted the sky orange and pink, so the two of us drifted to the room where Jesse would be staying. Our fingers intertwined and our lips curled into smiles. Words weren't important to us right now, only the fact that we were in each other's presence. After a few moments of silence, Jesse sensed the sun would set within minutes.

"I must say goodnight, I will be turning to stone soon, but you're welcome in my cabin anytime. I can listen if you need to talk but don't take my silence as an insult," he said with a smile.

I giggled, "I think I'll let you be tonight. I can talk quite a bit, and I don't want to scare you off."

"Never," Jesse said as he kissed me on the cheek. I was surprised he didn't kiss my lips. He was still giving me the time I thought I needed, but as I assessed my emotions I found no guilt or sorrow. I found excitement. I was ready to make the leap from my past to my present, and possibly future, with Jesse. With this thought, I kissed him. It wasn't a hot, passionate kiss, but a sweet kiss that said I was ready. Ready to be with him.

As I pulled away from the kiss, I looked into Jesse's surprised eyes. The kiss meant we could move forward.

I smiled again, this time with a more flirty expression. I winked and left him. Tomorrow we would be together and spend time getting to know each other. Jesse waved before shutting his door.

My smile stayed on my face until I got to my room. My thoughts stuck on Jesse and sleeping proved to be a difficult task with my mind racing. I decided to see if Alani was still awake. Best friends come in handy for new-love-sleepless nights.

On my way to Alani and Nalani's room, I ran into Hiu, almost literally.

"How's it going, Captain?" I asked.

"Good, I'm getting ready to hit da bocha," he replied. I noticed the towel and shampoo in his hands.

"Don't you have a shower in your quarters?" I asked.

"Yeah, but Alani had my junk in her bag, I got it from her."

"Oh, is she still awake? I was going to see her."

"Yeah, she be awake for a while. Are you doing okay?" he asked.

"I'm fine. I just need to talk to someone."

"Well, you can talk to me if you want," Hiu offered.

"I don't want to bore you with my girl talk, Hiu." An awkward energy threatened to surround us.

"All right, but you know I'm here when you need me," he replied.

"You, Alani and Nalani are the only ohana I've got. Where else am I gonna go when a vampire is trying to change or kill me?"

"I don't know," he said with kindness in his eyes. He turned to walk away, but I stopped him.

"Hiu?" she said.

"Yeah?"

"Mahalo," I replied.

Hiu walked back to me and gave me a hug. "Ko aloha makamae e ipo," he whispered.

I pulled out of the hug and glanced up at him. He was much taller than me.

"What does that mean?" I asked, but he just smiled a silly grin and waved as he continued walking down the hallway. I sighed. I would ask Alani what he'd said, but pronouncing the Hawaiian language was difficult and repeating a phrase like that would be next to impossible for me.

I found Alani's room and knocked on the door. Alani answered, "Ava! Hey, I was wondering where you'd gone. I thought maybe you were with Jesse."

"Shh," I said. "I don't want everyone knowing quite yet."

"Come in here, Nalani is taking a bath. So, there is something to know then, right?"

"Well, we are taking it slow. I kissed him a few minutes ago. I feel like I got that closure we talked about. Tom showed just how bad his ugly side is. I know now, in my head and my heart, he's nothing but a manipulative monster. I think—I know he killed my parents, and I'm plotting my revenge."

"It's good you've gone from being in love with the guy to wanting to kill him. That makes me feel a little better about the situation," Alani said.

I smiled. Alani was definitely the type to speak her mind. Her opinion meant a lot to me.

"I still don't know if it really was love or if I just got swept up in his blanket of charm, but it doesn't matter. Jesse and I can move on. And since I'm immortal, it eases some of the fears I had. I don't know if I want to be immortal, but I don't think I have a choice. Not right now anyway."

"Wait. You're immortal? Nalani didn't tell me that part. That's awesome!" Alani exclaimed.

"Yeah, weird huh?"

"A little, but that means you and Jesse are meant to be. You guys can be so happy together!" Alani said excitedly. She clapped her hands together. I think she was already planning our wedding in her head.

"After Tom, I still want to take things slow. It seems like that may be beyond my control, though."

Alani's bathroom door opened and Nalani stepped out. "Aloha, Ava!"

"Aloha," I replied.

"Tutu, did you know sirens are immortal?"

"Why, no I didn't. I guess that's something the legends left out," Nalani said. "Is this something you want, Ava?"

"Well, not necessarily, but I don't have a choice. It's in my blood. It's so strange finding out this way. I wish my mother would have been able to tell me."

"Your mother and father would both be proud of the way you're handling the news. They can't be here now, but they are always with you in your heart. Use them to strengthen your soul and you will go far. Your abilities are a great responsibility. I know you will use them wisely," Nalani said.

"What you did with the ocean was so cool!" Alani jumped in her seat as if electricity ran through her.

"Thanks, I didn't even know I could do that until today. It might come in handy. Anyway, I'm going to go to bed now. I think I'm finally tired enough to sleep. I will talk to you in the morning," I said as I stood up to leave.

"Aloha ahiahi!" Alani and Nalani said.

"Aloha ahiahi!" I replied.

I closed the door behind me and walked to my cabin. Sleep finally approached me like a silent ghost.

I thought about how things were going to be once we got back to Hawaii. The last time I spent days on the boat, I spent them wallowing over an undeserving man. I had two choices on how to spend the trip back to Hawaii. I could either take a mini vacation—because I really needed one—or I could learn more about myself and see just what I was capable of, because once we got to Hawaii, the challenge of conquering the vampires was going to begin.

My plan was to take down Psytech headquarters first. We would have to go in and kill as many vampires as possible. If I were lucky, I would get another chance at Tom, but he's too smart to be ambushed. We had to figure out how to lure Tom away from his drudges. He might be injured from the dagger I'd thrown at him, so he would increase his personal security.

Now that he knew I was aware of who I was, he would be on the lookout for any power I could use against him. Apparently pearls in the ears of human men made my singing useless. I would use my new-found ability to defeat him. He didn't know I had been given the power to control the ocean. The fact that he was a vampire meant he was a good swimmer, but whether or not he could beat the current I would throw at him was yet to be determined.

These thoughts threw any notion of a mini vacation out of my head. The sleep that had begun to approach me a few moments ago took a detour, and so did I.

I went out to the deck and to the back of the boat. I leaned over the railing and concentrated on the ocean and the sound and movement of it as the boat glided across it.

I lifted my arms and concentrated. I used the ocean to speed up the boat and push it farther toward our destination. I slowed it down again. I didn't want to push us off course, but the knowledge of my power comforted me.

I closed my eyes and tried to focus on the waves. With my fingers spread apart and palms up, I lifted tendrils of the water. They swirled and obeyed my every movement. I pointed in one direction and they followed my command.

I brought one of the tendrils up to me. I made it curl around my waist without letting it touch me. Then I made it form a little shield around me. Not sure that this would actually help during a fight, I returned the tendril to the ocean.

Then I got the idea to make a ball of water I could hurl at drudges. I focused again and lifted about a gallon of water into the air with my thoughts. I used my hands to form the water into a ball shape and then shot it out into the distance. It was too dark to see how far it went, but I was pleased to see my ability at use.

The ocean calmed as I released it in my mind. I decided I would practice again tomorrow and every day until we reached our destination. I wondered if Hiu had anything I could use as targets.

This power came naturally to me. I wondered if my mother had somehow given me everything I needed to be a siren without me realizing it.

"Okay," I said to myself, "Time for bed."

CHAPTER TWENTY-THREE

The next morning, I found everyone out on the deck eating breakfast. Nalani got up early and prepared ham and eggs for everyone. Hiu seemed to be focused on some maps and calculations.

"I don't get it," Hiu said to Jesse, "I turned the GPS on for just a minute this morning. We are farther along than we should be. We musta caught a current or something."

"Uh, I might be responsible for the current you're talking about," I said.

Hiu turned to me, "What do you mean?"

"Last night I was practicing with the ocean and I pushed the boat a little. I didn't do it for long because I didn't want to push us off course, but I wanted to find out if I could actually do it if I had to."

"Wow, so ass why I'm so futless. It was you!" Hiu exclaimed. "You good to have around, kama'aina."

Hiu's comments made me smile with pride. I didn't want the role of damsel in distress. I wanted the role of the powerful siren. "Hey, do you have anything I can use for target practice? A flotation device we can drag behind the boat or something?"

"What are you shooting it with?" Hiu asked.

"Water," I replied with a smile.

"Oh yeah, I got da kine you need. There some life preservers we can throw out there," he said. He disappeared to retrieve them.

"What's going on?" Jesse asked.

"I'm going to practice my ocean control. I think it's my best weapon against the vampires and drudges," I replied.

"That's a good idea. You should definitely try to get more familiar with your abilities, you never know when you might need them," Jesse said. He put his arm around my shoulder. I leaned in and gave him a little hug. After a short while, Hiu came around the corner with four life preservers attached to some rope. I rushed over to help him.

"I spaced them out for you, I tied some good knots, so you should be able to throw a lot of water at these and still keep them on the line. They're at 20-yard intervals."

"Thanks, Hiu!" I said. Hiu went to the railing and tied the end of the rope to it. Then he threw out the preserver that would be farthest and so on, until all four preservers were out. I thanked him again and went to the railing to concentrate. A crowd formed behind me as my friends all watched with curious eyes.

I wanted to try the water ball thing again, so I began with that. I gathered up about a gallon of water again. I formed the ball in mid-air. Then I flicked my wrists out toward the closest life preserver. The water ball almost hit it but was a little off. Everyone clapped anyway, and pressure built up in the form of my embarrassment.

I tried it again, but this time I focused even harder. With a flick of my wrists, I hit the life preserver with the water ball. Everyone clapped again. I decided to try to hit the second farthest one, and with my nearly infallible concentration, I did. I formed a fourth ball, and aimed for the third preserver and hit it. I was getting faster too. My aim improved as the fourth preserver took a direct hit. With each hit, my friends cheered me on.

My connection with the ocean grew stronger and stronger. The ocean seemed to anticipate my next command. This time, I drew up two water balls and shot one after the other. I hit the 40-yard and the 60-yard preserver. Then I tried three and hit the 40, 60 and the 80-yard preserver.

I manipulated the ocean like a sculptor manipulated clay. I made columns of water shoot out from the center of each life preserver. Each column reached a height of about 25 feet. Another idea came to me. I climbed over the railing and dove into the water. Some of my friends shouted my name, but I reappeared with a column of water supporting me. The water swirled around my waist and held me steady. Everyone clapped and cheered.

"Anyone want to join me?" I asked.

Jesse and Alani made their way to the railing and dove in. I used my connection with the ocean to lift them up as well. Jesse and Alani both laughed.

"This is crazy!" Alani shouted.

I made the columns gently set the three of us down safely on the deck of the boat and sent the water back out to sea. Hiu and the others came to meet us.

"That was gnarly!" Hiu hollered, as he came down the steps from the upper deck. Everyone else agreed in some way or another. All except Latoria who glared and rolled her eyes with crossed arms from farther back.

It didn't matter.

Empowerment rushed over me. My abilities gave me a close connection to the ocean, and also a close connection to my mother. If my mother could see me now, she would be glowing with pride. I couldn't let this part of myself go.

I was now a siren. At heart and by blood. I could not destroy this connection to my mother, and so I decided I would not give up my immortality or anything else connected to my ancestry.

I needed to inform Jesse of my decision. I needed to let him know where I stood on the issue before our relationship went any further.

I looked around. Everyone chatted with each other about me and my powers and things they thought I may be able to do. Jesse and Latoria were near the stairs. I approached them and received a hostile glare from Latoria as she turned and walked away. Jesse's expression was strong and stubborn until he saw me. It melted into a gentle and almost apologetic one.

"You are quite the young siren, Ava. With more practice, you can expand your abilities to the fullest. Of course, you must decide what you want out of life before you get too attached to your abilities."

I nodded, "That's why I came over here. I want to talk to you about a few things."

"Okay, let's go somewhere a little more private," he said. The two of us snuck away while Hiu pulled up the life preservers and Alani tried to describe to everyone else what it felt like to be held up by water. We found a discrete mechanical room and closed ourselves in.

"I just want to say . . ." I paused and tried to map out my words. We'd been so honest with each other since we met, I needed to continue. "If you want to be together, I'm ready. Yesterday and last night settled all my emotions, and I actually took time to think about us. I want to give it a shot, but before you tell me one way or another, my decision is to remain immortal as a true siren. I felt a connection with my mother today and I can't ever let that go. Without my knowledge, I think she groomed me to be a siren. It's coming so naturally to me."

"My decision will likely be to remain immortal as well. When I saw you out in the water, I thought you might decide this way. Your eyes said it all. If you hadn't come to this conclusion on your own, I would have begged you to do so. This is what you are meant to be. So, I told Latoria we must continue the search for a witch, but one with the power to allow me to remain immortal."

"Why did she seem so cold at the end of your conversation? Isn't that what she wanted?"

"She wanted to help me find a witch, but she did not want me to remain immortal. She wants me for herself. When I told her I wanted to keep my immortality she questioned my reasons. I told her I had found someone I wanted to stay immortal with and she put the pieces together. I'm afraid she will most likely be hostile toward you, but I made it clear that even if you weren't in my life I still had no romantic feelings for her," Jesse explained.

"What if we find a witch but she can't give you immortality?"

"Then we will decide what's better for you: an immortal who cannot protect you in the dark hours of the night or a man that can only protect you for the remainder of a human lifetime."

"You don't need to protect me, Jesse." I said.

Jesse put his hand on my cheek and kissed me passionately.

"I know I don't, but there's nothing I'd rather do for the rest of my life. Even if we get rid of Tom, there will always be another vampire seeking a siren to control. You're a rare treasure. Both as a kind and thoughtful person and as a supernatural being. I want to be on your side."

I melted into his arms and felt butterflies in my stomach. I kissed him and knew our meeting was fate. No one else made me feel this way, not even Tom.

By comparison, Tom was like an animal. Beautiful and majestic from a distance, but deep down, he was untamed. Jesse was exactly who he claimed to be. Although he was mysterious, I also trusted him, which is something I never had with Tom. Jesse was a true gentleman, not a lion in sheep's clothing. He was the kind of man that comes along once in a lifetime. He wasn't selfish, as I had first judged him to be. Jesse Sutton was someone I could possibly spend an eternity with. I felt it with every ounce of my being.

It was almost as if I were blinded by Tom. I've opened my eyes and he can't lead me astray anymore.

My thoughts settled and I pulled gently away from Jesse. I stared into his kind eyes; the eyes that had never betrayed me. He kissed my forehead.

"What are you thinking about, my love?"

"I'm thinking about you. What else would I be thinking about in a cramped control room on a boat in the middle of the ocean staring into the eyes of the best-looking man walking the planet?" I said with a giggle.

"Perhaps we should find somewhere else to go. Somewhere more romantic?"

"Well, I think we're eventually going to have to tell everyone about us. I already told Alani and Nalani probably has it figured out. Latoria knows too, so I guess we should tell everyone before gossip distracts everyone from the task at hand."

"I have a feeling Hiu will be disappointed," Jesse said.

"I suppose, but it's only a crush, he'll get over it," I replied.

"I think you underestimate his feelings for you. I believe he's in love. The way he watches you is intense," Jesse noted.

"That's because we're family," I said.

"I'm not so sure, but we can break the news whenever you want."

"I was thinking dinner time?"

"Sounds good to me."

The rest of the day went by fairly quickly. Jesse and I parted ways so he could try to contact his friend at NASA again and I could continue to practice my affinity with the ocean. I discovered a few new ways to manipulate the water. Among other things, I found I could create an arc of water and more than likely use it to sink a vessel if I desired.

Soon, it was dinnertime. Chicken and vegetables were on the menu. It was a fairly generic meal, but extremely tasty with the added herbs and spices. Halfway through dinner, Jesse and I decided it was time to tell the others about our relationship.

"Everyone, we want to announce something," Jesse said as he stood up. I stood as well. Everyone turned to see us, and Jesse continued, "I'm sure some of you are aware or at least suspected something was going on between us, but we wanted to put rumors to rest. Ava and I are seeing each other. We found a true connection, and we hope all of you can be happy for us."

"We're glad something good has come from this whole adventure," I chimed in, "We didn't want to leave you all in the dark, and hopefully you'll support our connection."

Everyone remained silent for a few seconds. Alani was the first to speak, "I'm so happy for you guys!"

Moana smiled and Nalani didn't look surprised, but I could tell she was happy for us. Hiu and Latoria were both upset. Latoria seemed furious while Hiu acted like he'd missed the last ride at an amusement park. His sad expression did not change once we sat back down. He was being quieter than usual.

Dinner finished without much more fuss. Alani pretty much ran the table conversation and, to my embarrassment, talked about mine and Jesse's imminent wedding and how cute our kids would be. Jesse and I had never talked about kids or getting married. Even before Psytech and the virus, I had barely ever given it a thought. I turned my head toward Jesse with a nervous expression. He seemed to be un-phased by the conversation. He politely handled all the comments and questions while holding my hand under the table.

Moana asked if Jesse and I were going to be cabin mates. That was another question that caught me off-guard, but Jesse was coy in his answer, "If Ava doesn't mind sleeping with a boulder in her bed, I would love to accommodate her."

I smiled. We'd already shared a hotel room. This wasn't much different. "I might need to consider that offer. Did you want to take my cabin, Moana? That way you don't share a bed anymore?"

"Well, if you don't mind, that would be very considerate of you."

"I think we might be living on this boat for a while. There really isn't anywhere we can go in Hawaii that's safe from the vampires, so I think it might be more comfortable for you," I said, "We can move our things after dinner or tomorrow morning if you want."

"The morning will be fine, it's not that I don't like rooming with Latoria, but these cabins are a little cramped."

I nodded but turned my attention to Hiu. He didn't seem to be listening. He was staring into space. Then his eyes shifted and stared into mine. He was hurting. After a moment, he abruptly left the table. I looked back at Jesse. He had been right.

"Go ahead," he whispered.

I went after Hiu. He was walking rather fast toward his cabin. He got to his door and I was right behind him.

"Hiu, wait!" I said.

"I can't wait, Ava. Not anymore. I've been waiting and waiting for you, but it's been a waste of time. I've waited too long."

"What are you talking about?" I asked him.

"Ever since we met I've been waiting for the right time to make my feelings for you clear. After your parents died, you seemed so distant, so I gave you time to heal. Then, you seemed to be coming around, but everything blew up in my face. The whole virus thing, Psytech, and the vampires. That bloodsucker, Tom. I wanted to give you your space, but I shoulda gone for it."

"Hiu, I don't understand. What did you say? The other night in the hallway, you said something to me in Hawaiian, what was it?"

"It was 'Ko aloha makamae e ipo.' It means you are so precious, sweetheart. You said thank you, and I was just telling you that you are too precious to me to let anything happen to you." Hiu paused and took a deep breath, "I'm in love with you, Ava. I always have been." Hiu finally admitted in plain English.

I was silent. I always knew Hiu had feelings for me, but the extent of it surprised me.

"Now you're in love with him and I'm left in the dust."

"We're family, I'll always love you, but I love you like a brother. I'm sorry that's all I feel, but it's the truth. I don't want to hurt you, Hiu."

"I know. It's not your fault. I just thought that maybe someday you would see me as more than a goofy guy that's practically your brother," Hiu explained.

"There's someone out there for you. I'm not the one. I'm sorry. I don't want you to waste your time on me. There's someone out there who will love you and you'll love her. You're one of my best friends and I don't want that to change. But, if you think it will be too painful to be around me, I will give you space. I can find somewhere else to go once we get to Hawaii."

"No. No matter how much I hurt, I can't let us split up. You're still ohana, and I will put aside my feelings and be the man I know I am. It's best that we all stick together," Hiu said.

"Okay, if that's what you want," I replied.

"It is, and I suppose that Jesse seems like a nice enough guy. At least you aren't with a vampire. If that were the case I'd be deeply offended that you'd rather be with a dead guy than me," Hiu said with a little smile.

I hugged him. I hoped Hiu would be okay. I didn't like to see him in pain and knowing I'd caused it made me feel even worse.

"If it doesn't work out, don't forget about me," Hiu said, half joking and half serious.

"How could I forget about you?" I asked. Then the two of us went back out to the deck, where Moana, Alani, Nalani and Jesse were still talking. The sun was beginning to set. It was almost time to say good-night to my knight in shining armor. Jesse looked up from the conversation as Hiu and I re-emerged. I'm sure he could tell our talk had gone better than the one he'd had with Latoria.

"Well, I'm sorry to leave you all, but it's getting to be my bedtime," Jesse said as he stood up from the table. The others said "goodnight" to him and he came to me. Hiu approached Jesse with his right hand out, ready to shake his hand. Jesse returned the gesture and they shook hands.

"I wanted to tell you guys that I'm gonna be supportive. But, as the only big brother that Ava has, I'm warning you not to hurt her. I realize you're stronger than me—and immortal—but I will figure out something bad to do to you if you hurt her," Hiu said. He had a joking expression on his face, but I knew he was serious.

"I promise you she's in good hands," Jesse replied.

Hiu gave a little salute and walked away, leaving Jesse and I alone for the first time since we announced our relationship.

"Wow, his mood turned around quickly," Jesse commented.

"Well, we had a little talk. I guess he likes you and he thinks you're the next best thing. If he can't be with me, then he's glad it's you and not some jerk or vampire. He's also the self-sacrificing type. He just wants me to be happy even if it means that he won't get what he wants. He's putting on a brave face. Inside he's still hurting and it's going to take time for him to heal," I explained.

"That's comforting. I wish Latoria were half as understanding as he was, but if she's willing to sacrifice our friendship because I've chosen you then that's her loss."

I smiled and peered out at the setting sun, "You better get in there. Do you want me to put a movie in for you?"

"Sure, put in your favorite movie. You're welcome to watch it with me."

"I might just do that," I said. "You get comfortable and I'll be back."

Jesse gave me a kiss and nodded, "I'll be waiting," he said with a smile.

I rushed off to get my copy of "Sherlock Holmes," the 2009 version. It was kind of old, but I was nostalgic. I'd seen the older television series and read the book series when I was a young girl, and when the new movies came out, I had been a teenager. Sherlock Holmes was a classic character that always retained his personality no matter what.

Soon, I was back in Jesse's cabin. I'd tried to hurry back to see him before he changed to stone, but unfortunately, he was already a perfect statue. He'd written a quick note that was left on the bed:

I thought you'd be more comfortable if I took the chair tonight.

Jesse

Knowing that he could hear and see me, I kissed his marble lips and said, "I hope you like older movies."

I pushed play and buried myself in the blankets on his bed.

CHAPTER TWENTY-FOUR

The next morning I woke just in time for Jesse to return to his human state. The sun came in through the small window in his cabin. The comfortable bed provided a haven while reality fell to chaos around me, so I opened up the covers and motioned for him to join me. Reality needed to wait a little longer for both of us. He smiled and jumped into bed with me.

"Good morning, beautiful," he said.

"Good morning," I answered.

Jesse snuggled up close to me. We looked each other in the eyes. He kissed my forehead and then my lips. I returned his kiss and smiled at him.

"I wish I could cuddle with you all night," I said as I ran my fingers through his hair.

"Me too," he confessed with a sigh.

I gave him another kiss to try to cheer him up. He scooped me in closer to him and pressed our bodies as close as we would go. Jesse kissed me with passion and I felt butterflies in my stomach. I wanted him even closer to me.

I rolled over so I could lay on his chest. Jesse put his arms around me and hugged me tight. We continued to kiss and more tension built up. I started to unbutton Jesse's shirt. Then I sat up as he helped me take my shirt off and ran his hands back down my ribcage and rested them on my hips.

I leaned over him and started kissing his neck and muscular chest. I could feel he was ready. I rolled over onto my back and he followed. He kissed me from above now. He helped me pull off my shorts and then took off his own pants. I pulled him back on top of me.

We synchronized with each other and moved to a rhythm known only to us. Jesse's strong body filled two needs: the need to feel safe and the need for pleasure. The passion between us swelled, and when we let it go, our worlds collided like two stars in the galaxy.

After making love, Jesse and I collapsed on the bed and cuddled. My smile would not go away and Jesse's smile remained as well. Jesse ran his fingers up and down my side. It tickled in certain spots, but I just wanted Jesse's touch. I rested my head on his chest and my hand on his abs.

"I've never been so in tune with another human being," I said.

"Nor have I," Jesse replied.

"Do we have to get out of bed today?" I asked him. I turned my head so I could see his face.

"Not if you don't want to, but they might come looking for us after a while."

"We could just lock the door and tell them to go away," I replied with a shrug.

Jesse smiled and kissed me. "What about food?"

"I am getting a little hungry. We should stock our room with supplies so we can hide away for days," I replied as I sat up and leaned over to kiss him again. The two of us took our time getting dressed for the day and eventually headed out to greet everyone. Breakfast had long been over, but leftovers of French toast and eggs lingered on the table.

Nalani and Moana were the only ones in the galley.

"Aloha!" they both said as Jesse and I entered.

We both returned the greeting and started to eat. Nalani offered to make fresh food, but we declined. I was too hungry to wait.

"So, I'm going to pack up my stuff after I eat and you can take my room," I said to Moana between bites.

"Thank you, that's nice of you," Moana replied. "Between us, Latoria is a little hard to be around now that you two are together."

"That's unfortunate," Jesse replied with a little frown.

"Well, it's not any of my business. I'd rather just stay out of it. Besides, there's more going on than silly drama. We have to figure out how to stop the vampires from controlling everyone," Moana added.

"Yes, we do. I've been thinking about what we are going to do. First, we need to find out when they are planning on going public. I know they want to make us all squirm and long for our technology to be back, but eventually they will reveal their plan. When they do that, the world will be even more chaotic than it is now," I explained.

"They aren't going to like us poking around. We are sure to have a few standoffs with them. We need to be prepared," Jesse replied.

"The drudges are going to be thick. Unfortunately, Tom knew something I didn't about sirens. Apparently, pearls in the ears of men will prevent me from using my voice as a weapon, but what he doesn't know is I can control the ocean. I intend to keep that under wraps for as long as I can," said Ava.

"Ah yes, I forgot about the pearl in the ear trick. Sorry, I didn't tell you," Jesse apologized.

"It's okay. I don't remember any songs that would help me anyway. It's like I need a siren tutor or something," I said as I put my head into my hands. There was so much I didn't know about being a siren. Jesse's stories had helped a little, but I sensed blank spaces that could only be filled by a siren who knew the secrets of our kind.

"Maybe we should try to find a siren who can teach you about who you are. It would be a great help and I'm sure you want to know everything you can about your heritage. Hawaii is bound to have another siren on its islands. It's definitely an ideal place for sirens to live considering there's no way to get away from the ocean," Jesse replied.

"If we can find one, that would be wonderful, but it's not a top priority. My main objective is to stop Psytech," I answered.

"Okay, so we need to somehow get into Psytech and get some information about their plans and how they created the virus," Moana chipped in.

The three of us continued to discuss possibilities of Psytech break-ins and things of that nature. We made little to no progress and we eventually gave up the subject. Everything would be touch and go once we got back to Hawaii. Plans of where we would stay lacked solidity. We would stick with the boat, just in case we needed a fast getaway, but beyond that, we didn't have a plan.

The next day came and went. Most of it was spent in silence as we prepared ourselves for what we would come up against in Hawaii. I practiced my affinity with the ocean more and started to play with different ideas I had. Hiu announced Perry had called him with news the other group had found a safe house and that Jesse's friend from Las Vegas had made it to L.A. They said they would keep in touch. He also announced we would get to Hawaii around 2 p.m. the next day.

Jesse and I continued our romantic ventures. We built a strong connection with each other. It felt natural and real. I slept in Jesse's cabin for the third night while he watched over me from his stone prison. Eventually, the morning of our arrival brought a dark cloud over all of us.

By eleven, the Big Island came into view on the horizon and the boat arrived in Hilo bay by one-thirty. There weren't many boats docked upon our arrival. We were informed that most people with boats went out to catch fish for the islanders and no space for night docking was available.

Hiu paid for an hour of docking so he could check the other docks for space. Everyone else seemed glad to be on land, but a weary look settled on their faces as they kept an eye out for vampires.

We split into groups to gather supplies. Moana, Alani, and Nalani went to get food and water. They had to at least try even though food on the islands had become even scarcer in our absence. Most of the supplies available were produced on the island. Stories of ranchers starting to butcher their cattle for food peppered conversations. Fruit grown on the islands also helped, but produce growers were careful to only hand out so much. Rumors of people breaking onto plantations and stealing fruit soon reached my group.

Jesse and I were sent to find household items while Latoria stayed to watch the boat. She had the most important job. Another dockworker told the group that islanders trying to get to the mainland, where things weren't as bad, were stealing boats. Jesse and I walked through town and noticed the same things we saw in LA; broken windows, abandoned stores, and cars that had been abandoned and then broken into.

"What should we do?" I asked.

"Well, I guess we could try to find a store that still has the owners watching over it. Maybe we can trade for supplies. Do you have anything on you we don't need?"

"No, but there might be some stuff at my house . . . if it is still intact. We'll need transportation, though. It's too far to walk," I said.

"No problem," said Jesse with a smile as he eyed a motorcycle.

"What is it with you and motorcycles?" I asked with a smile.

Jesse immediately went to the abandoned bike. It lay on its side, but Jesse's strength made it look like he lifted a bicycle. He hot-wired it with ease and the motor started with a low rumble. I grinned and hopped on the back.

"My sweet little criminal," I commented.

"Where are we headed?" Jesse asked.

I navigated him to my house. From the outside, it seemed to be unharmed. It was far enough away from downtown that most of the looters passed it up. Not to mention it was hidden away by plants and trees. Most people passing by wouldn't notice my small two-bedroom.

I no longer had my house keys, so Jesse picked the lock. I picked up on all the things he was doing that pointed to him possibly having a less than perfect record.

"Should I be aware of a criminal record before we go any further?" I joked.

"No record, but that just means I didn't get caught."

I grinned at him. "Actually, I'm glad you can do this stuff. It's a little bit of a turn on."

The lock clicked and my front door opened. Jesse motioned for me to enter. We walked into an undisturbed house. The last time I had been inside was when I'd come with Tom. I hadn't realized how long it had been until now. As I rooted around for things we could trade, Jesse took a look around.

"You have a whimsical style. So much nature in this house," he commented.

"It's mostly my mother's doing. Changing it just seemed wrong to me. It's traditional Hawaiian decorating with elements of the beach and such."

"I see that. So, did you find anything?" Jesse asked.

"I found some canned food Alani and Nalani missed the first time. It's not a lot, but we can find use for it. I found some candles we can trade. That dockworker said some people are losing power because they can't pay the power company. There's some camping supplies in that closet, knives are, everywhere," I gestured around me and continued, "My mother was an advocate for personal security. I'm going to gather up some of my personal stuff. I think there's soap and other toiletries in the bathroom," I said.

I didn't want to leave my house again. I took in the familiarity of my home and realized how much I missed it.

There were some things I didn't want to get stolen by looters, so I gathered up some of my mother's jewelry and my father's watches along with other keepsakes and treasures. I found a stash of batteries in my desk drawer and put them in with the camping gear.

"You know, I'm not sure we need to trade any of this stuff for anything, I think it would be best to hang on to the camping gear and candles and knives," Jesse said.

"I think you're right, but how are we going to get all this back to the boat?"

"I didn't think about that when I hot-wired the motorcycle. I guess we'll need to find a car."

I grinned. "I have a car."

"You do? Where?" Jesse asked.

"In the garage, silly."

"There's a garage?" Jesse asked.

I led Jesse to the back of the house where a garage with overgrown plants and vines covered the entire building. The doors were also covered with vines but weren't as thick. I took a machete from my camping gear and began to chop my way through the greenery. Jesse helped clear it. Finally, the two swinging doors were free. I unlocked the combination padlock and opened the doors to reveal a blue, four door, 1971 Chevelle with a white hard top.

"That is a beautiful car," Jesse said with wide eyes. He practically drooled over the antique classic. "Does it run?"

"I hope so," I replied. "I haven't touched it since my father died. He loved this car, and so did I. We used to take it for drives along the coast all the time. He worked on it himself."

I found the magnetic key holder under the driver's side door then unlocked it, hopped in, and unlocked the passenger door for Jesse. It was an automatic, so I put the key in the ignition and prayed for it to still work. I turned the key and there was nothing but the sound of a dead battery.

I knew it well. Then I remembered the portable jump-start pack I kept in the garage. I plugged it in, and after a few tries, Jesse and I got the car running.

"Yes!" I yelled when it came to life.

We packed up the portable jump-start pack along with the other items we found inside the house and headed back to the boat. Once we returned to the dock, we saw Alani and Moana waiting for us.

"We didn't know where you guys went," Alani said as her greeting. "You kinda worried us. Hey, is that your dad's old car?"

"Yep, we took a motorcycle to my house to gather supplies, then we realized a motorcycle wouldn't carry all this, so we started her up," I said.

"So did you guys find anything we can use?" Moana asked.

"We found some of my camping gear and batteries and candles and stuff. We don't have to use the energy on Hiu's boat so much if we use this stuff. We have to be more careful about the amount of energy we use, fuel is getting scarce," I explained. "We found some of my knives too. That might help against the drudges. We also found some canned food."

"Good. We didn't get much food. It's a good thing we stocked up before we left Jesse's house," Alani said.

The four of us started unloading everything into Hiu's boat. He had found a space on the original dock for us to stay for the night, but we would have to find somewhere else to stay the next night.

Nalani had made dinner for everyone and soon after Jesse had to retire to our cabin. I went with him, even though it was still early. I'd rather watch movies with my statue boyfriend than talk more about the problems at hand. I just wanted a break from it all. The time I spent with Jesse, even when he was in statue form, made me relax just enough to release some stress. With the recent events, I felt like a balloon inflated to the point of bursting, but when I was with Jesse, it seemed that some of the air was let out.

The next morning, Hiu had to find another place to dock the boat. Dock space was extremely limited, and his regular spot that he rented from before the virus crisis was taken when he left for California. A lot of the boats were out at sea during the day, fishing and trying to catch food to survive off of. With most of the big container ships out of commission because of the virus, food was getting scarcer on the islands. I hoped that we could somehow help everyone who was stranded on the islands. First, we had to get enough food to sustain ourselves, and then we had to get more virus blocking devices to the container ships. Revenge would have to wait, the people of the islands were more important.

Hiu was having a hard time finding a dock spot. Jesse and I had gone with him while everyone else stayed on the boat. Chaos surrounded us. Boats coming into port with fish were raided. Dockworkers tried to maintain order by shouting orders into the crowds, but their words were lost against the roar of people yelling and shoving to get to the fish. Fishermen traded fish for fruit and other food, but some of them had trouble keeping people from just taking the fish. Hiu, Jesse, and I tried to stay away from the swarms of people.

Even finding a dockworker that wasn't busy was a difficult task. Eventually, Hiu was ready to give up. We were all heading back to the boat when someone shouted Hiu's name. Hiu turned to see who it was, and a smile developed on his face.

"Kapono! Howzit, broddah?"

"It good. Just tryin' to keep working with this big mess. Where you been, brah?" Kapono asked.

"I went to LA. We just get back yesterday," Hiu said as he motioned to Jesse and I. "Ava, Jesse, dis Kapono. He's my good friend. He works the docks."

"Oh, man. Things are getting funny 'round here. I 'bout had-it with these lolo guys."

"Us too, we're trying to find somewhere to dock, but no can," Hiu explained.

Kapono nodded, "You won't find da kine here, brah."

"I starting to figure that out. Things aren't much bettah in town either. I don't know what we gonna do," Hiu said as he let him eyes wander through the crowd.

"I bet you just have to drop anchor somewhere, brah. No moa room anywhere. Lemme see if I can cockaroach you a spot," Kapono said walking over to another dockworker.

I watched him talk animatedly to the other man. Kapono was Hawaiian, like Hiu, but he talked pidgin constantly. Whenever he and Hiu were together, it was a blur of words I could barely understand. I had met Kapono before at Alani's house. I remembered he was an avid surfer. He had longer hair than Hiu, about the same length as Alani's, it was also dark, but a bleached streak near the front was his signature look. He and Hiu had the same build; the body of a surfer. They dressed much the same too, always wearing shorts and a wife-beater. After a few minutes, Kapono returned with a defeated look on his face.

"Sorry, man. I try, but no can. Dock manager say we full. No mo' notting."

"Ass alright, we figure something out, broddah," Hiu replied.

"I got a choke of hana to do, but if you stick around for later, I show you a spot to drop anchor bumbye," Kapono said as he and Hiu exchanged a handshake I assumed was exclusive to their group of friends. I'd never seen it before.

"Leddahs!" Hiu waved as the three of us made our way back to the boat. I thought about what Kapono had said. Maybe dropping anchor would be better than docking. It would make it harder for us to be found by the enemy. Docking meant records, and records meant we could be tracked down.

"Hiu, I think we should let Kapono show us a good place to drop anchor. It's probably better that we aren't easily found," I said as we reached the boat.

"I was just thinking that. What do you think Jesse?" Hiu asked. I was surprised Hiu would ask Jesse's opinion, but it made me smile on the inside. I wanted them to get along. An awkward relationship between them would mean more stress for me.

"I think it's smart to stay away from the crowds and riots. If it's secluded enough it should deter drudges and vampires as well."

"Okay, so we wait here for Kapono. He know dis island even bettah than me, and I know it well."

CHAPTER TWENTY-FIVE

After about an hour, Kapono showed up at the boat. Everyone was on board with the plan, so all we had to do was find a secluded area where we could drop anchor. Kapono and Hiu went up to the pilothouse and soon we set sail down the coast. To the south of Hilo, a black, rocky coast lined the ocean. Cliffs shot up from the sea like giant shadows. I always loved looking up at the cliffs from a boat in the ocean. They were majestic. A wonder of nature.

After a while of seeing only the cliffs, the boat slowed and a small break in the cliffs came into view. It was a recess in the cliff wall. If I hadn't been looking directly into it, I would have missed the inlet. Hiu directed the boat into the crevasse and revealed a beautiful secluded cove. There would only be two ways to see any vessel inside; either from directly above, or from the entrance on the east side.

Hiu and Kapono emerged from the pilothouse as everyone marveled at the beauty of the cove. "Well? What you think, brah?" Kapono asked Hiu.

"It most definitely is secluded," he answered.

Jesse looked around. I could see the wheels turning in his head. "Possibly a little too secluded. We could easily be taken by surprise," Jesse said to me. He tried to keep the concern between the two of us. Kapono wasn't aware of the problems we faced.

"I think I can handle that," I said.

Kapono noticed the exchange, "What you mean 'taken by surprise'?"

Jesse turned to Hiu. Hiu nodded and took a few steps toward Kapono and put his arm around him. "I think it's time you been enlightened."

Kapono looked around at everyone. He tried putting it together, but his mind didn't quite hit the right switch. "Are you guys fugitives or something? I no deal with fugitives, man."

"Well, kinda. But not from the law," Hiu said as he led Kapono away so that they could talk.

I knew he'd recruit Kapono into our group. I wasn't sure if that was good or bad. He'd be good to have around. He knew the island like the back of his own hand and he had connections. I hoped he didn't get too freaked out by the news of vampires in Hilo.

After Hiu explained to Kapono about Psytech and the vampires and everything else that had happened in the last few weeks, Kapono took Hiu's passion for vampire slaying to a whole new level. He knew the legends and didn't think they were real until we told him everything. Nalani issued him a protective ring, and he ate lunch with us. He was an animated character. Kapono talked with his hands a lot and always spoke well above the required volume.

"Man, it good to have another guy around. We starting to feel outnumbered!" Hiu said in a conversation at lunch.

"You gonna need another guy if you wanna fight vampires," Kapono replied, with a mouthful of food. "Dis some ono grind! Lau lau is da kine!" he said to Nalani.

She replied with a smile.

"So, you a siren?" he asked me.

"Yeah, I guess I am," I replied.

"You make ships wreck?"

"No, it's not like that. I can control the ocean and my singing can influence men to do things. I'm not very good at it, though. I just found out a few days ago," I explained.

"Huh. Dat gnarly!"

I smiled. "Thanks, it is kinda neat."

"One of deez days you gotta make some pumping insane waves for me to surf," Kapono said excitedly.

"I could probably do that," I laughed.

"Dis guy is one rippah," Hiu said.

Conversation took off. Subjects like surfing and kayaking came up. Kapono and Hiu entertained everyone. Latoria kept to herself for the most part. Alani seemed drawn to Kapono. I noticed once he came aboard, Alani acted a little different. Nalani joined in on the reminiscing and told us about all the trouble Hiu and Kapono got into when they were younger. Moana told a few stories of her own. Jesse and I relaxed on a bench and watched everyone else have a good time. We sat with our hands entwined and enjoyed the conversation and the cliff side.

The rest of the afternoon was used to catch fish and relax a little. I practiced my ocean control and Kapono expressed his wish to grab a surfboard as he watched me. He seemed genuinely excited to be part of the big secret. He was a nice addition to the group.

Numbers were welcomed as we prepared to take on a hoard of vampires and drudges, but secrecy was also essential. Kapono promised he wouldn't say anything to anyone, and Hiu cleaned out one of the rooms we used for storage so that he could stay on the boat if he wanted. The city of Hilo grew more chaotic each day and Kapono was especially grateful to get out of the neighborhood he lived in.

Kapono made plans with Hiu to get some of his things the next day and to gather up any supplies that might be helpful. Moana and Latoria made dinner to give Nalani a little break. They cooked the fish we caught earlier. I was getting sick of fish, but I didn't say anything. I was just grateful to have food.

I gazed out toward the ocean after dinner. Colors of pink and orange began to paint the sky. Clouds rolled in and the sun dipped toward the horizon. I dreaded the time that Jesse would revert to his statue state. I wanted to spend the night with him, not his statue. I knew that he could still see and hear, but I wanted to be able to lay with him in bed. Longing for something I couldn't have wasn't doing me any good, so I decided to make the best of the hour we had left.

"Hey, want to take a swim with me?" I asked Jesse.

"I would go anywhere with you," he replied.

The two of us told Hiu we were going for a swim and jumped off the back of the boat into the cool water of the crevasse. I spotted a cave earlier and led Jesse to it. We found the entrance and swam inside. The cave was partially underwater. Inside, it opened up at the top and let some sunlight in. Jesse found a boulder sticking out of the water for us to sit on. We climbed it together and sat with our feet in the water.

Jesse splashed me with a mischievous twinkle in his eye. I retaliated with my own little splash and he was prepared to do it again, but I stopped him with a few clever words.

"Don't make me use my powers on you. You can't beat me in a water fight!"

"I suppose you're right," he said as he splashed me again, but before I could even the score he put his arm around me and pulled me in closer. I looked up into his eyes and he kissed me. I forgot all about the little water fight.

"This is a beautiful place, but your beauty surpasses it significantly," he said to me. He kissed me again and my heart fluttered. We laid down on the big rock and started to make love.

I got the same feeling I did the first time. The feeling of being connected to Jesse in a profound way. It was like there was no one else on earth, and we were the only two people that ever had such a connection. Nothing compared to the intense bond between us.

We collapsed in exhaustion and smiled in ecstasy. The cave grew much darker. Jesse looked up.

"I suppose we better get back. Unfortunately, I must soon feel the wrath of the curse."

I hugged him before we got back in the water and swam back to the boat. We made it with only a few minutes to spare. I felt sorrow inside me as I watched Jesse's color fade to gray. His magnificence transformed into stone and I realized I'd been wrong when I thought his statue wasn't art. Now that I had spent more time with Jesse while he was human, I saw the passion I'd seen in his eyes only an hour before still present.

It was possible that our love had changed him and that the passion wasn't there back when I thought all I was looking at was a statue. It was also possible that our love made him appear as a true work of art only to me.

I thought about how Jesse carried himself when I first met him. He was reserved and rigid. A coldness kept him from opening up to everyone else around him. In the short time I had known him, I watched him go from that cold person to a warm and gentle one. He was almost brought back to life. When I met Jesse, it was as if he was dead inside. This made me wonder if I had done this. The Jesse I knew now was a wonderful man that still had a little mystery about him, but that was part of the reason I liked him so much.

I knew I could spend my immortal life with Jesse and still find out something new about him every day. The excitement of revealing someone's past, especially someone who has been around as long as Jesse, was the most romantic adventure I could ever dream of. I sensed he had a few skeletons in his closet, but somehow I knew that nothing in Jesse's past could make me think badly of him.

Anything Jesse had done prior to meeting me didn't matter. The only thing that mattered now was the fate of the world. Anything else had to be put aside.

I fell asleep thinking about Jesse and our future.

The next morning I woke to Jesse watching me sleep with a smile on his face.

"Good morning, my love," he said.

"Good morning," I said as I sat up and gave Jesse a kiss.

"You are so beautiful. I don't know how anyone could ever resist your charm," he said.

I smiled, "Where did that come from?"

"I was just thinking. I never had a chance. From the moment I saw you, I was yours."

I giggled then put my hand on his cheek and let it glide down his neck and onto his chest. "I thought about you last night. I realized I knew something was different about you the night we met. I've seen you change right before my eyes. You seemed so cold the night we met, and now your soul seems to have been revived."

"I never thought that I would fall in love, especially after the curse. It's amazing to me that a chance meeting could change my life so drastically. You're right. Before we met, my existence resembled that of an ordinary statues' existence. Living forever, drifting through time like an object that is never truly noticed and doesn't necessarily want to be noticed. Before you, I was just an object, and now I have my humanity back," Jesse said as he pulled me into his arms. "I have you to thank for bringing me back to life," he whispered in my ear.

A smile came across my face as I relaxed in his arms. We embraced for a while and then went out to breakfast. Everyone was already there. As usual, Jesse and I arrived last. Hiu finished up then went to pilot the boat back to town so Kapono could pick up his things. I thought today would be a good day for Psytech surveillance, so I brought it up to everyone else.

"We need to start some surveillance on Psytech. We need to get moving on them," I announced.

"Yes, we do," Jesse agreed.

"How should we do that?" Hiu asked.

"Well, we can't all go. Some of us need to stay with the boat," I said.

"There are eight of us. Four can go, four can stay," Hiu replied.

"Okay, but the group that goes will have to split into two groups. We will need some radios to communicate between us," I explained.

"I got da kine," Kapono said.

"Great! We'll need code words, in case Psytech can listen in," I replied.

"We'll figure that out, but who's gonna go and who's gonna stay?" Hiu asked.

"I think Jesse and I should go, and Kapono since he's got the radios, and probably you," I answered.

"Okay, let's just get to the docks," Hiu said.

Hiu and Kapono went up to the pilothouse and I followed.

I had an idea.

"I want to try something. I think I have enough control to get us out of this crevasse, I just want to try, but I wanted to get your permission," I said to Hiu.

"I trust you, Ava. I know you wouldn't try anything unless you knew it was safe, so go ahead."

I concentrated on the ocean and the cliffs. I focused all my energy on the ocean and the boat. I lifted my arms and created a swell beneath the boat and then used the swell to carry us out of the crevasse. The boat slipped through without even coming close to the rocky cliffs, and soon we glided into the open.

Hiu and Kapono let out a little sigh of relief.

I did too.

Then I turned over the boat handling to Hiu. Out on the deck everyone stood near the railing and pointed at the swell of water as it receded. Jesse had a proud smile on his face. Alani jumped up and down while she clapped her hands.

"That was awesome! If we were back in pirate days, you could throw an enemy boat against the rocky shore. We wouldn't even have to shoot cannons at them!" she said.

I laughed, "That's right, no pirates would want to mess with me!"

The rest of the short trip back to town was consumed with getting ready for surveillance on Psytech. Jesse and I would stake out the gate while Hiu and Kapono would try to get a look at the warehouses.

Once we found a dock we could use temporarily, Hiu, Kapono, Jesse, and I went to find transportation. I had my dad's old car put in a shipping container before we had left, and I was glad to see that it remained.

We drove to the café across the street from Psytech. It was the same one I'd gone to with Tom. I gave Hiu the keys to my car. They still had to stop by Kapono's place to get his things. Jesse and I decided to do their surveillance from the café. The owner's eyebrows smushed together as we walked in. I was amazed it was still open.

"Aloha!" I greeted. I tried to be friendly.

"I hope you folks won't be causing any trouble around here," the owner said as he eyed Jesse, who wore jeans and a black t-shirt. I realized he did seem kinda rough around the edges at the moment. I hadn't thought anything of it until now, but he looked good to me. I pulled my attention away from my boyfriend and back to the owner. He was an older guy, most likely in his early 50's. He was Hawaiian in origin, short, and stocky. I glanced at my own outfit before answering. I, too, wore a black shirt and jeans. I wondered if

I subconsciously dressed myself like Jesse or if it had been a coincidence.

"Oh, no, we just got back to town from LA and we just wanted some coffee, sir," I assured him. He relaxed his brows a little, but he still remained weary.

"Alright, but all I have is regular coffee. Everything else is gone," he said slowly.

Jesse and I each nodded and sat at a table. We watched intently out the window. There wasn't a lot of activity at the gate.

After a while, the owner became restless. Jesse noticed the owners' stares and soon got up to confront him. I glanced up at him with a question in my expression. He shot me a look of reassurance.

Jesse began talking quietly to the man while I returned my attention to the gate. I listened in on what was being said behind me.

"My partner and I are investigating the building over there," Jesse said as he flashed the man a very real-looking badge revealed to me by the reflection of the store window. The man's face turned to the building as he looked for something that would give him reason to believe Jesse.

"We have intel that they may know something about the virus," Jesse announced officially. I couldn't help but smile a little. I covered my mouth with my hand.

"Now, I need to know if we have your full cooperation," he continued. I had to try harder and harder to hold in my laughter. He sounded so serious. I watched in the window as the man shook his head in agreement.

"Yes, of course," he replied.

Jesse pulled out a small notebook from his pocket. "I'm going to need your name and address for our records," Jesse said, readying his pen.

The man recited his name and address as Jesse jotted it down. He flipped the notebook closed and continued to give the man more instructions.

"We will need you to keep quiet about our presence. You never know who might be working for the people in that building. If they find out we are here, they could move their whole operation, and I don't want any rumors going around, do you understand?"

The poor man nodded again.

"Just keep in mind that if you do happen to blow our cover, you could be facing some serious treason charges," Jesse said solemnly.

"You don't have to worry about me, sir," the man said. "I won't tell anyone you're here. I'm not the gossiping type. You folks can use my shop anytime!"

Jesse nodded and then returned to his seat. I passed him a disapproving glance and he incredulously whispered, "What?"

I just smiled. I'd tease him later for scaring the man to death.

Our attention finally focused back to the gate. I wished I had a camera, but I settled on just keeping a tally sheet of the number of people coming and going with time passages. I noticed that most of the outgoing traffic came at noon and most of it returned at one. Jesse was recording plate numbers, although I wasn't quite sure why. Our observation was momentarily interrupted when Hiu returned to deliver a radio. Jesse exchanged it for a list of code words.

For the most part, it looked like a normal business. Employees were coming and going, or so it would seem to the unquestioning eye. Finally, Jesse and I saw three semi-trucks enter the gate. Jesse radioed Hiu to let him know there might be some action at the warehouses, but he warned him to keep a good distance.

"What do you think is in those trucks?" I asked with a hint of morbidity in my voice.

Jesse caught on to my tone and answered, "Probably just more devices that block the virus."

I turned back, watching as each truck checked in at the gate. I hoped Jesse was right as the image of the shareholders in the coffin-like crates came to my mind. Although, if he was right, the vampires might be planning to begin the task of forcing people to sign contracts in return for the devices soon. Surely, that would be the next step for Psytech.

Hiu's voice came over the radio again, "We got brown ones."

"How big?" I asked. Brown ones meant boxes.

"Small," he replied.

"Told you, I'm always right," Jesse said smugly.

I smirked and rolled my eyes. Hiu and Kapono held their position while the trucks were unloaded, after that we called it a day. Jesse talked to the owner of the store once more to see what time he would be at the shop the next morning.

"I'm usually here at five and open by six, but I could come in earlier if you need me to," the man replied.

"Thank you, but that won't be necessary. We don't want anyone catching on to any changes. We will come back between seven and eight tomorrow morning," Jesse said with his official voice. Jesse then handed the old man some money for the coffee and sandwiches we had eaten plus a hundred dollar bill for his cooperation. The man thanked them while we walked out the door. We were to meet Hiu and Kapono a few blocks down.

Once out of earshot from the old man, I met Jesse's eyes with mine and said, "You're a man of many scandalous talents."

Jesse smirked. He tried to hide it, but failed miserably, "I don't know what you're talking about."

I began listing the things I'd seen him do over the past few days in question form, "Hotwiring? Breaking and entering? Posing as a CIA agent?"

"Don't forget, you posed as a CIA agent too!" he said as he tried to incriminate me.

I smiled. "I didn't show a fake badge to an old man."

"You didn't deny you were a CIA agent," Jesse teased.

"So," was all I could think to say.

"So if I go to jail, you're coming with me, honey. You're my partner in crime. Like Bonnie and Clyde," Jesse said as he gave a mischievous grin.

"Bonnie and who?" I retorted.

Jesse laughed, amused that I was clueless to his reference. "Bonnie and Clyde. A couple of famous bank robbers," he explained, "You know, they died in a storm of bullets back in the 1930's."

"I guess that shows your true age," I teased as we arrived at the car. Hiu was still in the drivers' seat. I decided not to kick him out. I felt the need to let someone else take the wheel.

"At least I'm not into old guys," Jesse retorted, lovingly, of course.

I just laughed. I didn't have a comeback for that one.

"What so funny?" Hiu asked as they climbed into the car.

"Ava likes old guys," Jesse replied.

"I do not!" I said childishly.

CHAPTER TWENTY-SIX

The rest of the car ride back to the boat was filled with playful jeering and teasing between the four of us. Kapono mostly made fun of Hiu since Hiu was the only one he knew. But he seemed to be fitting in with us easily. Once we put my car away and boarded Hiu's boat, the teasing came to a close and we started in on a more serious conversation and involved everyone else.

We all sat down to dinner and discussed what we should do about the surplus of virus blockers assumed to be in the warehouses right now.

"We should burn down the warehouses," Kapono said bluntly.

"We can't, brah. We need da kine for the container ships so we can get food flowing again," Hiu explained.

My mind tried to formulate a plan for the strike. The lot almost emptied between the hours of noon and one o'clock, but it was still too full for comfort. A night operation wouldn't work because we would need the advantage of Jesse's immortality, so that option was out. We needed one more day of surveillance before we could make the decision.

"I think we should watch them again tomorrow. We'll keep track of the cars coming and going. That should give us our window of opportunity to go in and take as many of those virus blockers as possible. We're going to need something besides my car to transport them."

"I can take care of that," Jesse said with a grin.

"I'm sure you can," I said.

"Okay, we've got a nice set up at the café across from Psytech. The guy thinks we're CIA, so he's letting us sit in his shop without a whole lot of questions," Jesse announced. "We'll watch tomorrow and the next day we'll strike. We're going to need either Latoria or Moana in on this too. The other one of you will need to stay back on the boat with Alani and Nalani."

"I'll go," Moana said. Latoria didn't seem eager to go on the mission with us.

"Alright, the five of us will set up a time to leave tomorrow night after we've done our reconnaissance," Jesse said. He glanced at Latoria, which turned my attention to her as well. She seemed to care nothing about what we talked about.

I hoped I wouldn't have to step up and say anything to her. Latoria's distaste for me was becoming more and more evident to everyone else, and I didn't know how to handle it. Catty wasn't something I did well, but somehow, politely asking Latoria to back off seemed cowardly. I didn't want to fight with Latoria, but at the same time I wasn't willing to extend the olive branch. Jesse was an adult who made his own decisions, and although I could see why Latoria liked him, I would not be so pouty in Latoria's shoes. Not with so many lives on the line.

Friendship was a terrible thing to throw away, and Latoria seemed content to do just that with her friendship with Jesse. A true friend would be happy he had finally found love, but Latoria was too wrapped up in her own grief to realize the friendship she put at risk.

Dinner finished after more conversation about how to get into Psytech and backup plans for where to meet in case of disaster. Hiu worked on sharpening obsidian and I practiced my ocean control while Jesse took inventory of the ammo and guns. Alani helped him. I remembered him saying Alani's training was almost complete the other night before his "bedtime." The sun was about to go down, so I put my practice on hold so I could say goodnight.

I saw Hiu and Kapono mimicking some moves they'd probably seen in action movies. They were all hyped up, but I knew deep down they worried about how things would end up.

I left Jesse alone after I turned the TV on for his entertainment. I told him I was going to practice some more and that I would return in an hour or so. I hated leaving Jesse alone when he was a statue, but I had to practice more to defend my friends. I made my way to the back of the boat and turned my eyes up at the sky framed by the cliffs that nearly surrounded us in the crevasse. It was clear, but a few clouds started to roll in.

I hesitated when I got to the back of the boat. Latoria leaned on the railing and faced the water.

"Latoria, I didn't expect to see you back here," I said as I tried to sound friendly.

The woman turned and scowled slightly at my presence. "I'm sick of sitting alone in my room."

"It's a beautiful night," I said. "I was planning on practicing a bit since it's not raining."

"I'll leave you alone. I don't want to get in your way. Unless you need an audience. In that case, I'll just fetch Alani or Jesse. Wait, I can't. He's a statue, and he'll probably be stuck that way for the rest of his life now that you're in the picture."

The harsh words hit me like a whip. I preferred the silent treatment to this kind of offense.

"Can't you be happy he's found someone to be with?" I asked, keeping up the diplomatic act.

"I would be happier if it wasn't with someone like you," Latoria sneered.

"What is that supposed to mean?" I snapped.

"First you barge into Moana's house, trying to rope her into your little crisis, and then you drag us into it. We were all perfectly fine before you and your drama."

"You think I enjoy the fact that the world is going to hell and I'm the one who found out about it first? I would much rather have gone through life not knowing anything about Psytech or vampires or sirens. But now that I have, I'm doing my best to adapt. You don't even have to be here, you could have stayed behind with Edison, Perry, and Kassidy. I'm going to fight. I will fight for humanity just as hard as I will fight for Jesse. You need to realize everything happens for a reason, and you and Jesse weren't meant to be," I said. The volume of my voice raised with each sentence.

"You ruined everything. I almost had him, and you took him away," Latoria yelled.

"I took no one that wouldn't have run away on his own," I said harshly.

Latoria began to cry. A tear ran down her cheek and caught the glint of the moon. Instant guilt flooded my gut.

"I'm sorry. I'm just stressed out, okay? There's a lot on my shoulders. I know Jesse cares about you, Latoria. He just wants your friendship. There's nothing that can change that. I know what he's going through because I'm going through it with Hiu. I hated hurting him. I think it hurt me just to say the words I said to him. Jesse is hurting too because he knows your feelings run deep. He doesn't want to hurt you and he doesn't want to lose you as a friend. I hope someday you understand Jesse and I have something special. I hope you can forgive me someday."

Latoria still had tears running off her face, but she seemed different.

"It's not fair. I've been trying to get him to open up to me for years. You come along and in a few days he's changing for the better. His heart was locked up tight, and I knew there was something just waiting to be awakened in him, but you got to it first. I don't understand why he can't love me," she said.

"We can't choose who we fall in love with and who we don't fall in love with. It's a natural thing that either happens or doesn't. There will be others for you, Latoria. I thought I was in love with a vampire. Turns out he's a monster. Jesse's no monster, but trust me, you will love again," I replied.

"I might be able to forgive you if that happens, but for now I'm too hurt to forgive either of you. I hope you're right. I hope I do find someone and all this will seem silly to me, but right now my envy will not let me forgive and forget."

"Fair enough, but can we at least be civil toward each other? There is much more going on around us than you and me. We have to stick together and stop Psytech. Agreed?" I asked as I held out my hand for a handshake.

Latoria slowly met my hand with her own and said, "Agreed."

She walked away.

I felt a little better about the air between Latoria and me. A pang of sympathy overcame me as I watched her walk away. I couldn't imagine what I would do if someone tried to take Jesse away from me. I would probably react much the same way as Latoria at first, but after a while I imagine I would have had the strength to contain my discontent for the person who stole my love for the greater good. I would be able to put others' needs before my own pitiful love issues, although I'd never get over Jesse. If we were to ever be apart, I knew I wouldn't be able to get past the pain it would cause.

The thoughts in my head swirled around. I made myself stop thinking about the possibility of Jesse ever leaving me. The hope that he felt the same way about me made me want to go to him now and confess my undying love for him. Unfortunately, now was not the best time. His stony circumstances would only frustrate me further. It wasn't fair that he had to return to his prison every night because he couldn't fall in love with the woman he was slated to marry all those years ago.

It was amazing to me that so many women had fallen for Jesse, yet I had been the one he'd fallen for. It was also very humbling. The fact that he could suddenly consider someone so insignificant to his existence for his one and only was a mystery to me. Jesse was a mystery in himself. There was so much I didn't know about him, yet I wanted to spend my life trying to unravel the secrets and stories that made him who he was.

After pondering over my relationship with Jesse, I decided to try to get a little practice in before bed. My abilities grew stronger and stronger every time I used them. The ocean's energy uplifted me. When I finished, I felt restful. I made my way to mine and Jesse's cabin and entered to find him still in his stony state, which was no surprise, but what did take me by surprise is the reaction of my heart at the sight of him.

His beauty was marveling. He'd taken off his shirt before settling in and his musculature showed even more than it did when he was in human form. I admired his six-pack abs, the smooth curves of his strong biceps and triceps, the firmness of his forearms and his bulging pectorals.

At that particular moment, he was the most beautiful thing I'd ever seen. His position on the recliner was cavalier. He reclined with one arm behind his head and the other on the armrest. His ankles were crossed and he was barefoot. His hair was in disarray from the swim we'd taken and the expression on his face was content. He didn't smile except with his eyes. The position contrasted sharply with the stance he used in the garden back in L.A.

I approached him slowly and realized he must have noticed my intense reaction. I smiled at him and kissed his cheek before saying goodnight and going to bed.

The next morning, I woke to the sight of Jesse's curious eyes. He touched my cheek with his soft hand. The softness of his skin always took me by surprise. He spent half of his time as a stone hard statue, yet when he changed back to human form, his skin was so velvety. A true contradiction to what one might think.

His infallible voice gently greeted me, "Good morning, my love."

"Good morning," I responded with a smile that reached every part of my body. My excitement of seeing Jesse so close made my fingers and toes tingle. Adrenaline coursed through me as I brought my lips to his. His pleasant reaction pulled me in even closer, although I wasn't sure if I had made the move myself or if he'd pulled me into his arms.

More than likely it was both. Our embrace ended too soon, and Jesse looked into my eyes again.

His curious gaze grew more intense, and I could tell he tried to form a question in his mind. I waited patiently while he gathered his thoughts.

"Last night, you came in looking . . . different. You've never looked at me in that way. For the first time, an overwhelmingly pleasant emotion came over me while in my stone prison."

I felt myself blush, "I was just caught off guard," I tried to explain, embarrassed that he noticed my reaction.

"I was in the same place you left me," he said slowly.

"I know. I was expecting that. I wasn't expecting your . . . divine appearance to catch me off guard," I explained.

"What do you mean?" he asked, clearly confused by something I'd said.

I remembered how wonderful he looked on the recliner. He was just as wonderful today and every day, but for some reason it had slammed into me last night as I returned from practicing. "I guess I hadn't let it set in."

"Let what set in?" Jesse asked, prying for more information.

"How absolutely gorgeous you are," I finally said.

Jesse let out a short chuckle. His hand made its way to my cheek again and let his fingers brush along my jawbone. I shivered with the sensation. "You are more beautiful than anything I've seen in this world and I've seen almost everything. I can't imagine my appearance would even compare to yours. There's more to your beauty than mine. Your beauty comes also from within. Your heart and soul radiate an energy that blows me out of the water, for lack of better terms."

I smiled shyly. I wasn't sure if I quite agreed, but the words were flattering all the same. Then I remembered my conversation with Latoria. The exchange was something Jesse should know about, "I talked to Latoria last night."

Jesse's brows lifted. "Did you?"

"Yes. We spoke about you. She was angry. I let some angry words slip as well, but in the end we agreed to disagree and to be civil toward one another. She said someday she may be able to forgive me, for taking you from her, but only if she could come to the realization that it was meant to be," I summarized.

Jesse's expression showed fury. "She has no right to hold anything against you."

"It's okay," I assured him, "I get it. I'm a girl too. If I were in her place I'd feel betrayed too. There's no rhyme or reason for it. It's just jealousy. Envy is fortuitous as part of the many complex human emotions."

Jesse's expression lightened slightly. He understood.

"You are so perceptive. You're not blinded by anything. It's something that has drawn me to you since we first met," he said. He ran one of his hands from my neck to my shoulder, the other hand rested on my leg. We sat across from each other on the bed. His eyes followed my fingers which were moving up and down his muscular arm.

"I don't know. I felt blinded by Tom."

"But you still left. You knew you couldn't stay with him no matter how you felt. Part of you saw what he really was."

"Jesse, I want to tell you something," I said. He switched his gaze to my eyes and readied himself for whatever I wanted to speak about.

I continued when I knew he was listening intently. "I want to be with you, for the rest of my immortal life. There is nothing that would make me change my mind at this point. My heart is in your hands and yours alone."

Jesse smiled, "Ava, you brought me back from my numb existence. I can't tell you what would happen if I ever lost you. To me, it seems I would turn to dust. My life is nothing without you, my humanity depends on you. My heart, whether it is stone or not, is yours to keep."

Truth shone through in each word he spoke. I was weary about the possibility of getting hurt, but the fact that we had such a strong bond—stronger even than the one I thought I'd had with Tom—made me disregard any doubts I had. I looked into his eyes and said the words I'd been afraid to say until now, "I love you."

Jesse's expression was pleasant. "I love you too, Ava Tanner," he said. His lips kissed my forehead and then my lips. The energy between Jesse and I had been supercharged.

Our intimate moment was soon interrupted by a knock at the door.

I went to answer it. Hiu stood outside along with Kapono. "Hey, are you guys almost ready?" Hiu asked.

"Yeah, we'll be ready in a few minutes. Do you want us to meet you in about 10 minutes on the deck?" I asked.

"That works! Hele on!" Hiu said with a wave.

I was relieved Hiu seemed to be sticking to his word about being supportive. Jesse and I prepared for day two of surveillance.

We packed a few guns and obsidian weapons. Jesse was sure to bring his fake badge again. He showed it off to me before putting it in his pocket. I rolled my eyes with a disapproving gaze and a smile.

CHAPTER TWENTY-SEVEN

As soon as we were ready, I went to open the cabin door, but Jesse stopped me. He pulled me into his embrace and held me for a moment.

"I can't get over how beautiful you are," he said before he kissed me and then slowly and gently released me.

The rush of adrenaline made me stumble. I caught myself and looked at Jesse with a confident smile.

"You are too much. Your kisses make me . . . flutter. It's like I can't think straight or walk straight after I kiss you. It's like I lose all motor skills."

"I must have quite the effect on you," he said with a grin.

"Don't get a big head," I replied as I stepped out into the hall. We walked to the deck and met Hiu and Kapono. First, we retrieved my car and drove to the café again. The owner was prepared for us and saved the table next to the window so we could watch the gate. There were only two other people in the café. One ordered coffee to go and the other sat at a far table.

I eyed the man at the far table. He looked normal enough, but then all drudges and vampires looked fairly normal. He wore khaki shorts and a blue short-sleeved, button-up shirt with sandals. He sure wouldn't be doing any running in them.

I pushed my suspicions to the back of my mind and settled down with Jesse at the table. Hiu and Kapono went to their spot from the day before and were reachable by radio again.

I took out my tally list from yesterday and began counting how many cars entered the gate and how many cars left again. Jesse jotted down plate numbers.

"Why are you recording plate numbers?" I finally asked. It had bugged me a little since yesterday.

"So we can keep track of who's in and who's out. I'm also putting a star next to the more extravagant vehicles. Those will most likely belong to vampires. Drudges will be driving the less expensive ones," he explained.

"Have you noticed a black Audi? I haven't been paying attention to cars—just counting," I said.

"I saw one yesterday, but I've yet to see one today. Why?"

"It's Tom's car," I stated bluntly.

I didn't want Jesse to ever think of Tom as competition. I knew it was silly to think that he would be jealous of the man who tried to kill me, but I couldn't shake the feeling that there was more than just one kind of rivalry between Jesse and Tom.

I continued my tally. During the time no cars came or went, we cross-referenced our notes and made a list of when more drudges occupied the building compared to times there were more vampires at the building. At the end of our reconnaissance, we found that most drudges cleared out during lunch, but vampires were around most of the day. Leaving for lunch wasn't a necessity for vampires.

The owner of the café was very attentive. Jesse gave him more money before we left. He explained that we may or may not be back tomorrow. The man graciously took the money and thanked us before he walked us to the door. Hiu and Kapono waited a few blocks away again, so Jesse and I strolled along the road and took our time to breathe in the wonderful air.

It rained overnight and the air was fresh with floral undertones, the way it always was in Hilo after a rainy night; the way it had been the day I planned my escape from Tom. I started to wonder if I would ever get Tom out of my head. It wasn't that I missed him or anything, but the memories surfaced more often than I expected.

I hated Tom and had no desire to see him again until the day I brought his life to an end. I hated that the memories of the time I spent with him remained in my brain. One day, life wouldn't be so hectic, and I would be able to replace my memories of Tom with memories of Jesse.

As Jesse and I reached Hiu and Kapono, Jesse stopped me just before we got to the door and gave me a kiss. He opened the door for me and closed it after I stepped in, then went around to his own side. Hiu and Kapono talked about what they saw from their point of view.

"There wasn't much going on in the warehouses today. At least, nothing we could see," Hiu reported.

"Yeah, the trucks from yesterday are still outside. They unloaded some boxes, but not all da kine. They were using warehouse one," Kapono added.

"That makes sense, that's where they're most comfortable. It was the original warehouse they used before the takeover," I said.

"Right, so tomorrow we'll be targeting that warehouse," Jesse replied.

The four of us were in agreement. I suddenly became worried about making it out of the warehouse alive the next day. Vampires weren't necessarily the problem, we had rings to protect us, but drudges with guns would be a problem.

"I think we need to try to get some bulletproof vests," I said, "For you two and Moana," I added.

"You need one too," Jesse replied.

"I'm immortal. I'm not the priority."

"You can still get hurt. You may not die from a gunshot wound, but you'll still feel it as if you were human," Jesse explained.

"I will heal, they may not," I argued.

"Guys, no need to get futless, I know where to get da kine," Kapono said. "We only need choke kala!"

Jesse's face conveyed confusion. Pidgin was something he wasn't quite used to. "He knows where to get some bulletproof vests, but we need a lot of money," I whispered.

"Ass what I just said," Kapono said.

"I have plenty of money," Jesse replied.

"Tell me where to go, brah," Hiu said. Kapono gave him directions and soon enough we arrived at a run-down shack. I was a little suspicious about our surroundings. We were in a part of Hilo known for rough and tough natives.

Kapono led everyone to the opening of the shack, and knocked on the wooden frame. There was no door. A voice from inside called out, "Howzit!"

"It's Kapono, I brought some friends," Kapono called back.

"Native or haole?"

Kapono glanced back at the rest of us and called back, "Both."

"Komo mai," said the deep voice.

Kapono lead us inside. A rather large Hawaiian man sat at a makeshift table in a chair much too small for him. I guessed he was at least 300 pounds, but much of it was muscle. He examined our bunch and his gaze lingered on Jesse. He stood up as his head came within inches of the low ceiling.

"What you need, brah?" he asked Kapono.

"We need vests," he answered.

"I got da kine, how many?"

"How many you got?" Kapono asked raising a brow.

"Seven or eight," the man replied with a shrug.

"We'll take them all," Jesse spoke up.

The man looked at Jesse and gave him a little bit of a scowl.

"How much?" Jesse asked, unphased by the intimidating man.

"Fifty-five hundred. Cash," he answered.

"Done," Jesse said. He took out a giant wad of cash and handed him most of it. My eyes nearly popped out of their sockets when I saw the amount of money he had. I certainly hadn't seen him pack that this morning.

Kapono's large friend took the money and counted it quickly. He went to a spot in the rickety wooden floor and pulled up a few loose boards. Under them were eight vests. They were high quality; something the military would use. I'd seen similar ones in a warehouse I managed for the military in my time at Herrick-Peyton. Each of us grabbed two, but Jesse wasn't quite finished.

"Have any guns?" he asked.

"I got a few," he answered.

Apparently he was a little more trusting of Jesse because he went straight to a cabinet and opened it to reveal a small arsenal. There were about seven rifles and around fifteen handguns. Ammo filled the bottom shelf, which was almost overflowing. Jesse walked to the cabinet.

"I'll take that one, that one, and those two," he said, pointing out two assault rifles and two handguns. "And a box of ammo for each," he stated with money in hand.

"One noddah thirty," he said.

Jesse handed him the rest of the cash from his pocket. The man counted it again and slipped it into his pocket with the rest of the money.

We each grabbed a gun and a box of ammo along with our two vests. Jesse thanked him in the Hawaiian language and nodded his head. Kapono's friend replied with his own, "Mahalo."

"See ya, brah!" Kapono called on their way to the car.

The man just waved and called back, "Kipa hou mai," before returning to the confines of his shack.

"Kipa hou mai" meant "come visit again" in Hawaiian. I assumed that Kapono's friend most definitely wouldn't mind making that kind of money in again.

Once everyone got back into the car, I turned to Jesse. "You know, you really shouldn't be waving that kind of cash around, people will think I'm a gold-digger."

"Well, I am old, but unfortunately for you, I won't be dying anytime soon," he replied with a grin.

"I can't believe you were walking around with 85 hundred dollars in your pocket," I said.

"Don't forget about the 15 hundred I gave to the owner of the café," he said.

"Ten thousand dollars? You had ten thousand dollars in your pocket? What if someone would have mugged us?"

Jesse laughed, "I'd like to see someone try to mug me, an immortal with special skills, and you, a siren. That would be a good show," he continued laughing.

I rolled my eyes. "I still think it's crazy. What if it had fallen out of your pocket?" I countered.

"Then I suppose I would've had to go back to the boat for more," he smiled.

"You're crazy," I said.

"Crazy in love," he whispered into my ear.

"That was gnarly, brah, I never saw Nahele deal with a haole before," Kapono commented.

"Intimidating guy, but I guess business is business," Jesse replied.

"You lucky, brah, that moke don't even talk to haole, most of the time. He only talk to natives and kama'aina. It good ting he didn't bus you up," Kapono explained in amazement.

"Who's up for some ice shave?" Hiu asked as we passed a sno-cone stand.

"Sounds ono!" Kapono replied.

I thought it would be a good morale booster to bring back to everyone else. "Let's get some for everybody," I added.

Soon, we arrived back at the dock and unloaded the gear we'd just procured. Back on the boat, everyone was happy to see more guns and our new vests. The ice shave reminded me of better times.

At dinner, the plan for the next day was solidified, and everyone had their part. Alani, Nalani, and Latoria would stay at the boat. They would have a radio, and if anything went wrong, Alani could pilot the boat to our secret spot.

In town, Jesse would find a truck to load the devices into and Hiu, Kapono, and Moana would drive it. Jesse and I would be the first through the gate to create a distraction so that the others could get in and load up the truck. When they loaded all they could, Jesse and I would get them out and follow soon after. If they had drudges or vamps on their tail, we'd lead them away from the docks and the truck full of devices. We'd all be in contact by radio.

I hoped everything would go to plan. I didn't want anyone to get hurt. With the ocean being about five blocks from the Psytech building, my powers may not work, and that worried me a little. The river was nearby, but I didn't even know if the river would be susceptible to my influence. Dinner wrapped up as I thought all of it over. Jesse and I withdrew to our cabin.

"What's wrong, my love?" he asked.

"I just don't want anyone to get hurt tomorrow," I explained.

"We'll be fine. We have plenty of guns and daggers. Everyone has protective jewelry and a bulletproof vest," he replied.

"I know, but bullets don't just hit the vests. I'm not even sure if my powers will work," I said.

"Even if they don't, we'll be okay," he reassured.

"I hope so."

Jesse could likely tell I was still worrying. He went to the stereo system that was in the cabin and pulled out a CD. He waited patiently as the ancient CD player came to life and finally opened its disk holder. Then he pushed play, and the sound of tango music filled the room.

"Do you tango?" he asked as he held out his hand.

"I know a few moves," I said before taking his hand.

He spun me into himself and out again. I smiled. His moves were fluid. I hadn't danced the tango in a long time and I was out of practice, but his confidence flowed into me and soon I kept up with his steps. The dance was the most romantic one of my life. I felt myself floating from one end of the room to the other with more ease than I thought possible.

He dipped and twirled me. Our steps were perfectly mirrored and quick. The song came to an end, and as Jesse dipped me one last time, he kissed me passionately.

Jesse brought me upright and pulled me out of his kiss. I was smiling at him and trying to catch my breath. His glance switched to the window which was getting darker and darker. I looked out the window as well and then back at him.

"I wish we could continue our dance, but it seems we've run out of time," he said desolately. His voice was thick with sorrow and regret.

I sighed, "That's too bad. I'll miss you, Jesse."

"I'll miss you too," he said as he sat in his usual chair and pulled me into his lap.

"I'm going to practice for a little while, but I'll be back soon," I said.

"Don't stay out too late. We have a big day tomorrow. We strike at 12:15," Jesse reminded me.

I stood up and gave him one last kiss before I walked to the door. His grasp lingered until I exceeded his reach and then he smiled at me before once again, turning to stone before my eyes.

I wanted to work on my speed and accuracy. Tomorrow would put my abilities to the test, assuming I could even use them. The river was the closest body of water to the Psytech building. However, it wasn't actually part of the ocean and I didn't know if I could influence the river water. The moonlit crevasse revealed something I hadn't noticed before. There was a thin waterfall barely visible in the dull light streaming from the top of the cliff. I realized that if I could manipulate the water coming from the little waterfall, that I should be able to manipulate the river water.

I focused on the waterfall and zeroed in on the sound and the path of it as it fell freely from the cliff edge. I lifted my hands and tried to catch the water in mid-air before it hit the ocean water below it. My success provided relief. The water slowly built up into a ball and I hurled it at the cliff side. The water exploded on impact and trickled down to the ocean waves.

My connection to the water was weaker than my connection with the ocean water, but I could still use it to help me defeat drudges and at least stun the vampires. I was more at ease about the ambush we planned for the next day. After practicing a little more, I gained confidence and found that sleep came on easily now that I knew I could do everything in my power to keep my friends safe.

The next morning I woke early, just before the sun came up. I watched from the bed as Jesse came back to life.

"You're awake already," were the first words he said to me.

I smiled at him. "Well, I can't sleep in every day," I said.

Jesse stood up from his chair and came to me. I was eager to kiss him and I could tell he was too. Today our kisses were different. They were more urgent as with the cloud of dangerous uncertainty just over our heads.

"Everything will be okay," he said as if he'd read my mind.

I nodded and we began to prepare for the day. I put on my khaki cargo capris and a black tank top with my black jacket. I wore tennis shoes and pulled my hair up into a loose bun to keep it out of my way. I watched Jesse as he put on his clothes. He wore a black t-shirt and tennis shoes with gray cargo pants.

I couldn't help but think we were preparing for war, but then I realized I wasn't far off. Stealing the virus blockers would most definitely start a war between us and the vampires. Revenge would follow us as we flee from the Psytech building.

After we dressed, Jesse and I met everyone else on deck. Jesse divided the guns and ammo, Hiu got the shotgun; his favorite, and Kapono and Moana each got a pistol. Moana also had a rifle. Jesse and I each had a pistol and Jesse took a rifle. Latoria and Alani had two rifles and a pistol between them. Nalani refused to use a gun, she was old-fashioned and she'd never used one before. She did, however, take an obsidian dagger. Everyone else had at least one dagger as well. Hiu gave me the obsidian throwing spikes he'd been working on. I had six in all and they were neatly held in a sheath I could strap to my belt.

Jesse laid out the plan one more time. We'd get in through the main gate and cause a commotion in the parking lot. When most of the vampires and drudges were busy with the distraction, Hiu, Kapono and Moana would get in through the same service gate Hiu and I used the first time. They'd pull the truck in and load up all they could.

Moana was the best shot, so she'd be the lookout and take care of any stragglers that weren't preoccupied with Jesse and me. After the devices were loaded onto the truck, we'd receive a signal and the five of us would make our escape and get to the dock.

Alani, Latoria, and Nalani would guard the boat and if needed. Alani would pilot the boat to the crevasse.

When the plan was finalized, we went on our way to find a pick-up and another motorcycle. Jesse spotted a pick-up near the docks with a "FOR SALE" sign. It was perfect for our needs and it even had a topper. There wasn't a phone number, so Jesse and I went into the nearby store to find the owner. The others waited in the car.

Inside the outdoor sports store, we found two men, one behind the counter and one in front of it, chatting like they'd known each other for a long time. Jesse put on his easy-going charm and approached them.

"Aloha, I'm wondering if either of you know who owns that truck out there. It's got a "FOR SALE" sign, but I didn't see a number," he said.

The man in front of the counter spoke up, "That's my truck. You interested in buying it?" he asked.

The man wasn't Hawaiian in blood, but I could tell he had been on the islands for a long time. He was probably a rancher.

"Yes, as long as it runs. How much are you asking for it?" Jesse said in a friendly tone.

"I'm asking six thousand for it, and she runs great," the man replied.

Jesse took another look at the truck before making a counter offer. "How about five thousand cash right now?" Jesse asked.

The man thought for a moment. He turned his gaze toward his truck, and then at Jesse who pulled out his money. After a glance toward the man behind the counter and a nod from his friend, he agreed.

"I'll take it," he said. He held out his hand for a handshake. Jesse shook his hand and then gave him the cash. The man counted it and pulled out his keys and then tossed one to him.

"I just gotta get some things out of the cab," he said.

Jesse and I followed him out and soon he'd retrieved his belongings and we were on our way to find the next item on our list: a motorcycle.

"Why don't we see if that one is still at my house?" I asked.

"I did like that Ducati," Jesse said with a smirk.

Jesse and I lead the way to my house in the truck while Hiu and the others followed in my car. Once we arrived, I found that my house was still untouched and the motorcycle was still in my driveway. I decided to put my father's car back in the garage for now. We wouldn't need it today.

It was about eleven o'clock. Moana had brought sandwiches for everyone, so we ate and went over the plan again—just to be sure everything went smoothly.

After we ate, we all put on our bulletproof vests. Hiu, Kapono, and Moana piled into the truck, and Jesse and I hopped on the motorcycle. My heart began to race as we sped toward the Psytech building. My nerves jumped all over the place and I struggled to get a hold of them.

Finally, I focused on the nearby ocean and used its strength to steady myself. Hiu and the others got into position while Jesse and I found a place in the alley near the café we'd used for surveillance. The plan was coming together.

CHAPTER TWENTY-EIGHT

We waited for noon to come around, and watched as the drudges left through the gate. At 12:15, Jesse radioed the others to tell them we were going to make our move and to be ready for the next signal. The outgoing gate was beginning to lift and Jesse seized the opportunity. He threw the motorcycle into gear with a flick of his wrist and raced across the street to get through. I held on tight as adrenaline coursed through me. I was still in control of my nerves. I used the adrenaline to my advantage and made myself act quickly once we were through the gate.

Almost immediately, the guards were coming out of their booth with guns drawn. I recognized that they were the same security guards that Herrick-Peyton used, but they were different somehow. Their expressions were blank. Emotionless.

None of the men acted scared or angry. They were like zombies. I decided quickly that I didn't want to hurt them if I didn't have to. Jesse had his assault rifle drawn and I had my pistol.

"Put your guns down and place your hands on top of your head!" one of the guards shouted robotically.

Jesse and I didn't move. Soon, a crowd formed around us. Jesse kept me behind him, away from any bullets that could fly toward us. Most of the men in the crowd were vampires. There were a few drudges, but only a handful. I wore my ring, so the vampires were forced to keep their distance.

Jesse and I started assessing the crowd so we could pick out the vampires from the drudges. It was easier than I anticipated. Most of the vampires were dressed in suits while the drudges dressed more casually.

"What do you want?" a voice called from the crowd.

I recognized it quickly. It was Tom. I turned to face him and pointed my gun straight at him. I knew it would do nothing but stun him, but that would give me time to reach for my throwing spikes.

"I'm here to kill you. Or don't you remember the promise I made you back in California?" I asked.

A few drudges stepped closer and Tom laughed. Jesse pointed his gun at them. At this point, the guards weren't a threat. In the distance Hiu, Moana, and Kapono quietly made their move. The distraction had worked.

Tom stepped forward. His stride was calm and controlled. He stopped at the border of my protective force field. I felt the ring push him away.

"You can't kill me. You're greatly outnumbered, you're pointing a useless gun at me, and I've got drudges who will step in front of any dagger you throw at me. So, what do you really want?"

"I want you to die," I replied.

At that point, everything seemed to happen at lightning speed. I pulled the trigger and shot Tom right in the chest. He flinched and the bullet ricocheted and hit one of the drudges in the back. Jesse started shooting his fully automatic at the crowd. Some hit vampires and ricocheted, others took out drudges. The vampires reacted, and jumped high into the air. They wanted to get to us, but my ring prevented it.

I reached for my throwing spikes as Tom called for the guards to fire. I threw one at Tom, but his speed evaded it. Jesse moved behind me to shield me from the bullets that were coming from the guards. He was about to shoot back when I noticed he would most definitely kill them.

"Don't kill them!" I shouted back as I grabbed for another spike. I threw it at Tom but hit another vampire with it. I watched as the vampire shriveled up and his soul was sucked into the obsidian.

"They'll shoot you if I don't," Jesse replied.

"No! They're innocent! There's still a chance for them!" I yelled back. Then I focused on the nearby river. I beckoned to the water.

A thick, steady stream weaved through the air, and the vampires watched as the water swept the guns away from the guards. Tom's eyes followed the stream of water, to the river and he caught sight of Hiu, Kapono and Moana stealing the virus blockers. He yelled, "They're stealing the virus blockers! Go stop them!"

With the guards incapacitated, and most of the drudges dead, Jesse and I turned our attention to the vampires. Jesse took out his dagger and started a fight with one of them. I used the water to try to push the other vampires back and give Hiu, Kapono and Moana a little more time. It didn't take long for Jesse to finish with one vampire and move on to the next. He moved like a Special Ops agent. He struck with precision and force. I wondered where he got his training.

Once I got the vampires a safe distance away from the others, I took out my remaining four spikes and started throwing them into unsuspecting vampires. I hit two and they shriveled up like the first. Tom was practically dancing around the lot to avoid getting hit. The other two missed and landed on the concrete. One broke into pieces, the other slid under a vehicle. I had one more chance to kill Tom: my dagger.

I kept my eye on him and waited for him to slip up. Tom made his way to a dead drudge and pulled a gun off the lifeless body. I watched as he took aim, but the bullet wasn't for me as I expected. It was for Hiu. I looked at Hiu and the others. A few drudges were fighting with them and they didn't see Tom with his gun pointing straight at Hiu.

I screamed and hurled my obsidian dagger at him. It didn't fly straight since it wasn't meant for throwing, but it was too late. Tom fired and the bullet hit Hiu in his neck. The dagger I threw made contact with Tom's arm. At the same time, Jesse barreled into him with his own dagger, but it melted away like it had at the gas station. Tom had bloodstone on him and it rendered the dagger useless.

My rage grew, and I conjured up a fierce ball of water and threw it at Tom with all I had. Jesse scrambled to find another dagger, but they were all out of reach. Tom recovered from the blow and yanked out the dagger that was in his arm and disappeared with lightning speed into the alley.

I turned to Jesse. His face was solemn and he nodded toward Hiu.

My gaze followed his and I started running to the others. Moana and Kapono were both kneeling over him. Moana was in hysterics and Kapono was trying to stop the bleeding.

Tears welled up. I paused a moment to get myself under control so I wouldn't turn into a blubbering mess like Moana. Then I brought water from the river to wash his wound.

"W-we have t-to get him t-to a hospital," Moana sobbed.

"Ava, if we get him to the ocean you may be able to heal him. I've seen it done before, but it must be ocean water to heal him," Jesse said.

I nodded, "Let's get him out of here then. Kapono, get Alani on the radio and tell her to get the boat ready. You will probably have to drive too," I said, as I glanced at Moana.

"Moana, get in the truck, you are going to have to . . ." Jesse's voice was cut off by a deafening gunshot from right behind us. I felt a sting of piercing pain in the right side of my lower back and my stomach. The bullet went through and through. I collapsed on the ground as blood flowed out of me at an alarming rate.

Jesse was at my side in an instant and took me into his arms while Kapono shot the injured drudge that was lying on the ground with his gun pointed at me. The drudge laughed hysterically until the shot rang out.

I looked at my hand. There was a lot of blood on it. I couldn't move.

I heard Jesse's voice, "Kapono, can you ride a motorcycle?"

"Yeah, brah," he replied.

Jesse tossed him the keys, "Get to the boat and get ready for us. Moana, get in the back. You are going to have to calm down and get in the back with Hiu and Ava," Jesse commanded.

Moana did as she was told, but she was still sobbing quietly. I felt Jesse pick me up and put me in the truck, then Hiu was next to me in a flash. Jesse sped out of the parking lot and broke the gate at the main entrance in the process.

In only minutes, we were at the dock. Jesse pulled Hiu from the truck and ran him to the boat and quickly came back for me. Latoria and Kapono were unloading the virus blockers and taking them to the boat. Jesse grew impatient and finished the job himself carrying four times the amount that any normal man could.

He obviously didn't care about being discrete right now.

I was grateful there weren't many people around. I felt faint and looked over to Hiu, who was about to fall unconscious. He was losing a lot of blood. Suddenly my adrenaline kicked in and my pain became unimportant. I slid myself over to Hiu. I lifted his head in my hands. Jesse was at my side quickly.

"Tell me what to do," I commanded.

"Ava, you have to heal yourself first. You cannot heal him unless you're at your best. You must use what strength you have left to heal yourself," Jesse explained.

"He'll die before I'm healed," I shrieked.

"No, not if you concentrate and heal yourself first."

I took a deep breath and concentrated on the ocean. I brought water up to myself and spun it around my waist.

"You're doing well, just concentrate on the healing powers of the ocean," Jesse said.

I focused in on the ocean and imagined it taking away my pain and mending my wound. I heard Alani gasp and I looked down to see I was healed. The whole thing only took a few minutes.

"Ava, this won't be so easy. He's not an immortal, so it will take much more time and effort to heal him," Jesse said.

I nodded and shifted my focus to Hiu. I prepared myself by steadying my emotions once more. I brought the ocean water up on the deck of the boat and focused on its healing abilities. I tried to channel the energy into Hiu.

He was pale and unconscious. I could tell he'd lost a lot of blood.

Jesse had been right. It took much longer to heal Hiu than it had to heal myself. I worked for over an hour and took a short break every 20 minutes or so.

The breaks weren't my idea. Jesse told me that healing takes a lot out of a siren and that in order to keep it up I'd have to take breaks. Finally, after becoming smaller and smaller, Hiu's wound closed and he had been healed.

I was drained and weak after all the power and energy I'd exerted.

"You should lie down," Jesse said to me.

"Hiu hasn't woken up yet," I mumbled.

"We will watch after him, you must get some rest. You may be immortal, but you are not invincible. You need your rest," he repeated.

"If anything happens, wake me up," I said.

"I will," Jesse promised.

I went to mine and Jesse's cabin and laid down. I fell asleep almost instantly.

CHAPTER TWENTY-NINE

I dreamt I was back at Psytech. Tom was there and it was dark out. He was across the lot from me, staring at me with feral eyes. No one else was around. He started running toward me at lightning speed, but somehow, in slow motion from my point of view. I could tell by the surroundings that he quickly approached, but I seemed to have all the time in the world to react. I pulled an enormous ball of water from the river and readied myself to hurl it at him with a dagger floating in the center of it, but before the opportune moment came, I was wakened from the dream.

I opened my eyes to see Alani sitting at the side of my bed. I glanced at Jesse's chair. He was in it, already turned to stone.

"What time is it?" I asked. I was a little disoriented.

"It's almost midnight," Alani answered.

I sighed and slumped back into my pillow. "Is Hiu alright?"

"He's fine. He woke up soon after you fell asleep. He tried to thank you, but you were out like a light. No one could wake you. Jesse wanted to wake you before he turned to stone, but you wouldn't budge, so he asked me to stay until you woke up to make sure you were okay," Alani explained.

"I had the strangest dream," I replied, "I dreamt that I went to Psytech and was about to duel with Tom, but I woke up before I could see the ending."

"Well, I'm just glad you're okay," Alani said before she pulled me into a hug. "Thank you for saving my brother. Jesse said the bullet hit an important vein and that even a good doctor may not have been able to save him," Alani said quietly.

I could tell she was trying to hold back tears.

"He's my brother too," I said, "I will make it right. Tom isn't going to do this ever again. I'm going to kill him. I want to do it right now," I said as I pulled the blankets away from me.

"You can't go right now, it's dark out. Jesse won't be able to go with you, and you'll be more vulnerable. You need your rest. I want revenge too, but the next battle will have to wait."

"I can kill him by myself," I replied, "My vengeance is enough."

"No, you can't go by yourself, I won't let you. Wait until daylight. You need protection, I wouldn't be able to handle losing you Ava," Alani pleaded.

"I'm immortal. I'm not going anywhere," I said as I stood up.

"So is Tom, but there are still ways to kill him. There are ways to kill you too. I can't let you do this. I will wake up Kapono and make him keep you here somehow," Alani said as she crossed her arms in front of her chest.

I looked at Alani's worried face. It was clear that she wouldn't let me go without a fight.

"Okay, I won't go," I said. I was lying, but only because I didn't want Alani to cause a scene. "We'll come up with a plan in the morning," I said.

Alani raised a brow as if it had been too easy to convince me to stay.

"Okay," she said, "I'm gonna go to bed. You should go back to bed too. Aloha Ahiahi!"

"Aloha Ahiahi!" I called back. Alani closed the door behind her and I turned off the bedside lamp. I waited a few minutes, to make sure that everyone had gone to bed. I turned the lamp back on.

Jesse's stone face haunted me. He knew what I was doing. There was no doubt about it. He couldn't stop me, not right now.

I felt a little guilt as I threw on my clothes and tennis shoes. I grabbed two daggers and a gun and quickly strapped them to my belt.

"I love you, but I need to do this," I said to Jesse before I kissed his marble forehead and quietly slipped out the door. I was careful not to walk near anyone's cabin door. Finally, I made it to the back of the boat and brought the water up to me, and made it carry me off the boat and out of the crevasse.

Soon, I was using the ocean to carry me toward Hilo. I imagined it was what surfing felt like. It was a rush and sent more adrenaline through my veins. Soon, I neared the part of the coast I knew was close to Tom's house. I came to shore a few houses before his so I could slowly sneak onto his property.

I crept across the neighbor's yard. I could see lights on in Tom's house. I tried to see if he was alone. After a few minutes, he passed by a window, another burst of adrenaline coursed through me. I closed in on the house. I was careful to remain unseen until the last possible moment. I'd make him come outside, and then blast him with a ball of ocean water carrying a dagger before he would know what hit him. I was behind a bush just outside the window. I peered inside to find that he was alone.

There was a motion sensor attached to the back door. I got myself into position and tripped the sensor. I conjured up a ball of water, placed a dagger inside, and waited for him to come out.

Tom was quick to respond to the sensor, and as soon as he opened the door, I hurled the ball at him. The dagger was heading straight for him. It was a direct hit that slammed him backward into the house. I ran after him then stopped in the doorway.

Tom was lying on the floor with water everywhere and the dagger was starting to melt away. Tom sat up and glared at me. He flashed his fangs.

"That's three bloodstones you and your friends have ruined," he said. I took out the other dagger and gripped it fiercely in my hand.

"You almost killed my friend," I spat at him.

"Almost? Damn. I was hoping he would die. There are too many hospitals around here. I'm glad to see you've recovered. Although, I'm sure your wound still impedes you. I watched as my drudge tried to do his duty. It's too bad your friend killed him, he would've made a good vampire guardian. He took initiative," Tom said.

"No wound," I said as I lifted my shirt, "I'm at my full potential."

Tom smiled, "You are a powerful siren. I've underestimated you. Too bad you won't stop hiding behind that pathetic protection ring. We could have a real battle on our hands."

"If you discard any bloodstone you have, I'll take off my ring," I said.

Tom smiled his sly grin and reached in his pocket to take out three small red and green stones. He tossed them at my feet.

"If that's how you want it," he said.

I took off my ring and dropped it on the stone path as I prepared myself once more. I knew I didn't have his speed or his strength, but I would use the ocean as my strength and I hoped that my reflexes could keep up with him.

Tom slowly stood.

I formed a ring of water around my waist and spun it around me like the rings of Saturn. The obsidian dagger was still in my hand. Suddenly, Tom disappeared from sight. I sent the ring of water bursting outward. I heard Tom's body hit the ground from behind me, but he was up again as soon as I turned around. He dashed straight toward me and the two of us hit the ground.

I tried to stab Tom with the dagger, but his strength was enough to push it away from himself and he tried to cut me with it. I felt the cold, hard edge just under my jaw and a trickle of blood ran down my neck.

"Siren blood . . . a delicacy," Tom said as he brought his lips closer to my neck and licked up some of my blood.

I struggled against his hold to no avail. I focused on the ocean again and called on it to give me strength. I felt myself becoming stronger and I pushed the dagger and Tom away from my throat.

"You can't win. I'm stronger and faster. All you have is a silly dagger and a few drops of water," Tom said.

I called on the ocean water once more and hit Tom with as much force as I could. I kept it coming. A powerful stream formed in midair. It was like a firefighters' hose constantly hitting him with extreme pressure. I didn't let up, and the water finally pushed Tom off of me and against the house.

Paint started to peel off from the pressurized water. I stood at a safe distance and watched as Tom struggled to fight back. I saw my chance and threw my last dagger into the stream. I let it carry the obsidian into his heart.

Once the dagger hit him, I returned the water to the ocean. I turned back to Tom, with the expectation of seeing him withered and shrunken, but he had tricked me.

The dagger had melted away—he was still wearing a bloodstone.

I looked around for my ring. I couldn't see it anywhere. All the water I'd thrown around had washed it into the grass.

"My turn," Tom said before he jumped up and tackled me. We rolled to the muddy ground and he grabbed me by the throat.

"This is your last chance. You either join me or die," he whispered before having another taste of my blood.

"I will never join you," I said as loud as I could with his hand around my throat.

Tom squeezed tighter, "I guess I'll have to kill you like I killed your mother then."

That was all the motivation I needed. My wrath conjured up a tsunami in the nearby ocean.

I felt my spirit leave my body to fuel the gigantic wave. The wave headed straight for Tom and my body. As my spirit came closer to my body, I saw myself from above and noticed my eyes were glowing blue. Tom noticed my eyes as well and he looked up just in time to see the wave coming straight for him. The moment the wave hit Tom, my spirit reentered my body and caused an underwater electric shock to jolt Tom off and away from me.

The water carried him out to sea. I sat up and watched as Tom tried to fight the current, but I could see he was getting nowhere. I regained my strength then stood, and ran toward the water and dove into a cyclone I'd formed to carry myself out to where Tom was, which was already about a mile from shore.

I finally neared him and towered over him in my column of water. He glared up at me with hate in his eyes.

I smiled at him from my watery perch, "Hell hath no fury like a woman scorned. Remember that. Next time I won't make the same mistake I made tonight, and I'll have more obsidian."

The water holding me up began to spin faster and faster. The sky above me clouded up. An electric feeling went through me as I lifted my hands to the sky. I looked up to the clouds and pulled energy from them into myself, then turned my gaze back on Tom and shot a bolt of lightning from my hand. The jolt blew him out of the water and down again. I then washed him farther out to sea as an act of spite.

Once he was out of my sight, I formed a mirror out of water in front of me.

I could barely see in the dim moonlight but as I looked at my reflection in the water, I saw my eyes were still glowing but becoming dimmer. I watched in amazement as they faded back to normal. I concluded that it was a side effect of my spirit leaving my body. At least, that's what I thought had happened.

I returned the makeshift mirror to the ocean and returned to the boat the same way I'd left. I quietly crept back onto the deck and sent the ocean back to its normal state. The sky was turning lighter in color and soon it would be sunrise. I thought about Jesse and rushed back to our cabin to show him that I was okay.

Once inside, I made myself known to Jesse. I let my eyes connect with his and sat on the bed. I knew he would probably be angry with me. I only hoped Jesse could forgive me. I watched out the small window as light spilled in and then Jesse changed back to his human form and leaped from the chair. He tackled me on the bed in a warm embrace.

"Don't ever do that again!" he said harshly, but with undertones of love in his voice. "You have no idea how anxious I've been. What were you thinking? You could have been killed."

"I'm fine," I said, "I just needed to get revenge, but it slipped through my fingers again. I was so close. He tricked me."

"Tell me everything," Jesse said as he pulled me out from his arms and stared me in the face. Then he noticed something, and I watched his expression as it changed from worry to anger.

"He had his hand around your throat!" he almost yelled.

My hand went to my neck and I stood up and went to the mirror. There were bruises where Tom's hand had been just under the small cut. The ocean water had washed the blood away.

I turned back to Jesse. His anger was tacit.

"Yes, but I created a tsunami. It was so surreal. My spirit left my body and propelled the wave toward him, and when the wave hit him, my spirit returned and sent a jolt of electricity into him and then he was washed out to sea. My eyes were glowing in a blue color. It was so strange. I think it must have been a side effect of the whole spirit leaving my body thing, but I followed him to send him out even farther.

It was then that I discovered something else. If I try hard enough, I can shoot bolts of lightning from my hands," I explained.

Jesse was still silent.

"Please say something. I'm sorry I worried you, but I had to do something. I had to get him back for hurting Hiu. I just couldn't let that go unjustified," I pleaded.

"I know you felt that you needed revenge, but what you did was dangerous. I didn't wait all this time to find you just so you could be killed by a lowly vampire," Jesse lectured.

"I'm sorry. You're right. It was reckless, but now I know I have this incredible new power, and I can use it to defeat them," I explained.

It seemed I was forgiven. Jesse's expression lightened and he took me into his arms again. He held me tightly. I didn't want him to let go, and I knew that he didn't want to let go either.

"I love you, Ava. I don't want anything to happen to you. I'm glad you found out more about your abilities, but it could have come at a high price. A price I'm not willing to pay. I won't sacrifice you for victory against the vampires, I won't do it."

"I love you too, Jesse. I wouldn't sacrifice you either. I know how you feel, and I understand that I worried you beyond belief. I hope you can forgive me," I said.

"Of course, just don't do it again or I'll have to handcuff you to the bed at night," Jesse said with a grin.

I smiled mischievously. "Why not get out the handcuffs right now?"

Jesse grinned again and pushed me down on the bed. He playfully pinned my wrists down above my head. Then kissed me sweetly and gently before releasing my wrists and bringing his hands down to my rib cage. He lifted up my tattered shirt just slightly. Our reconciliation was interrupted by a knock on the door.

I groaned. I didn't want to be bothered at the moment. The lack of sleep had caught up with me and I just wanted to enjoy Jesse's presence before taking a well-deserved nap, but I allowed Jesse to help me up and I went to answer the door anyway.

"Hiu!" I yelled excitedly, "You're okay!"

I grabbed Hiu and pulled him in for a hug. He smiled and hugged me back.

"Thanks to you!" he replied.

"Hiu, I would do anything for you. I'm just glad that I could heal you," I replied.

"Me too," Hiu laughed. Then he noticed what Jesse had noticed before and his expression turned grim, "What's that on your neck?"

My hand automatically went to my neck to cover the bruise. I was embarrassed. I didn't want everyone to know that I'd tried to take on Tom by myself.

"I went to get revenge on Tom, because of what he did to you," I relented.

"Is that a bruise in the shape of his hand?" Hiu asked with outrage.

"Yes. Don't worry, I've already been lectured about the stupidity of what I did," I said with a glance toward Jesse.

"On the positive side, I did find out that I can shoot bolts of lightning from my hands and that I can create a tsunami."

Hiu shook his head, "Dat don't excuse it, you no mo' start beef with a vampire by yo'self. What happen to him?"

"He's still alive. He tricked me, I thought he had no bloodstone on him, but it turns out he did. Unfortunately, he'll live for a while longer," I said.

"Well, I think we need to lay low, at least, for a few days. People in town are going to be talking about everything that happened. There's no way the events of yesterday went unnoticed," Jesse chimed in.

"I agree. They all gonna be talkin' story," Hiu replied.

"Me too. Let's get some breakfast. I'm suddenly starving," I said as I pulled Jesse and Hiu in the direction of the galley. The three of us arrived in the galley where everyone gathered to enjoy a peaceful breakfast.

BONUS

READ CHAPTER ONE OF MOONSTONE

DORIN

I stood in line at the upscale hotel while two busy front desk clerks tried to check in impatient guests. I stood fourth in line and the woman second in line caught my eye. She was a healthy thin with long blond hair pulled back into a loose ponytail. She had bright blue eyes and held her head high in confidence as she patiently took in the aesthetic of the lobby. Meanwhile, I enjoyed the aesthetic of her long legs.

I judged from her black skirt and blouse that she was a business woman. I'd never found a business woman sexy before, but something about her drew me in.

Finally, the man in front of me doing a funny little dance lost his patience and walked toward the bathrooms.

That's when I first caught the intoxicating scent of the woman in black. I closed my eyes and let the urge to attack her then and there pass. Not now, Dorin.

Now third in line, I had a limited amount of time to make conversation. As I stepped forward, I hit a wall.

She wore only one piece of jewelry--a ring that would make things difficult--not a wedding ring, but something much more ominous. I felt the force inside pushing me away. She acted as if she was unaware of its power over me. Of course the first woman to pique my interest would be wearing a protective ring. My luck was nothing if not bad.

"That's quite a unique ring you're wearing," I stated. I had to test the limits.

She looked up at me with her big blue eyes and smiled.

"Thank you, my grandmother gave it to me. She carved it herself from a seashell," the woman replied.

The force was even stronger after I made my presence known--it strengthened the wall between us. Not because she was afraid, but because I wanted to taste her blood and the vampire spirit inside the ring knew it. The spirit warned my subconscious mind to stay away, therefore physically pushing me away from her. The fact that I couldn't harm her because of my curse was the only reason I'd gotten so close to her to begin with. If I wanted to have my way, the ring would have to come off.

The curse was only a small problem. Once she kissed me, she would be mine to take.

The woman finished checking in and it was my turn. I watched as she went out to her car to grab her luggage and I timed it right so that we ended up taking the elevator together. I was careful to stand at the other side of the elevator so the ring would not noticeably affect me. I made small talk--even though such trivial conversation annoyed me to know end--and it turned out we were going to the same floor.

"So, where are you from?" I asked her.

"New York City. I drove down here for a meeting today. I'll probably stay the weekend and then I'm headed to Miami on Monday."

"That's funny. That's where I was planning on ending up. Well, Miami and the Palm Beach area. I'm taking my time. I don't want to get there before spring break is over," he replied.

"That's exactly why I'm staying the weekend. I want to give the spring break crowd a chance to clear out."

The elevator opened on the third floor and we stepped out. I let her go first. We walked down the south hall together. Our rooms turned out to be across the hall from each other.

"Looks like we're neighbors," I said as I fiddled with the door key--I couldn't stand plastic cards in place of a real key, but the world changed and I had to do the same.

"Have a good night," I called.

"You too!" she replied.

Once inside my room, I decided to try out a talent that I had recently developed. X-ray vision wasn't as simple as peering through a wall. It was more like a bat's sonar. It took incredible concentration which is something that would end up making me thirstier than I already was.

The ability consisted of simply hearing the sounds in another room and using the reverberations of those sounds as they bounce off objects to get a picture of what was in the room. It worked better if there were a constant noise--like a television. Luckily, that was the first thing she turned on. The channel she selected was a news station.

AILA

When I closed the door to my room, I little butterflies fluttered in my stomach. My 'neighbor' was good looking and had a sexy accent to boot. It was an accent I couldn't quite place, something out of Europe, most likely South Eastern Europe. Refocusing myself, I turned on the television to CSNBC and began to unpack. I filled the drawers and hung my important blouses and skirts.

"Now to make adjustments," I said to myself as I walked to the alarm clock and set it for seven. Then I turned my attention to the thermostat. It was a touchy touch screen, but eventually I found my nails did the trick. I liked the temperature to be precisely seventy degrees.

I took out my laptop and set it up on the desk. It waited for the moment I needed to do reports. Work on the weekend wasn't required, but I had work to do before my vacation started the following week. My cell phone charger hung from my suitcase. I plucked it out and set it on the end stand table.

I grabbed my toiletries and headed for the bathroom. The contents of my make-up bag fit perfectly on the counter. Next, I removed my hair brush from the bag and placed it on the counter for easy access in the morning.

The ice bucket was ready to be filled, so I grabbed it and headed to the hallway. Once I opened my door, I was surprised to see the good-looking man was also emerging from his room.

"Well, hello," he said, "I wonder if you could possibly help me. I was just on my way to the desk. The thermostat in my room seems to be erratic or perhaps it's even broken. I know you don't work here, but personally, I think it's me. Perhaps someone with a better grip on American technology can help."

"Oh, yes. I think I could help you with that. I was adjusting mine and I found that fingernails make the perfect tool," I replied.

He chuckled and glanced down at his well-groomed nails, "That would explain it. I have none to speak of," he said waving his fingers. "Would you mind setting it for me?"

I hesitated. I wasn't sure about going into a strange man's room, but the pocket knife in my jacket reminded me I could take care of herself. I smiled and agreed to help him. He opened his door wider to let me in. His room was a mirror image of mine. I found the thermostat and started toying with it.

"What would you like it set on?" I asked.

"Oh, about seventy, I'd say," he replied.

"That's funny," I said as the thermostat beeped at me, "That's exactly how I set mine."

He chuckled again. "What a coincidence."

"Well, I should get going. I was headed to the ice machine," I said with a smile.

"Of course, don't let me keep you. I'll walk you out," he replied.

I walked into the hallway and glanced back at him. He smiled at me and said, "By the way, my name is Dorin."

"I'm Aila."

"Thank you for your help, Aila. Would like to join me for dinner at the steakhouse across the street--as a thank you for helping me out with my troubles?" he asked with a charming smile and hope in his eyes.

My confidence broke and I averted my gaze. I thought I might melt if I kept looking at him. I took a second to think it through.

"That would be nice. I was planning on going there anyway. What time would you like to go?"

"Around seven?" he asked.

"Great, I'll see you at seven."

"I'll pick you up," he joked.

Moonstone is available to preorder and will be released on February 1, 2016.

Go to: www.kaylacurry.com/moonstone-preorder/ to preorder from your favorite retailer.

WHILE YOU WAIT...

Fall into my other novel, *Where the Carnies Are*.

It's Free for my VIP Readers. Go to:
www.kaylacurry.com/vip-reader-sign-up/ to sign up.

ABOUT THE AUTHOR

Kayla Curry's creative mind never sleeps. Literally.

At night, her active imagination produces dreams all night long. It's those dreams that provide much of the inspiration for her stories which have a little Victorian charm mixed with a fairy tale flair.

Her works include *Where the Carnies Are, Obsidian (Mystic Stones Series #1)*, and many short stories.

She lives in North Platte, Nebraska with her husband and two sons and she plans to keep writing and creating for the rest of her life.

ACKNOWLEDGEMENTS

Thank you to my wonderful editor, Samantha and my book formatter Jason. You guys are amazing!

Thanks to my family, friends, and ARC readers. Couldn't do this without you. I appreciate your support.